THE STEP BACK

stretched tight over my chest and ribs, the muscles long and sinewy even after two years of weight lifting. My sharp features, on the other hand, were finally beginning to mellow into an adult's face. I checked the mirror to reaffirm it—the freckles dimming, chin rounding, eyebrows filling. If it kept on this way, I thought it might even be a handsome face one day, though the moment I turned from the mirror it seemed to rearrange itself into the old patterns—my mouth filling with braces, ears flapping out, cowlick standing up.

London still hadn't come home by the time the sun went down. I had been going to the sliding door every twenty minutes to call and whistle and clap, my voice cheerful at first, then pleading, then angry. For a few minutes the burnished light slid up the foothills until they wore golden crowns. Then the shadows deepened. The watery-blue sky slipped over a purple horizon, and the first stars came out overhead.

I was starting to worry, but only mildly, because beneath the worry was the belief that life offered only setbacks and lessons, not real peril— you missed a shot so you could make a more important one later, you lost your dog so you could experience the joy of its return. It was hard to believe otherwise when the air felt so mild, when the terrain beyond the house was so familiar and benign. Here was the deck where I'd had my earliest birthday parties, the lawn where I'd hunted Easter eggs, the hills where I'd led Charlie on our "expeditions," warning him to stay back from the rattlesnakes I pretended to see so that I could twirl my pocket knife into the dirt. I thought of all the versions of myself I'd left in this landscape, then wondered, as I often did, about the version that lay just beyond its horizon: Who was he?

"Ed." My father touched my shoulder. He was holding a fresh drink. "We're having a family meeting."

"Good." I slid the door shut. "I'm getting worried about London."

In the living room, my mother was on the far end of the sectional sofa, her makeup stripped, blotting at her red eyes with tissues. Charlie sat nearby in sweatpants, watching her fearfully. My father gulped his drink, then ushered me in, and I realized we weren't there to talk about the dog.

2

That summer I wanted to play basketball all the time, every waking moment, and my teammates—ex-teammates now—mostly obliged. They were almost as eager as I was to get outside, peel off their shirts and let the sun wash their shoulders. We met at this court or that court or drove in a caravan searching for one that was available. Then we played for hours, cutting and jumping, knocking hips, grappling for position, sprinting, colliding, sweating and swearing, slapping fives and arguing about fouls and walking off injuries. It was a sophisticated game, with screens and back-cuts, picks and rolls, box-outs and close-outs, help and rotation, so that whenever a shot went in (or not), and whenever a miss was rebounded (or not), and whenever a ball was blocked or stolen or tipped or recovered (or not), we knew we had all played a role in it, that we had failed or succeeded together.

In this fashion we won and lost, we overcame and were overcome, and then we changed teams and tried again. We kept at it until there was nothing left in our legs, until our throats and lungs ached with fatigue, and then we collapsed into the shade, gape-mouthed, sweat dripping from our chins. We gulped Gatorade, tore at Velcro, yanked laces, tugged off shoes and braces and sweatbands, peeled socks that had been doubled and tripled for blister prevention. Then we sat with our legs splayed, talking and laughing, enjoying the cool air between our toes and the serenity of exhaustion and the last few moments of closeness before we disbanded.

I'd never felt as good on the court as I did that summer. The only time that came close had been the last game of the season, when I'd gotten the start for being a senior. By the time the coach had subbed in the real starters, the score was 7-2 and I'd scored all seven. The first two came when I beat everyone down the court on a fast break, the next two when I tipped in an offensive rebound, the last three on a long-range shot from the top of the key. I still remembered what it felt like, holding my follow-through as the ball splashed through the net and the other coach called timeout. The real starters had skipped over from the scorer's table to mob and congratulate me, and the crowd had cheered the seniors off the court. When I let myself glance at the bleachers, I saw Charlie there beaming at me, clapping wildly like everyone else.

One day, Russo showed up before a pickup game at the junior high court. He was the coach, a short bald man with razor-burned cheeks and a hard belly that sat in his lap like a curled cat when he squatted to draw up a play. It also forced his legs wide apart when he demonstrated a good defensive squat for a lazy player. Sometimes he made such demonstrations on the sideline during games, tugging at the knees of his slacks, his face crazed. To make substitutions he yanked us from the bench by our jerseys and flung us toward the scorer's table. At halftime he shouted and stomped and broke clipboards over his knee. Otherwise he was a kind and earnest man who hosted spaghetti feeds and preached to us about family, because that was what he said we should be.

And we were. We helped and tolerated each other the way family would, both on and off the court. We tutored Danny Shea into eligibility. We drove to parties late at night to pull Val Lambright away from the alcohol and marijuana that otherwise might have kept him from graduating, let alone coming to practice. When Andre Dennis had his power turned off we washed cars until we'd raised enough to have it turned back on, and when his mother lost their house, we housed him.

And that was why everyone, as if by agreement, dropped into defensive positions as soon as Russo arrived, slapping the ground to show the depth of our crouches. We shuffled around as if performing old drills, calling encouragement to each other, eyes bulging with mock intensity. Russo loved it. He laughed and teased us with instructions, his face glowing. Then, as if on a whim, he called, "Hey, Garrison."

I rose from my defensive stance.

"Walk with me," he said.

I followed him off the court and around the corner. We strolled by the aquatic center, where screaming kids flung themselves down the slides, the air pungent with chlorine. Russo clasped his hands behind his back and looked at the sidewalk. "I hear your parents are divorcing."

I confirmed it with a tone of world-weary acceptance.

"What happened?"

"My mom moved to Maryland."

"Why?"

"She's from there."

"I mean why'd they split up?"

I swabbed my face with a shirtsleeve, not wanting to say the reason. It seemed obscene to discuss it, and anyway, I wasn't sure it was true. "My opinion," I told Russo, "is that she probably had an affair."

"An affair? What makes you say that?"

I shrugged. "Things don't add up."

He was staring at me like he expected more. I shrugged again.

"And how do you feel about all of it?" he asked.

The truth was that it didn't seem to have much to do with me. I was leaving. "It's a little weird," I told him, "but I don't care much."

"That's not true, is it?"

"It's not worth complaining about. Lots of people have divorced parents."

"That doesn't mean it isn't hard on them. Divorce can be tough for kids."

"I'm not a kid."

He moved aside for an oncoming pedestrian, then faced me on the sidewalk. "Maybe not," he said. "But when you're young, you bring your past with you whether you like it or not. You don't figure out what to do with it, it can bend your whole life the wrong direction. You get what I'm saying?"

I'd been conditioned to take Russo's advice seriously. When you were heaving from ladder sprints, you had to believe in his counsel of discipline and commitment to line up again and wait for his whistle. But this time I didn't see how it applied to me.

"I appreciate the concern," I told him, "but I'm leaving for Berkeley in like a month. The one to worry about is my brother. He's only thirteen. He's got a lot of growing up left to do."

Russo seemed to stop himself from saying something, then relented, his voice low and eager. "How tall is he now?"

"My height."

"You been working on his post moves?"

"He's got them down. I'm going to start him on ball handling. I think he could play the wing."

We looked at each other brightly, excited about this prospect, then started down the sidewalk again. "Keep an eye out for him," Russo said. "He probably needs your help in all this."

"I know. I am."

"And let me know if there's anything I can do."

"Thanks, but like I said, it really doesn't bother me." A long truck was angling itself through the intersection ahead while other cars waited. "You want to know what does bother me, though?"

He gave me a look like he was all ears.

"Our dog ran away, and nobody seems to care. Nobody even looks for him except me. We don't know if he got hit by a car, or if someone else took him in, or if he's living in the hills, or what. He could be anywhere. But you ask anyone about it and they look at you like you're crazy." I lowered my voice and said, "That's what bothers me."

"Grief can do funny things to people," he responded. "Give them time."

The guys were trying to dunk when we returned. Kyle Andrews swooped in and threw the ball off the back iron. Andre Dennis turned the ball over for a finger roll. Seth Feldman did the Air Jordan pose, barely brushing the bottom of the net, and everyone laughed. When the ball finally careened my way, I carried it to the top of the key. They cleared out of the way for my attempt, but I just held it on my hip. "Shoot for teams?" I asked, and they all got in line behind me.

***

The only time I couldn't play basketball, besides the nights I bussed tables at Il Grappa, were Sunday mornings. That was when my mother called. It was an event I had come to dread, but I didn't know what would happen if I wasn't there to pick up. It was strange to fill my mother in about my life, and to be filled in about hers. The first part was tense and formal, like going to a dance with a girl you barely knew. I could never think of what to say. Was my old Corolla running okay? How were all my friends doing? Had I read any good books lately? I searched for answers longer than a word or two, but my mind was blank, and peering into it for full sentences was like peering into a bleak arctic desert for something other than ice. My car was fine, my friends were fine, the books I read were fine. Everything was fine, and what more was there to say?

The second part of the call was worse, her monologue about the new life she was establishing in Maryland. She'd adopted a cat, she said, and enumerated all the cute and funny things it had done, then started giving play-by-play commentary of what it was doing right at that moment. She was taking a spin class, she said, and proceeded to describe it in painstaking detail, the instructor and the other spinners and the burn in her legs and *everything*. It was boring—never in my life had I been so bored—but also, it defied my understanding of her in a way I had trouble tolerating. My mother, allowing cat hair on her Burberry Tartan Straight-Leg Trousers. My mother, sweating in a gym. My mother, roaming a big-box bookstore, wearing an earpiece, asking customers if they were finding everything they needed. My mother, burying her head between some other woman's legs. I couldn't even get a picture of her on the other end of the line, standing there in Maryland.

Every once in a while she had to ask if I was still there. I would say yes, and she would continue the monologue. Then one time she got to talking about the things she missed in San Seguro—the kinds of trees, the churros stand on Broad Street, the quality of the sunshine, us boys. When she asked if I was still there, I stayed silent, pivoting the receiver from my mouth and breathing quietly as she said, "Ed? Ed? Oh, shoot. Ed?" Then she was silent too, and for a couple minutes we listened to the susurrus of the long-distance wire.

"Those things didn't leave," I finally answered.

After my turn was over, I carried the phone to Charlie, and Charlie pressed it to his face, smiling sheepishly like the child he was, already oblivious to my presence. "Hi Mom," he would say, voice deep, and by then I would be headed downstairs. Sometimes I could hear him laughing even from the living room, and I would have to go outside to shoot baskets. I often found myself wishing I could call around for a pickup game, but there was no way to do it with the phone tied up, so I just kept spinning myself passes, squaring my feet, driving up and launching the ball from my fingertips and holding the follow-through, trying to stay in the moment, to keep my mind from wandering into places I didn't want it to go.

When basketball was over, though, or when I was lying in bed at night, staring at the glow-in-the-dark stickers that still speckled my ceiling, my mind went there anyway. I saw my father kissing my mother in the kitchen. I heard the way they signed off from phone calls with a casual, "I love you." I remembered Charlie and me bursting into their bedroom on Christmas morning to find their two sleepy smiles on their two adjacent pillows.

And then suddenly I would be back in the armchair the night of the family meeting, facing them. There was my mother, pitched forward, knees together, the tissue box in easy reach on the coffee table. There was my father on the opposite side of the sofa, lounged back into the overstuffed cushions, cradling his drink against his stomach. And there was Charlie, slumped between them, looking at me in fear and confusion, as if I was in on it.

For a long time nobody had said anything, until finally our father exhaled audibly through his nose—an impatient, irritated noise. "Go ahead," he'd told our mother.

A battle was unfolding in her face. She looked at the ceiling for several long moments, waiting for whatever was inside her to pass. "I can't do this," she said finally.

"So don't," he said.

She looked at him, then at Charlie, then at me, as if for encouragement. I gave her my look of determination, the one I gave Russo as he made his pregame speeches about discipline and effort. She nodded at me, seeming to draw courage from the look, and her expression settled into one of resolve.

"Well," she said, and spent a moment watching the five fingertips of one hand bounce against the five fingertips of the other. "I'm sure you boys remember how hard a time it was for me when I was in Maryland, taking care of your grandmother and then handling her estate. What you probably couldn't tell was where the difficulty was coming from, exactly. Being there gave me a lot of time to step back and think, and one of the things I thought about—well, it was something I've spent most of my life trying to ignore. It's gotten very hard to ignore it lately, though, and I'm at the point where I can't do it anymore."

She flexed her back into a rigid, unnatural posture. "You're both old enough now," she said, "to have experienced certain feelings, probably about girls. Certain romantic feelings. Right? You feel a pull toward them, and it's nothing you have any control over. It's just there inside you. Do you know the feelings I mean?"

She looked at each of us, and we each nodded.

"That feeling you have," she said, "I have it too. Toward women, I mean." She leaned forward and examined us. "Do you understand what I'm saying?"

This was my mother. What she was telling us seemed so absurd it was almost funny.

"You're gay?" Charlie asked.

She dipped her head. "I haven't always known what to do about it. It's something your dad and I have talked about a lot lately," she said, and looked at him. He was holding his drink, jabbing the ice cubes with a tiny straw, sunken into the plush cushions as if he'd like to be swallowed by them, to disappear into a cocoon of paisley fabric and stuffing. He gave a slow nod without raising his eyes.

"And the conclusion we've come to," she said, "is a mutual decision. Isn't it, honey?"

Our father looked at her, and his eyes contained nothing except submissiveness and humiliation. "It's a mutual decision," he said.

"We decided it would be best if we weren't married anymore."

She closed her mouth and leaned back, giving us an opportunity to react, though the only reaction that occurred to me was to worry about Charlie. He watched her with a crumpled expression of fear and confusion I knew well. It was a look he had turned on me often as a kid—coming in from Little League tryouts after letting two ground balls go between his legs, asking if it was true that babies came from certain anatomical insertions, telling me about the "bullies" who made fun of his size. The look meant he needed me to interpret his troubles for him, and it was the best part of being a big brother. I sometimes told him ghost stories I'd picked up from library books just so I could watch his eyes go wide beneath tensed brows and then answer his questions about whether they were true. When he turned the expression on me now, I gave him back my look of determination, the same one I'd given my mother, though it didn't ease any of the fear from his face.

"You probably have a lot of questions," our mother was saying, "so let me tell you that as far as logistics go, your dad will stay here in the house. I'm going to move back to Maryland. It'll be nice for me to be near your aunts and uncles, and also to be near the capital. There's some important advocacy work being done there that I'd like to join, things that were unimaginable in the days of Stonewall, although we still have a long way to go—a *long* way. Do you boys know who Matthew Shepard is?"

My father said my mother's name. She looked at him, and her face lost some of its intensity.

"In any case," she continued, "you'll keep living here with your dad. We don't want to disrupt your lives any further than we already are. But I'd like you to visit me every summer, and every other Christmas, and any other time you feel like it. Do you think you can do that?"

Charlie nodded. When she turned her eyes on me, I nodded too, though it took great effort. I didn't like suddenly having obligations in Maryland.

"Also, please understand," she continued, "that I've loved your father a lot. In many ways I still do. That's one of the reasons this is so hard for me, but—" She groped for words, then finally raised her palms and let them fall, a gesture that meant there was nothing else to say.

"But what?" I pressed.

"But I suppose all I can do anymore is follow my heart."

It was the kind of cliché she usually abhorred, and it seemed too an easy escape. "You haven't been following it already," I asked, "with Dad?"

My father made a choked noise like some of his drink had gone down the wrong pipe, though the drink was resting on his stomach. He put a fist to his mouth and leaned forward, his eyes clenched.

When the noise came again he stood and walked out of the room, bobbing on his bad leg.

My mother watched him leave. "Some things are acceptable now," she said, turning to me, "that weren't acceptable when your father and I first got married."

"Like what?"

"Have you seen the legislation coming out of Vermont?"

"What does legislation have to do with *Dad*?"

"I just mean that times have changed, and so have people's view on things."

This seemed so far beside the point that I wasn't even sure how to interrogate it. The best I could do was, "So what?"

"So it's opened new opportunities for people like me."

"And all this time you've just been faking it? With Dad?"

"I was never faking anything."

"Then why do you suddenly want to leave?"

She raised her palms and let them fall into her lap, where they rested like injured birds. But her expression was answer enough. It was a look that said she didn't want to consider the question, at least not in front of her children. It was a look of secrecy.

She turned to Charlie and said, "Tell me how you're feeling about this."

He shrugged, looking at his lap, but it was easy to see that he was barely holding himself together. I felt compelled to speak for him when our mother offered the same question to me: "How are you feeling, Ed? You seem angry."

"I'm not angry. I'm worried about Charlie. He's the one who has to finish growing up without a mom."

Charlie covered his face. His chest heaved and he made awful snuffling noises. Our mother slid over and moved a hand up and down his back, an awkward motion because he was already taller than she was. His size made it easy to forget how young he was. "It's not true," she murmured. "It's not true. I'll always be your mother."

She looked at me and repeated herself, though this time it was more like a reprimand: "I'll always be your mother, Ed."

But I had already been delivered into adulthood. I didn't need a mother. And anyway, she was the one upsetting Charlie, not me. I'd only pointed out the truth about what she was doing to him, and it didn't seem right for her to offer consolation about it. It only emphasized what she was taking away. I wished my father was there to offer him better consolation, but there wasn't anybody to do it but me.

"Come on," I told Charlie, standing up. "Let's make some flyers for London. We can post them around the neighborhood."

But Charlie stayed where he was, convulsing in our mother's arms, lost in some internal landscape of despair. I put out my hand, offering an escape.

"Charlie," I said. "Come on, Charlie."

He just kept crying. He didn't even look up.

"I could use the help," I told him. "Come on. Please? Charlie?"

He didn't respond, and I knew that if he ignored me one more time I'd go wild with the same sadness that was consuming him, so I went off to do it by myself.

Since then I hadn't offered my help, and he hadn't asked.

3

When it came time to enroll at Berkeley, I had a wild idea. Even though my parents' faculty positions gave me tuition discounts at state schools, they had encouraged me to cast a wide net with my college applications. "You never know where opportunities might arise," my father had said. I had taken the advice and applied to schools of various sizes and affiliations all over the state, some I barely knew about, gaining acceptance everywhere except my first choice, Stanford. Now I did a little more research into these other schools and found that one, Sequoia College, way up on the northern California coast, was not only Division III, the lowest level of collegiate athletics, but also had a last-place basketball team.

I never entertained the idea of playing basketball beyond high school because I'd barely played in highschool. But that was only because Russo hadn't understood what I am capable of. I was no star, not like Charlie could be, but hadn't I fought the starters tooth-and-nail in practice? Hadn't I always held my own during our summer pickup games? Hadn't I shown what I was capable of the last game of the season, when I'd scored all seven points before getting pulled? Plus, I would've been impressed if I hadn't improved from playing so much all summer. And anyways, what kind of bums finished last in a Division III conference? It was a long shot, but at Sequioa College I thought I had a chance of making the team.

I chewed the idea over for a few days, not mentioning it to anyone. Then my mother called one Sunday morning and asked me about move-in dates at Berkeley, and I finally found a response longer than a word or two. I told her how much basketball I'd been playing, how much better I was than the coach gave me credit for. I even invented some dazzling compliments from my friends. Then I explained the lowliness of Division III athletics and the miserable team at Sequoia College.

"That's something you want to be part of?" she asked. "The lowest of the low?"

"It's better than nothing."

"Berkeley isn't nothing. It's the best public university in the country. Do you know who they've got in their English department?" She listed a few names I didn't recognize.

"Sequoia has an English department too."

"And Berkeley will have all kinds of intramurals you can sign up for."

"It's not the same."

"Maybe not, but you need to think about your future, Ed. I know you enjoy your sports activities, but the college you attend can have a major impact on your life, and I don't think it's a choice that should be influenced by hobbies and diversions."

I bristled. Basketball wasn't a "diversion," and it wasn't hers to dismiss. "I guess I'm just following my heart," I responded, then found myself grinning as her silence spread before me. As it dragged on, though, I grew afraid that I'd said something irreparable. I was about to ask if she was still there, but she spoke first.

"Have you mentioned this to your father?"

"I haven't decided anything yet, Mom. It's just an idea I had."

"Promise me you'll speak to him before you make any decisions, okay?"

After passing the phone to Charlie, I lay on my bed, still trying to explain myself to her. I *did* think about my future. I didn't *want* to give up Berkeley. But I didn't want to give up basketball either. I loved basketball in a way that was hard to explain—something about it balanced me, made me feel like myself. I always thought I had no choice about giving it up, but maybe I did. I didn't expect my mother to understand. How could she, all the way from Maryland? If she were still around, she could tell me what to do, but she had forfeited that privilege when she'd left.

I went to my father's study to talk to him about it. I preferred his more indirect guidance, his long strings of questions rather than advice, a style that stretched back to at least first grade, when I'd asked him for help writing a love letter. He'd been chopping garlic for dinner but put the knife down and wiped his hands on his apron before taking me to the kitchen table and asking in a measured voice, "What kind of help?" The gist of my response was that I hoped he would come up with a few poetic gems I could plagiarize. When he asked what such a gem might consist of, I said anything that made a girl fall madly in love with me would be perfect, thanks. He asked what made a person fall madly in love, but of course I didn't know. "Well," he followed up, "why do you love her?" That was easy. She was nice. But what did being nice mean? And why did I think she acted that way? And why did it make me fall in love with her? And how could I earn a similar response?

I didn't remember my answers, or what I'd ended up writing in the letter, but I remembered being six years old and smelling the sharp odor of garlic while my father guided me through the paradoxes of love and self-interest.

His office door was closed, as usual. Behind it I could hear him tapping the keyboard. I was reluctant to disturb him, but I knocked, then knocked again. Finally, I cracked the door and peeked inside. He sat facing away in a globe of yellow lamplight, silhouetted by the blue computer screen, typing in staccato bursts. The blinds were drawn, giving the room a dim, subterranean look. It smelled of coffee and stale breath and hot electronics. On the desk, open books were stacked on top of each other like birds coupled in flight. Other books were spread over an end table, spines straining around pencils, pages cluttered with flags of scrap paper. Stacks rose from the floor around him. It looked like there had been a landslide on the armchair.

"Dad?"

The typing stopped, but my father remained perched at the edge of his seat, fingers on the keys. Then he let out his breath and turned. His stubble was coalescing into a scraggly beard, and from the watery distance in his eyes I could see that he had already helped himself to the whiskey bottle standing beside the teacup on the desk. "I'm right in the middle of something, Ed."

"I need to talk to you."

He lifted the cup to his lips, not realizing it was empty until his vigorous tilting produced no liquid. "Give me thirty minutes," he said. "Thirty minutes is all I'm asking."

I shot baskets in the driveway for thirty minutes and then went back in, but his door was still closed. I made a tuna sandwich on sourdough and ate it with potato chips and ginger ale, listening to Charlie eke out slow solos on his guitar upstairs. I did the dishes that had been accumulating in the sink all week, surprised at how long it took. When I was finished, the study door was still closed, the keyboard still chattering.

I went up to Charlie's room instead. It was silent inside, but when I pushed the door open I found him sitting on the floor wearing big earphones, an empty CD case in his lap. He looked at me with frightened eyes, then lunged for his stereo and threw the CD case in a drawer and mumbled, "Get out of my room," though I was only standing in the doorway.

"What are you listening to?"

"Nothing."

I walked in, ignoring Charlie's protests, and opened the drawer. The album cover showed a hollow-eyed man wearing a white latex suit that gave him breasts and ambiguous genitalia. "Marilyn Manson?" I said. "You like this crap?"

"I'm just listening to it."

"The guy is a freak, Charlie. Look at him."

"I already have."

"Those kids who shot up Columbine last year? This is what they listened to."

But he had stopped paying attention. He was looking away with hard eyes, waiting for me to leave.

"Anyway," I said, "I was wondering if you'd feed me the ball for a little while. I want to work on a new move."

"I don't feel like it."

"I'm trying to get this new move down because I think I'm going to try out for the basketball team at Sequoia College instead of going to Berkeley."

"Why?"

"What do you mean *why*? It's a chance to play college basketball."

"What's so great about that?"

"Are you serious? It's college basketball. Plus, it's like Coach Russo says. A team is a family, and I'm going to need one of those next year."

"You already have a family."

"Yeah, except for Mom. And Dad too, pretty much. Hey, maybe I could redshirt and keep my eligibility for a fifth year, then transfer to whatever college you end up playing for. We could make it part of your recruitment. Be teammates for a year."

He slipped the headphones back over his ears, and it made something in my chest go jagged.

"Look, will you just come feed me the ball for a little while? I'm sorry I embarrassed you about listening to Marilyn Manson."

"I'm not embarrassed. I can listen to whatever I want."

"Are you coming or not?"

"I said I don't feel like it."

"Please?"

He didn't answer.

"Fine." I tossed the CD case at him. "Have fun with your boyfriend."

Instead of practicing the move on my own, though, I called Sequoia College, just to see if it was even possible to enroll there so late. A man with an East Indian accent asked how he could be of service, then assured me that it wasn't too late. Some of their fall classes had already filled, he said, but they would be happy to have me. I smiled at the phone, shook my head, breathed a few airy laughs into the receiver. *Happy to have me.* I could tell from the man's voice that it was quite a coup, stealing a student from Berkeley, and I was embarrassed to feel so wanted, so appreciated. I assured the man that my decision was based solely on athletics, but I hadn't made up my mind to go through with it until that moment.

***

I'd applied to the school only because of its name. Our family had once visited the giant redwoods and sequoias inland from the Northern California coast, and I could still remember the vertigo and astonishment of it. We'd tried a couple short hikes, but our father's limp and our mother's hatred of exercise kept us from getting very far, so mostly we drove down bumpy avenues, Charlie and I leaning from opposite windows, looking up. Otherwise we relaxed at the campsite, our parents cooking and reading and enjoying slow games of Scrabble and chess. Charlie and I were content to pan for gold in the stream, search for four-leaf clover, pile dead wood into a teepee, poke the campfire with sticks, all the time surrounded by the giant trunks whose scale never seemed to diminish. At night Charlie and I giggled ourselves to exhaustion in our separate tent and synchronized our watches for midnight snacks, though more often than not, Charlie would wake fearfully before midnight, hearing what he thought was a mountain lion or grizzly bear. When his worrying finally spooked me, we would both go charging for our parents' tent, where everyone was safe.

At the end of the trip our father had handed his camera to a stranger and lined us up in front of a tree trunk as wide as a building, older than Jesus. The photo was supposed to go on our Christmas card, but we ended up using one he'd snapped upon our arrival, Charlie and me in the middle of a road, gazing in amazement at the distant canopy while yellow light fell around us. A copy of it had been on the mantel until our mother left, and it was probably responsible for my notion of a dim campus secluded in these forests, a quad full of sword ferns and giant clover, edged by wooden footbridges, everything smelling of pine and campfire and cold mineral water.

And so I felt hopelessly stupid when I followed my father's Volvo into an asphalt-blighted town called Conrad Park, a low expanse of car dealerships and appliance repair shops and discount grocery stores with hand-lettered signs in the windows. We stopped for lunch in a café that looked like a commercial office with a grill added in the conference room. The TV inside was tuned to a program that showed a man draped in camouflage kneeling by a dead elk and gesturing at the arrow standing up from its shoulder. My father glanced at me several times, but he didn't say anything about Berkeley, and neither did I. We'd said all we needed to when I'd broken the news.

"College of the *what?*" he'd responded, though he'd heard me perfectly well. He'd been waiting for a frozen burrito to heat, leaning against the kitchen counter and looking into space while the microwave droned.

"Sequoia College," I said. "Like the big trees?"

"Ed, you got into Berkeley. You barely have to pay tuition. I'll bet every single student at this college of the—"

"Sequoia College."

"I'll bet every single student would give their right arm to trade places with you."

His vehemence startled me. I had expected the kind of dispassionate conversation I was used to, in which we tested ideas without allegiance to them, each of us asking questions, switching sides, complimenting new perspectives before we set to work testing their integrity. And it was with the hope of restoring that kind of calm and reasonable exploration that I answered, "It's like you said, you never know where opportunities are going to come from, right?"

"I meant *financial* opportunities. Scholarships. Prizes. We might not have the resources that some families do, especially with your mother gone, but the one thing we do have is our tuition discount. But it's only good at state schools."

"What if I paid tuition myself?"

"Do you have any idea how much money you're talking about? It would be an incredible waste—and burden. And for what? Just to try out for a team that you're probably not even—Ed, are you really good enough to play in college?"

These were so unlike the responses I'd expected from him that my only reaction was defensiveness. "Don't worry about that," I told him.

"Is anyone else from your team playing in college? The *starters*, for instance?"

"None of them are trying out for a team this bad."

"Listen to yourself. This is what you want to mortgage your future for?"

To me it seemed more like a return on investment. I knew it would involve sacrifice, financial and otherwise, but the rewards of joining a college team seemed much more valuable than anything as abstract as imaginary figures on some future balance sheet.

The safety I'd always felt talking with my father, however, was gone. By staking out one side, he had staked me to the other, and each criticism he lobbed over the border fell on me like a personal insult. It was as much an objection to this new style of conversation as a statement of my intentions when I announced, "It's my decision."

The microwave beeped. My father had been standing pinned against the counter, gripping it with both hands, but his expression loosened as he cast a glance toward the steaming burrito, as if weighing his hunger against his disapproval. When his eyes came back to me, they had nothing in them but blank resignation. "Do whatever makes you happy," he said. "That's the way the world operates these days, apparently."

Now, on campus, my father could remind me of his arguments just by glancing around. The lawns were brown and dead, baking under a hot August sun. Runty saplings were staked to squares of dirt that looked no more capable of absorbing water than the cement from which they were cut. Hot waves of doubt broke over me, pushing trickles of sweat down my ribs, but it was too late to change anything, so we traversed the campus in a competition of productivity—navigating the checklist for parking permits and keys and identification cards and facility tours, my father working hard to make himself useful while I worked hard to show I didn't need any help.

At the bookstore, while I tried to comprehend the system for locating texts, he harrumphed over the selections for the literature courses, then warned, "This fellow Rivaldi, I'd stay away from him." I allowed him to help me select sundries at the Wal-Mart, hangers and laundry detergent and pencils, but I refused to let him pay. Instead I handed over the little cash left from my loans, a sum so big it made the few bills in my wallet seem as inconsequential as play money.

After that he relented. He had his own classes to prepare for, he said, and I was glad to see him go. I was sick of waiting for this small, sedentary man to drag his lame foot from building to building, sick of watching other families step off the curb to pass us. He rolled down the Volvo's window before pulling away but just sat there in his idling car, looking at me through sunglasses.

"What?" I asked.

"My boy." His mouth bent and his voice turned husky. "In college."

***

I stood in line for an hour to meet with an adviser. She was a quick-talking woman who greeted me kindly before looking over my registration form, then asked if I had the necessary prerequisites for the literature courses I'd selected. I said I didn't know, they'd just sounded interesting. "Your first term can be a bit of an adjustment," she said, and encouraged me to get some lower-level requirements out of the way. I took the advice, though I wasn't worried about adjustment. I'd been in college classrooms since I was a kid, Charlie coloring beside me while I watched my parents, trying to follow their lessons until an unexplained reference threw me. Everything that followed would always seem as meaningful and esoteric as a secret knock. My whole life I'd been eager to peek behind the door it opened, which was the reason I'd signed up for all the lit courses.

My roommate, Ezra, was pale and gaunt with black eyebrows that grew together. His sinuous hands seemed suited for drawing music from grand pianos, but he used them for nothing, as far as I could tell, except punching at his video game controller. I often woke to the frantic tapping in the morning and fell asleep to it at night. Ezra seemed timorous and insecure when he spoke to me but had no problem cackling into his headset with unrestrained rancor or shouting obscenities so profane they shocked even me. By the end of the first month he was gone, leaving behind only a flattened bag of Cheetos, and I enjoyed the privilege of living alone. It was a relief, but some nights I glanced at the stripped mattress across the room and wished the college would fill it.

My lower-level courses were held in windowless concrete shells that looked like old multiplex movie theaters. I had one class in a trailer with latticework around the bottom and wallpaper inside patterned to look like wood. The instructors mostly reviewed elementary concepts I was already familiar with, though they delivered them with warnings and exhortations, as though it was difficult material that they doubted we could grasp.

And indeed, the other students seemed barely capable of following instructions. My composition professor, a bony woman who wore shawls to class and had a streak of purple in her hair, gave a long lesson about how to write introductions without resorting to summary. Afterward, during an exercise in which we were supposed to practice these strategies, the other members of my small group insisted so adamantly on writing the kind of summary we were supposed to avoid that I broke from them and did it on my own, correctly. The instructor applauded when I read it aloud, but this kind of thing didn't win me many friends. I longed for basketball season.

I made an appointment to visit the coach, Rick Carmichael. He was a square-jawed, well-proportioned man in his forties who had once been the body model for an infomercial exercise contraption. He shook my hand over his desk, then sat with impeccable posture, slicing the air at his chest with little karate chops as he explained that the team didn't have any formal tryout sessions, per se, but that if I was interested in playing I could start attending the team "shoot-arounds"—he fingered quotation marks into the air—every weekday at three. These were just some drills and scrimmages to stay sharp, nothing he, the coach, knew too much about, since he, the coach, could not have any involvement, per NCAA/NAIA season-limitation regulations. He paused to flash his white, winsome smile. "The older players run things," he said. "Show up and tell them you're interested in walking on. They'll set you up."

He offered his hand, adding, "Of course, we'll have to trim the roster to twelve when the season begins."

The next day, I was so eager and nervous that I dressed down in my dorm room more than an hour early. I put on my best mesh shorts and a mesh jersey I'd picked up at a summer camp. I agonized over ankle socks or knee-highs. Then I replaced the jersey with a T-shirt, not wanting to look like I was trying too hard. I selected ankle socks, two per foot, and then pulled out the new high-tops I'd bought with my summer wages for this specific purpose, taking a moment to enjoy their aroma of fresh upholstery. Once dressed, I set my feet in a wide stance and dribbled a ball in slow figure eights around my ankles until the kid below me banged on the ceiling. I stood there a few moments with the ball in my hands, flipping it back and forth. I figured I might as well head down early. It would be good to spend some time handling the ball, shooting, making sure I was sharp. I wanted to make a good impression on my new teammates.

It was a mild day, the sun a high, heatless lamp, the parking lots awash with twinkling glass. The shrubs were starting to turn, their leaves fluorescent like sour candies. The students I passed had messy hair and grubby sweatshirts that broke the impression that this was all just a summer camp, soon over. At first the girls on campus had spent afternoons sunbathing in bikinis, the boys running for Frisbees with their shirts off, everyone traveling in packs with their sunglasses on, flip-flops snapping, smelling of sunscreen. Now it was clear that we were here for the long haul, for purposes other than fun, and it made me happy to remember my own purpose.

I entered the artificial light of the gym with its odors of floor varnish and stale sweat. The walls were lined at the bottom with stacked bleachers, at the top with big panels of acoustic material. The high ceiling was full of steel rafters and angled spotlights, dim above the hanging lamps that buzzed and flickered inside their wire cages. It reminded me of getting off the bus and walking into another school's gym with my old teammates, all of us in collars and neckties. I dribbled the ball a few times just for the sound of it, the single beat thumping in the big empty theater, my favorite sound in the world.

I had worked up a light sweat by the time the other players started to arrive. The first few carried their gym bags to the far side and got busy preparing themselves, stripping sweatshirts and sweat-pants, applying kneepads and sweatbands, taping fingers, tightening laces, talking in low voices and laughing. I was doing work under the hoop, flipping the ball in with my right hand, then my left, not letting it touch the floor, trying to look casual, unconcerned, oblivious to their presence while I watched them from the corner of my eye. I ranged out for jump shots, silently cursing myself each time I missed.

More players came. Some were stretching and some were thumping balls around, trying out lazy spin moves, changing direction with low oblique dribbles, draining set shots from long range. They all wore matching practice uniforms, crimson mesh shorts and crimson mesh jerseys. Before I knew what was happening they had started a lay-up drill at the far end, two lines facing away from me, players swooping in from one side to kiss the ball off the glass, players from the other side tearing it from the net and firing it back out.

I watched them in a paralysis of longing and embarrassment, not knowing how to join. They all looked big and fast, and I started to appreciate the difference between high school and collegiate athletics. I was both relieved and terrified when the drill dismantled and one of the players came jogging down, locking eyes with me in a way that meant he had something to say but didn't want to shout across the gym. He was Black and much taller than me, his arms covered with dark tattoos. He looked old, like a real adult. "Hey," he said kindly, and I was about to return the greeting when he continued, "the college team uses this court for practice on weekdays."

Somewhere behind the buzz of panic lay the calm knowledge that I only had to say, "Yeah, that's what I'm here for," and I would be invited to join them. But at the moment I was looking at myself though this other player's eyes, and I had to decide in an instant whether I wanted to confirm that vision or correct it, whether I wanted to be some random kid shooting by himself in an empty gym, not knowing better, or to risk further humiliation by announcing that I did know better, that I'd thought I was good enough to join them. The rest of the team was already in three rows along the baseline, facing me, the men in the middle holding balls against their hips, ready to run, waiting for me to clear out of their way. They looked comfortable, familiar with their drill and with each other in a way that clearly excluded me. I heard myself say, "Oh, okay," and then I was walking off the court in a confusion of shame and disappointment.

4

I called Berkeley, but it turned out that transferring was different from enrolling. Besides, I had already taken out the loan, and I didn't like the idea of wasting all that money. Who knew if my father's tuition discount still applied, or if he would still be willing to help me after the big fuss I'd made?

I tried calling him once, but Charlie answered and said he was out. It made me nervous, Charlie there by himself, and I had to remind myself he wasn't a little kid anymore. I asked him to tell our father I had called, then added, "It's not like the movies, you know. It isn't all parties and fun in college."

"It isn't in eighth grade, either."

"I know. That was the year Jeff Armbruster grew his hair out and ditched me. Remember him?"

"Yeah. He always said I was too slow to ride bikes with you, and you always listened to him."

"You *were* too slow. You were a little kid."

"Not my fault."

"Plus, Jeff Armbruster was my only real friend for a couple years. When he started going off with the smokers, I remember looking around the cafeteria and thinking, well, maybe I just won't eat lunch anymore."

"Did you?"

"No. That was about the time I joined the basketball team. But for a couple weeks I remember scarfing down my sandwich by my locker, then spending the whole lunch period reading magazines in the library. That's kind of what college feels like, actually."

"So come back."

"Home? I can't. Besides, most of my friends are gone. Mom's gone. Dad practically is too."

"I'm here," Charlie said.

I paced from the window to the closet. "Is it pretty awful?"

"Not really. I get to do whatever I want."

I kicked my shower sandals. Eighth graders shouldn't get to do whatever they wanted. That was just what I'd meant about growing up without a mom. "Well, don't do anything stupid," I said.

For a moment he didn't respond. "Thanks for the advice," he said, then hung up.

My father never called back, and I didn't know whether to blame him or Charlie for it. I called once more but nobody answered, and it made me feel so terrible that I didn't try again. Just the idea of the phone ringing while Charlie listened to his headphones and my father clicked his keyboard was enough to make up my mind to stay.

I found myself wishing I could ask my mother what to do. Unlike my father, she offered solutions instead of perspective. When my front teeth had come in so large and protuberant that the other kids started calling me Mr. Ed, my father only asked frustrating questions about their inner lives, whereas my mother told me to shrug and respond, "My teeth can be fixed but your personality can't." When that didn't work, she said we would just have to go ahead and get my teeth fixed, and she spent the next two summers teaching extra courses to pay for the orthodontia that accomplished it. That was her personality, to tackle each small facet of a problem as it arose until the whole mess was behind her. But I couldn't stand the idea of her offering that kind of advice from Maryland, or the idea of having to offer her gratitude in return.

***

That weekend I recruited some acquaintances for a pickup game. They showed up to the court wearing jeans, collared shirts, hiking boots. They dragged along other friends, men with ponytails, women wearing jewelry and sandals. During warmups they launched ridiculous shots, finding each more hilarious than the last. They called trite phrases to each other like kids on a playground—"I'm open!" and "he shoots, he scores!"—nobody knowing they should be embarrassed about it, except me. During the game they dribbled with slow, mechanical stiffness, heads down, drifting toward an open spot that held no advantage, then stopped, made a few wild pump fakes, and waited for someone to relieve them of the ball. The defenders bumbled around on locked knees, allowing plenty of room until the player was done dribbling, and then attacked with a sort of stiff-armed bear hug from which the player with the ball leaned away with increasing desperation. When I got the ball, I passed to someone else. On defense, I just stood there with my arms out. It wasn't a real game.

The next week I tried playing at open gym with other castoffs, but it was an impersonal, anonymous brand of basketball. You didn't say hello. You didn't know anything about your teammates. Nobody really cared if you played well. You won or you lost, and then you disbanded without saying goodbye.

I saw some of the college players around campus. I didn't recognize their faces but knew who they were from their height, their posture, their clothes, their expressions of indifference, as if what happened off the court didn't count. They were at the dining hall, at football games, at the library and the bookstore, on sidewalks and at parties and riding in old cars with their long legs folded up. They walked with languorous strides and slouched in their seats, faces cool, tranquil with higher purpose and fatigue, always together in twos and threes. I watched them with something like lust until my feelings of jealousy and exile forced me to leave whatever arena I was at that moment occupying.

For a couple weeks I considered my options. I could become the team manager, a position that would allow me to collect towels and distribute water bottles and haul equipment off the bus. But the team probably already had a manager, and anyway, it seemed beneath me. I thought about finding a major that would give me a career in sports business or sports medicine, but the results seemed too distant. I thought about becoming one of those superfans who painted their faces and led the crowd through chants, but it wasn't my personality.

Instead, I joined the student newspaper. The editor, Patricia Caldwell, was a round-faced woman whose eyes shone with irony and wit. She said she was thrilled to find a new sports reporter. Didn't I know how hard it was to find jocks who could spell? I laughed uneasily, but in truth I was relieved that I still fit the designation.

Patricia had me attend the weekly reporters meeting in a one-room Quonset hut at the edge of campus, barely big enough for its makeshift conference table and the newspaper-making paraphernalia that surrounded it. On one side was a bank of desktop computers, on the other side file cabinets and a huge printer, along with several relics from pre-digital production: a light table, a paper-cutter, a case of X-Acto knives. Patricia introduced me to Gilbert Platt, the sports editor, a husky, unshaven student in a Steelers jersey. In a low monotone he told me that sports writing was a lot like rocket science, then gave me a long blank stare.

He assigned me women's soccer, and I constructed my first article around the formula he had described. I was proud of it, so I was surprised when on production night the copy editor touched her

French braid and said, "It's not as bad as it looks." She held up three pages, bleeding red ink, which I finally recognized as my article. "It's really good for a first try," she added. With patience and solicitude and many tender, apologetic smiles, she showed me my buried lede, inappropriate quote tags, violations of numerical style, usage problems, lapses in objectivity, unanswered questions, inadequate number of sources, and other problems. I came away feeling battered but grateful. It was more than I'd learned in any class.

By the time winter sports rolled around, I had improved enough to earn my preferred assignment—men's basketball. This allowed me to attend the team's practices, enter their locker room after home games, even visit players' dorm rooms and apartments, as long as my notepad was open. I got to know the team captain who had thrown me off the court that day, a senior named Kenyon Cook. I liked his formality during our interviews, the way he turned away from the laughter of his teammates and let his face settle into a sober, thoughtful expression as he considered my question. I also liked A.C. Sullinger, a dazzling point guard who had played Division I his freshman year before transferring to Sequoia. He said he cared about academics more than basketball and preferred the forest to the city. I wondered what academics and forests he was referring to, since Sequoia didn't seem to offer much of either. My favorite of favorites was a sweet-shooting lefty named Knute Buhner, a talented freshman who'd come to Sequoia because he was shameless on defense, the kind of player who might score thirty points but give up forty. He joked about it during our interviews, along with everything else that came up. There were times he got me laughing so hard that I forgot the list of questions on my notepad, or that I had to leave once I exhausted them.

I didn't think any of these players recognized me from that day in the gym, but even if they did, it hardly mattered, because I'd handled the situation so well. I thought about the episode often, feeling the danger of it, and I was grateful that I had trusted my instincts, that I had walked away rather than trying to get involved.

They would think I was a gym rat, a lover of the game, a reporter who also played a little, not some deluded failure who had given up Berkeley to watch them practice lay-ins.

The only one who knew for sure was Coach Carmichael, and at first I was embarrassed to be in his presence. But he treated me so kindly, so much like an extended member of the team, that I quickly got over it. He referred to the players by their nicknames, as if I were on those kinds of terms with them as well. He got me a seat at the courtside press table during games. He gave me his home phone number for nights I was on a deadline, and when I called him there, he answered.

***

One weekend Patricia Caldwell had a little get-together in her apartment, a low-key affair featuring wine coolers and cheap hors d'oeuvres, all the lights blazing. She'd invited the entire newspaper staff, reporters included, and I found myself playing a drinking game with a few people I didn't know and gulping sweetened alcohol more quickly than I should have. When the game ended, I drifted into conversation with the girl sitting next to me, a columnist named Brittany Mercer. She was a senior, slim and well-tanned, her bleached hair styled to look like ramen noodles. She was telling me that she hated when people complained about divorce. "It's like, oh God, big deal, everyone gets divorced now," she said. "I'm always like, do you have any idea what's been going on in Bosnia? Have you ever heard of apartheid? Matthew Shepard gets killed and our President gets impeached, but no, please, tell me about how awful your parents' divorce was."

I watched her lips move and melted with agreement.

When she asked why my parents had split up, I said I suspected my mother of an affair. "You should ask her," Brittany said. "I did. I asked my dad straight up if there was another woman, and he was like, that's not the point. And I was like, no, that pretty much *is* the point."

"At least you were asking your dad."

She looked at me, confused.

"About whether there was another woman."

Later, she put her hand on my knee, and the next thing I knew we were lying in a carpeted hallway as discreetly as we could, swirling our tongues in each other's mouths. Afterward I offered to walk her home. It was drizzling and very dark between the orange pools of lamplight but that didn't stop us from pushing each other against truck cabs and alley walls, the soft rain wetting our faces and the smell of her hair closing over us.

When we arrived, Brittany mentioned that her roommate was gone. I thought it meant we could continue making out, but it turned out to mean much more. It was my first time, though I didn't tell her that. I just followed her lead and did what my body told me to, not knowing if it was right or wrong and not caring. Mostly, I was astonished at my luck and overcome by desire. Afterward, naked and sated, I lay awake for many hours, running my fingers through her sticky hair, counting the jewels that climbed the rim of her perfect ear, stunned that the world could feel so right.

***

In the days that followed, I couldn't stop thinking about Brittany Mercer. I knew it had probably been a fling, but if she had selected me for a fling, why not more? The problem was that I wasn't sure how to pursue her. In high school there had been a certain protocol, but trying it with a college senior seemed about as wise as wearing your letterman's jacket around campus.

I tried to court her more like an adult, and I hoped it was only because I was doing it incorrectly that she reacted with such frigidity. She was always busy, always retreating, and so I kept trying out new tactics—putting my hand on hers at the reporters meeting, calling to ask how her day had gone, trying to start conversations about Slobodan Milosevic and Nelson Mandela after an afternoon of research at the library. I'd learned about Matthew Shepard too, but it seemed too horrific to talk about. Two years earlier he'd been beaten, dragged behind a truck, and set on fire for being gay. Besides, Brittany was suddenly indifferent to all of it.

Then one evening I stopped by her apartment to ask about her plans Saturday night, thinking I might try taking her to dinner. "Look," she said, leaning against the doorway, "you're a sweet kid." But then she only let out her breath, her eyes sliding away.

"I think you're sweet too," I said.

"Saturday I'm going to a house party."

"Do you want me to pick you up?"

She closed her eyes. "Sure. Come around nine."

I arrived at nine sharp. Brittany looked slim and cold in her little black dress, which explained her air of distraction, I thought. She spent the drive with her arms folded around her, looking out the window, telling me only where to turn, and then walked quickly from my car. I followed closely, knowing better than to press my luck with questions.

We came to a place where people were thronged in the yard, holding red cups and cigarettes. We made our way through them to the sweltering inside, where lights flashed and music thumped. After we'd filled our plastic cups with the pineapple-clotted brine in the bathtub, she headed straight for the dance floor. I danced nearby, but she kept moving away from me, grinding provocatively against other men. At first I chose to be secure enough to not let it bother me, but finally I couldn't take it. I went to refill my plastic cup from the bathtub.

I carried the drink to the back porch, where a few people in baggy clothes were passing around a joint. I'd never seen one before, having had too much at stake during high school to risk getting in trouble, but I knew what it was from the way they held it in pinched fingertips, pencil-wise, sucking the coal bright. Why not hold it like a cigarette, I wondered, tucked in the crotch of two straight fingers? Some of the guys had thin beards and tattoos.

The women had long hair and wore things like thermal shirts and flannels. They all seemed wise and sophisticated and casually beautiful. I didn't understand what they were talking about, but I knew I didn't want to be standing alone if Brittany came looking for me, as I hoped she would.

Then the guy next to me was saying, "Hey," and jabbing the joint in my direction, and I didn't know what to do. I took it, scissoring it between two fingers like a cigarette, afraid of looking like a poser if I mimicked them too precisely. I drew smoke into my mouth without inhaling, the way Val Lambright had taught me to handle a cigar after we'd won the conference title our junior year. Then I passed the joint on and breathed through my nose, waiting with distended cheeks for the drug to take effect. After a time, I noticed that everyone was watching me, so I blew out the smoke, sighing with relief as they had.

They all lost it. They were doubled over, slapping their knees, wiping their eyes, coughing. Some guy squealed, "Fucking *jocks!*"

I gulped my punch until it was gone, then turned and walked to the bathtub for another refill, my limbs trembling. By the time I returned to the dance floor, muttering all the things I should have said, Brittany had her mouth locked on someone else's. He was an Asian-looking guy with muscular shoulders, his sleeves pushed up to show lumpy biceps, his hair spiked stylishly. He was shorter than Brittany, so she had to tilt her face down to meet his mouth, and for some reason that was the most upsetting part of the spectacle. Something dangerous stirred inside me, some wildness. I joined the dancers, still muttering, and long after the bathtub punch was gone, long after Brittany had left with the guy, I danced, sweating and breathless, driving away the women I approached, not caring.

The next morning, waking alone in my coiled sheets—mouth swampy and forehead pounding—I could still feel the wildness stalking inside me. It produced such an agitation of restlessness and energy that all I could think to do was lace up my basketball shoes and run. I went around campus twice, coughing and spitting, drenched in thick sweat. But even as I came upon my dorm a second time, I didn't feel like stopping, so I ventured out again, clomping down sidewalks in parts of town I didn't know, my legs heavy, the cramps stabbing hard, my lungs making outrageous demands. When upsetting images sprang to mind—Brittany's face tilted down, bumbling defenders in hiking boots, Matthew Shepard losing his flesh—I ran harder. As the physical pain rose through me, the images became remote, irrelevant, until finally they had nothing to do with me.

After that I ran several times a week. I wore my swishing basketball shorts and the heavy high-tops I'd bought for tryouts, and I took it slow and easy, keeping my breathing under control. I explored the different sectors of Conrad Park, traversing its cracked boulevards and weedy residential streets and poorly maintained little parks. I ranged out to the strip malls and diners, the pawn shops, the locksmith, the adult store, the check-cashing businesses with blinking neon signs. I went by the bland concrete vaults of a storage facility, a manufacturing plant that belched white smoke, a welding bay where the torches were streaks of blue light behind windows tinted black. I circled a wrecking yard, its butte of used tires protected by concertina wire.

And then I began to range out further, into places I didn't think existed in Conrad Park, wooded hills where no lines were painted on the roads, vast neighborhoods where mansions sat stylishly on manicured lawns. I found a pasture with horses and a little marijuana plantation. I found a dirt trail that took me onto a bluff where in the distance I could see the rocky coastline and, beyond that, the sparkling immensity of the ocean.

My mind wandered while I ran. I saw London running excited circles on someone else's lawn, Charlie practicing post moves in the driveway by himself, my father offering open-ended questions to students indistinguishable from me, my mother lying in bed with a blank-faced woman. These visions came to me unbidden but without danger, playing across my mind like swallows over still water. I always came back through campus feeling different, as though I had experienced something that set me apart, and I found that I could gaze at the other students like zoo animals—curious creatures that I liked very much, as long as they couldn't hurt me.

***

My mother was still making her Sunday morning calls, and although I had plenty to say now about my new life, I kept my answers as brief as possible. No, I hadn't tried out for the basketball team. No, I hadn't heard of Proposition 22. No, I hadn't met any girls. It was too painful to elaborate, and I started to dread the ringing phone. So when a few guys from the dorm began congregating in the lounge on Sunday mornings to watch football games, I was happy to join them, partly because it was nice to be around other former athletes, even if most of them had been linemen or wrestlers, and partly to escape my room, my telephone, my mother. She left messages, but I didn't bother calling back. We never really talked anyway—we just traded information. She was mistaking that for a relationship, but I knew better.

Then one day I was drinking from the vat of spiked coffee the guys had smuggled in when another political ad came on, this one supporting the proposition my mother had mentioned. It would make same-sex marriage illegal in California, which confused me. Wasn't it illegal already? Either way, it made me wonder why my mother had to go all the way to Maryland to get involved in political advocacy. Why wasn't she here, fighting Prop 22? Weren't there plenty of gay people in California? I remembered her look of secrecy when I'd asked her about it during the family meeting, then got to thinking about what Brittany Mercer had said about confronting her father.

By halftime I was tipsy, and while the other guys piled out the front door, I trudged up to my room, stumbling once. I found my mother's phone number on the list I had compiled before leaving town, and my heart thumped as I stood at the window listening to the line ring.

When my mother picked up, I said, "So, who is he?"

"Who's who?"

"The man you left Dad for."

Outside, the guys were trying to pelt each other with a Nerf football on the quad's dead grass, their breath tumbling up into the sunshine.

"Maybe I wasn't being clear," she said.

"Oh you were clear all right but I can see through all that."

"Did your father tell you there was someone else?"

"No. But if you hate men so much then how could you have ended up married to one in the first place? If you hate men so much then how am I alive at all?"

"I don't hate men. Is that what you think?"

One of the guys was writhing on the sidewalk with his hands between his legs while the others fell over laughing.

"All I'm saying is that it doesn't add up," I told her. "You don't spend twenty years happily married to a man if you're a lesbian. Either you're lying about being a lesbian, or you've been miserable for the last twenty years and lying about that."

"Sexuality isn't like a light switch, Ed, where it's either on or off. There's a whole spectrum of—"

"I'm sick of all that. I just want an answer to my question. Who's in Maryland?"

The guy who'd been on the ground was chasing the others into the street, football cocked by his ear. He kept pump-faking, and the one he was chasing kept ducking and recoiling. The others dispersed and circled back, trailing ragged clouds of laughter.

"All right," my mother said, and there was a finality in her voice that iced my stomach. "I wasn't intending to hide anything from you. I just didn't think it was necessary to give you every last detail, and I didn't want to overwhelm you with too much all at once. But I can see that you're struggling with all this, so maybe honesty is the best policy."

I turned from the window and the room changed shape, as if I had taken two steps back from every direction.

"It's true that I met someone while I was here last year," she said. "It wasn't something I ever planned on, but it happened, and afterward it was like something dormant inside me my whole life had suddenly woken up. It wasn't something I had any control over. It wasn't a conscious choice. I hope you know that."

So many bad feelings rushed through me that I didn't even know what they were.

"Also, I want you to know that this wasn't just—I'm in love with her, Ed, and I hope you'll be able to see that, rather than just fixating on her—role. She's a special woman. She's brave and supportive and she's been through a lot. She's got two kids of her own—no father, not ever—and she works as a technical writer, which means—you know how everything comes with instructions and warnings and things like that? She writes those. She's also a voracious reader and very funny once she comes out of her shell. Her name is Jane."

The name opened a cool little recess of scorn that I was relieved to enter. "What's her last name?" I said. "Doe? Is she *plain*?"

My mother blew a long breath from her nostrils. The air roared in the receiver. "I know this must be hard for you. It isn't easy for me either, you know."

"It's not hard. It's just the most inconspicuous name I've ever heard. It's the kind of name you'd make up if you had to make up a name on the spot."

"I'm not making anything up."

"Well then, it's just like I thought. You *did* have an affair."

"It was more like a discovery, Ed, and to be perfectly honest with you, I'm proud of myself for it."

"When you get married, you don't get to be with anyone else. That's what marriage means. So what if it's a woman? You still broke your promise to Dad. You're still a … a … an *adulterer*, and so is this Jane, and as far as I'm concerned—"

But my mother was making strange noises, so I stopped. After a time I realized she was crying. I turned to the window, shame and satisfaction wrestling inside me. The guys were walking back toward the dorm, tossing the ball, and suddenly I wanted nothing more than to end this conversation and join them, to lose myself in the noise of the football game, the dry heat and old upholstery of the dorm lounge, the stupefying alcohol.

"It gives me a lot of pain," my mother said, voice tight, "to know what I'm putting you through."

"Well, that's probably as it should be."

"I hope you understand better someday."

"I understand now," I told her, then pressed the button to hang up, though I continued to stand there, looking down at the pattern of tiny holes where sound escaped. I felt like smashing the phone into the wall but instead I lowered it gently into the receiver, turned off the ringer, and then didn't touch it the rest of the term except to conduct interviews for my basketball articles. I knew I was probably missing calls from friends, but I didn't want to talk to them either. I wanted people to just leave me alone.

5

When I left campus for winter break, however, I wanted nothing more than to play basketball with all my old friends. As I sped down the highway, low morning sunlight flashing between the coastal pines, I imagined the switches, the mismatches, the help defense, the extra passes, the last few plays before an early dusk closed over us. It spread so much warmth and anticipation through me that I had to turn up the radio, roll down the window, and shout lyrics into the frigid wind. I pretended they were there in the car with me, Kyle Andrews and Seth Feldman and all the rest, and I did silly dance moves for them, shimmying my shoulders, pumping my fists, twirling an invisible lasso. I pointed at other drivers, serenading them behind two layers of glass.

Fog was slipping in from Monterey Bay. I plunged in, and the sun became a pale dish. Water vapor greased the windshield. Road signs appeared suddenly, blurred by the mist. The oncoming cars were preceded by auras of light and then disappeared in a swirling red miasma. When I pulled into the driveway, I found an obscure figure drifting around on spread legs, undertaking some laborious jumping motion. I cut the engine and heard the slide of ball bearings, the clatter of wood on asphalt. It was a skateboard, and the figure was Charlie. He wasn't having much success getting the thing off the ground but didn't seem to mind. I got out and stood watching him, then grew tired of waiting for a greeting and carried my bags to the house.

"You should be working on your post moves," I told him as I passed.

Inside, it was quiet and dim. There were no Christmas lights, no tree, no decorations of any kind. I went to my father's office, knocked on the closed door, and waited, listening to the scrape of a chair and several rounds of throat clearing. Finally the door opened, and the man behind it was only vaguely familiar. He had kept the beard, which was now bushy and trimmed at the neck and startlingly gray. It made him look like somebody's grandfather. He seemed to be waiting for me to say what I wanted.

"I'm home," I said.

"So you are. Welcome back."

After a moment of hesitation, we undertook the unfamiliar task of hugging and executed it badly.

"Why isn't any of the Christmas stuff up?" I asked.

"Oh, I didn't have the energy for all that. I thought you boys were probably a little old for it anyway."

"Maybe I am," I agreed. "But what about Charlie?"

"Go ask him."

Charlie looked different too. His face had elongated further, making his chin prominent and giving him a doleful appearance. His acne had worsened into a swollen mask that his fingers were constantly excavating. His hair was shaggy, and he covered it with a flat-billed Giants cap, a style I didn't understand. Growing up, my friends and I had developed elaborate strategies to give our bills a perfect curve. He had also grown another two inches. He stood patiently while I stretched the tape measure from the floor but then shrugged off my congratulations about being the tallest member of the family, his aching face locked with boredom. "Can I go now?" he said.

"Wait. How do you feel about not having any Christmas decorations up?"

He was already heading for the stairs. "I don't care."

"Not even about a tree?"

"Why should I?"

He didn't mean it as a question, so I didn't respond, but I didn't understand everyone's sudden indifference. Even last year we'd huddled around the glowing tree on Christmas Eve to sip eggnog and read the same children's books as always. Charlie and I had both been over six feet tall, and our parents had been stiff and uncomfortable on the floor, but it had rekindled some of the magic and excitement of the holiday. So had the other routines—waking at seven the next morning, shuffling into the family room together, seeing the cookies reduced to crumbs and the stockings lumpy with tangerines. "Santa was here," our father had said, grinning and winking, pretending it was all for irony, because admitting otherwise would have ruined it, just as it would have ruined it now to explain all this to Charlie.

I stood in the living room, not knowing what to do with myself, while he clomped up the stairs. A moment later his door clicked shut, and he started playing the same guitar chords as always, with the same halts and hesitations. He hadn't improved at all. There was something so depressing about that—the lack of improvement—that I had to lace up my basketball shoes and go for a run, clomping around the neighborhood half-blind in the milky fog.

***

The next morning the sky was white. I spooned cereal into my mouth at the sliding door, looking at the brown-pelted foothills, wondering what had happened to our old dog London. When Charlie dragged himself downstairs at noon, I harassed him about playing some one-on-one in the driveway. "You'd *kill* me," he kept saying, even when I reassured him that he was taller, he was more talented, he was still playing. I relented when he told me he had a game that evening and didn't want to tire his legs.

It was in Atascadero, forty minutes away, but I was dying to see him in action. I made the drive, then sat in the bleachers like a proud parent, warm tendrils of nostalgia reaching into my chest as I watched the teams run through warmups and smelled the popcorn and listened to the eighth-grade band belt out a brassy, disjointed rendition of "Louie Louie."

Atascadero had a player Charlie's height. He wore a T-shirt under his jersey and had to keep tugging it down over his soft belly. During the game he lumbered up and down the court with a stricken, asthmatic expression. When the ball came his way, he didn't seem to know what to do with it. He was the type of player Charlie should have dominated, but Charlie didn't seem interested in exerting that kind of energy. On offense he flipped up lazy hook shots rather than deploying the arsenal of post moves I had helped him develop. He tried to reach over other players for rebounds rather than fighting for good position. He parked himself in the key and got called for violations. After possession changes he jogged down the court beside the big kid, trailing the action. One time he walked, trailing even the big kid, who, without Charlie there to bother him, rebounded his own miss three times, then finally put the fourth one in. Atascadero ended up winning by six, a gap Charlie could have easily closed on his own. I was appalled. What was it about failing that gave him so much pleasure?

The next morning I took out my phone list and got busy calling old friends, trying to organize a pickup game, but I got parents on the line who told me my friends wouldn't be home until Tuesday, or Friday, or next week. I got answering machines that announced the family was vacationing in Palm Springs or visiting relatives in Ohio. The friends I did make contact with said my name with skeptical voices, as if they didn't believe it was really me. When they asked how I was liking Berkeley, I only told them, "Things are good." When I brought up basketball, they said they had plans with their families. Others said, "Oh God, all that running? I'm not in the best shape." Cory Orford had made the football team at Fresno State, and even though the season was over and he was only a third-string receiver, he was prohibited from pickup basketball because of the injury risk. "I could get kicked off the team for even *being* there," he said. I told him I understood. I didn't want anyone getting kicked off his team.

Eventually I managed to round up four other guys—five including me—and I had the idea of bringing Charlie, who would give us enough for three-on-three. I imagined teaming up with him, an easy fluency between us from all our years practicing together. I would feed him in the post, where he would gauge his defender's position and then punish it with a drop-step or mini-hook, or finally deploy his step-back and witness its effectiveness against players as big and quick as he was. If they double-teamed, he could kick it out to me, and I would pop the jump shot. Afterward we would point to each other and high-five. It would be just like our drills in the driveway except it would count.

We agreed to meet at the Mission court, but it had to be right away because Seth Feldman had an optometrist appointment. When it was all set, I clapped once in celebration, then jogged upstairs to wake Charlie, though I found him already awake, making a beeline for the bathroom, his hands stuffed in the pockets of his pajama pants. When I said his name, he stopped and gave me a low, edgy look, as if I'd just caught him at something shameful. "I was about to take a shower," he muttered.

I remembered what it was like to be thirteen, hurrying to the bathroom with my hands shoved in my own pockets, trying to hide what was between them. "Listen," I said, "I'm meeting some friends for a pickup game. We need one more for three-on-three, and I told them I'd bring you."

"I'm not good enough to play against college guys."

"Sure you are. You're almost at high-school level and still going up. I was barely at high school-level and I've gone down."

"You played varsity though."

"You could make varsity as a *freshman*, Charlie. It won't be as easy as playing against eighth-graders, but you'll do fine as long as you play hard. Plus, it's just for fun."

He kept his hands in his pockets and gazed toward the bathroom.

"It's a special experience, playing with these guys," I said. "It's hard to explain. That's why I want you to come, so you can see for yourself. Also, we need you. You're the sixth guy. Help us out."

"Can I shower first?"

"Just hurry. We only have a couple hours."

He walked in, then gave me a suspicious sidelong glance before pushing the door closed, using his foot rather than taking his hands from his pockets.

I found my old outdoor ball, a cheap pimpled thing that went *toing!* when it bounced. I carried it to the driveway and did some form shooting, concentrating on my arm slot and my wrist snap, trying to find the old groove. I was concentrating so hard that at first I didn't realize what I was smelling. It arrived faintly, like the occasional whiff of beach salt that would sometimes ride ten miles inland to tickle your nose and vanish. But it was a distinct smell, a smell I recognized—honeyed and green but also sour. I stood for several long moments with the ball at my chest, getting a taste and then losing it, trying to name what it was, until I happened to glance back at the house just as a white billow blew from the bathroom window upstairs. I watched it disperse against the blue sky, heavy feelings unbraiding in my chest. Then I dropped the ball, its strange hollow beat growing faster and fainter as I stormed toward the house.

Upstairs the shower was running but without the wet slapping sound of someone bathing—just a steady empty hiss. From my knees I saw a towel stuffed beneath the door, but the odor leaking from the doorframe was unmistakable. I stood, pounded, and right away the toilet seat thumped and the water flushed. "I'm getting in the shower!"

"Hurry up!" was all I could think to holler.

Back in the driveway, I tried to concentrate again on the shooting, to lose myself in the simplicity of motion, but I kept glancing up at the bathroom window, now shut. Marijuana wasn't the worst thing in the world. I had even tried a little myself that night at the house party. But it hadn't put me in danger of getting suspended from school or kicked off my team. It hadn't been first thing in the morning. I wasn't in eighth grade, and I hadn't just been invited by my brother to participate in something sacred. Everything I offered, he turned it to acid and flung it back in my face. Somebody needed to teach him what it meant to be decent, and apparently there was nobody to do it but me.

When I went inside again, he was in the kitchen, unwrapping a cereal bar. He reeked of cologne. His eyes were pink and glassy, shifting around the room while he waited with cool distance for his big brother to say his piece.

"I hope you're ready for a real game," is what I told him.

***

The Mission was the color and texture of pumice, freshly tagged with graffiti. It crouched at the back of a big Mexican-style plaza. The fountain at the center was dry, just a small concrete pool with a spout at the center, pointed up. During the summer a bloom of water rose from it, and the pool was littered with pennies and ecstatic toddlers. As we walked by, I considered mentioning the many times I'd watched Charlie play there in his underwear, but I didn't want him to think he was off the hook. I carried my cheap rubber ball in silence, and Charlie trailed a few paces behind.

Behind the Mission was a pedestrian avenue and then a small park with a little half court on white concrete—no lines painted, no net on the hoop. Seth Feldman, Val Lambright, Danny Shea, and Tyler Osbourne were lounging on the park benches in various poses of relaxation, shoes unlaced, elbows resting on basketballs, chatting in low voices and smiling. I was surprised they weren't on the court, warming up and shooting, but my surprise barely registered as I floated toward them on a beam of nostalgia and affection.

"He didn't like the Smirnoff but it got him talking," Feldman was saying. He had shaven the black, pharaoh-like tuft from his chin, which sloped weakly beneath his overbite. Lambright, whose buzz cut had grown into a helmet of dirty-blond curls, said, "Yeah, he wouldn't shut up about his dick not working."

I stood with my brother, grinning, waiting for them to acknowledge me with the same enthusiasm exploding in my own chest, but they just continued on. "No, he said it worked fine but he couldn't feel it," Feldman said, and Lambright said, "Yeah, yeah, yeah. But you know how he found out?"

Danny listened with his fingers laced behind his coarse orange hair, face turned to the sky. "How?"

"Nicole gave it a little test drive for him right there on the cot with the thingy pulled around them."

Oz leaned over his knees and rubbed his knuckles, which were etched with something dark like engine grease. "I should've skipped work and gone with you guys."

"Work is work," Feldman told him.

"Yeah but I still should've."

The conversation lapsed for a moment, and I took the opportunity to ask: "Who was this?"

Lambright craned his neck and squinted at me, as if I had said exactly the wrong thing. "We're talking about Andrews."

"Yeah? Where is that guy? I left a bunch of messages on his machine."

Oz dropped a gob of spit between his shoes. Danny lifted his orange eyebrows and looked away. Feldman said, "Still in the hospital."

"Hospital? Why?"

Feldman glanced at Charlie, as if to consider the audience, then lowered his eyes, took a deep breath, and explained the shore break, the spinal injury, the wheelchair. "It was right out there at Del Oro," he said. "You know how it gets when the tide's going out. I guess he was actually really lucky. If it was his neck he wouldn't have been able to use his arms to swim back."

I could hardly believe what I was hearing. Andrews had been in my Cub Scout troop, on my Little League team. We had built a catapult out of Popsicle sticks and rubber bands for the fourth grade science fair and had played cribbage on team bus trips in high school. He was a close friend, a player who, like me, had often spent the whole game swaddled in warm-ups. He was freakishly athletic and could have been a great basketball player if he hadn't had so many other interests. In the spring he did a few jumping events for the track team, and so all winter after basketball practice he would drag big wooden boxes out of the equipment room and spend half an hour on plyometrics. I couldn't imagine him in a wheelchair. It was the worst thing that had ever happened to anyone I knew.

"When was this?" I asked.

"Few months ago," Lambright said, and Feldman said, "No, it's been six weeks, because that was our second visit, and we're the third group. We made a rotation," he explained, "so that every week he has people there with him."

"Why didn't anyone tell me?" I said. "I would've visited Andrews."

"We tried," Oz said.

"You're kind of tough to get a hold of," Lambright said with the same squint of disapproval. My eyelids tightened as I remembered turning off the ringer to my dorm phone. My stomach knuckled, making me want to fold myself over it, but instead I turned and punted my basketball, which also helped. How could I have failed to see that this group might still be bonded by forces other than basketball? The ball came down on the pedestrian avenue, took a huge leap, and disappeared behind a raised cornice on the Mission roof.

When I turned back to the group, Charlie was pressing his palms over his mouth, his face red, his eyes gleaming with laughter. Anger flamed into my chest. "You think this is funny?"

He shook his head but didn't change his expression or remove his hands.

"Someone gets paralyzed, and you think it's a big joke?"

"No." The word came out surly, and for a moment Charlie mastered his expression, shaping it into a look of scorn and boredom. Then the smile slipped back into place. "I can't help it," he said.

"Yeah? And why's that?"

He just stood there, battling the muscles in his face, exerting some control around the lips but none around the eyes. He looked like a child who had been caught eating something, and now, mouth full, was trying to charm his way out of punishment. Maybe that worked with our father, but someone had to show him he couldn't go around doing whatever he wanted at other people's expense. Marijuana wasn't an excuse. Neither was age. They were reasons to set him straight.

"Shoot for teams?" I said, walking away.

The first three to make shots would be on one team, the leftovers on the other. Lambright made his. Charlie was next, and his shot fell so cleanly through the netless hoop that to an untrained eye it might have looked like he'd missed everything. I stepped up and chucked a pass at the backboard that ricocheted straight back to Feldman. He pushed the ball into my chest. "How about you shoot for real?"

"I did," I said, and went to the back of the line.

Feldman took a few dribbles, then shot and missed. Danny stepped up and made his, and the teams were set.

"I got Charlie," I said.

                    ***

I could tell he wasn't used to playing against someone his own size. He kept calling for passes up high, and I kept tipping them away.

When he did manage to get his hands on the ball, I stripped it, leaving his fingers curled into the empty space the ball had just occupied, or I swatted his lazy shot back into his startled face. On offense I backed him down, pounding my shoulder into his chest, gaining ground inch by inch until I was under the hoop, and then flipped the ball in without any trouble.

He tried giving a little back. He slapped my wrists and shoved me, but he didn't know how to do it in a way that made a difference. On defense I began to deny him from receiving passes at all, fronting him in the post, sticking close as he jabbed and circled, trying to get free. After a few minutes he slowed down, and after a few more he stopped. He stood far from the hoop, hands on his hips, watching his teammates pass and drive, his red face washed with sweat and frustration.

"What's the matter?" I asked. "Need another cereal bar?"

Lambright said, "Take it easy, would you?"

But I didn't feel like taking it easy. I felt like I was finally making something very clear to my brother.

The next time I got the ball, I paused, making sure Charlie had a chance to set himself on defense before I blew by him and scored. The next possession I squared up and paused even longer, just to let the inevitability sink in. Charlie went into a deep crouch, his jaw knit, his eyes aimed at my waistband, something I had taught him.

"That's good," I said. "That's my center of gravity. Shows you where I'm going. But it won't do you much good if your reflexes are slow. Do anything to slow yours down?"

When I made my move, he lunged, and I accidentally clipped his shoulder and sent him spinning to the pavement. The two other defenders converged at the hoop and clobbered me.

"Foul," I said, carrying the ball to the top of the key.

"You all right?" Danny asked, offering Charlie a hand. Charlie looked at his elbow, then let Danny yank him up.

His teammates began to shift over every time I got the ball, double-teaming me, punching it from my hands or forcing me to pass.

On offense they set screens for Charlie, forcing me to switch onto someone else, and my teammates guarded him loosely, even letting him score a couple times. The second time he used a confident-looking step-back that Feldman complimented, giving him a high-five. A warm pride crept through my chest, and I wondered if Charlie felt it too.

Then, on a broken play, after a loose ball had careened off the hands of two other players, Charlie scooped it up in the post with me defending him, a forearm pressed into his lower back to communicate the staunch defense I intended and to prepare myself for another step-back. Instead, he executed a spin move so quick and graceful it left me falling forward, guarding nobody. It was a move I had taught him to deploy against overly aggressive defenders, which was exactly what he'd just done, and recognizing it filled me with both joy and humiliation.

Both of these sensations persuaded me, in the instant I had to react, to pay Charlie the compliment of a hard foul. It was an overmatched defender's last resort, an acknowledgment that he was beaten, an active surrender, a deep bow. But it was also a punishment. I turned and swept my hand across Charlie's elbows, which were raised toward the hoop, ball perched on his fingertips, and the whole structure collapsed sideways. Charlie went to the concrete in a heap.

"Foul," I admitted.

The other players were already closing in on me, yelling, "Jesus!" and "He's just a kid, man!"

Charlie got up and walked off the court, eating up ground with long strides, grit clinging to his sweat-soaked T-shirt.

"Hey!" I called after him. "Charlie!"

He didn't stop, so I jogged over. "We're right in the middle of a game," I said.

He kept walking, eyes locked straight ahead, mouth small with anger.

"I'm trying to show you something, all right? You don't just throw in the towel when things get hard. You have to keep going. I'm not just talking about basketball. Do you hear me?"

If he did he gave no sign of it, and it ignited the same wild sadness as every other time he declined my help. I cupped my hands around my mouth and called, "Hey! Earth to Charlie!"

"Fuck off!" he shouted, bursting into tears, and broke into a run. I watched him recede across the plaza—knock-kneed, heavy-heeled—so stunned that all I could do was bark a single, incredulous note of laughter. Other notes followed, and I found myself holding my belly as it emitted this strange, painful noise.

When I turned back to the court, they were already playing two-on-two without us. "Sorry about that," I said, but they just kept playing. I watched them a while, not knowing what else to do. Finally I gathered up my water bottle and keys.

Nobody said goodbye.

6

Clouds came. The weather turned cold. On TV, the local news-woman stood in a fur-lined parka, head turned to show viewers the novelty of breathing steam. At the mall, shopping for Christmas gifts, I overheard people talking with excitement about the possibility of snow, mentioning the few wet flakes that had fallen a decade earlier and spreading rumors about a recent dusting on the grade. Then one day, the sun came out and eased everything back to mildness.

Christmas morning, I woke before sunrise without meaning to. I smashed my head between two pillows, then finally went down-stairs. There were no stockings, no lights, no smell of pine, nothing at all to indicate what day it was except the little pile of gifts where the tree usually stood. They were wrapped poorly, except the ones that had come through the mail from our mother, which sat like shining reminders of what we'd lost.

It was after eight when my father came down. I was watching TV, finding comfort in an old Christmas movie that played on a twenty-four-hour loop, but I quieted the volume and listened to him move through the kitchen, open cupboards, grind coffee. Then his footsteps receded, and the office door closed. The silence and stillness of the house returned, and I understood for the first time why some people hated the holidays.

It was almost eleven when I heard Charlie move to the bathroom upstairs. The shower ran for half an hour and then he came down reeking of cologne. My father must have smelled it even from his office, because he emerged to holler, "Good God, Charlie. A little scent goes a long way." But then, after some banging around in the cupboards, they both came into the living room, Charlie gripping a bouquet of red licorice, my father holding a steaming mug.

Charlie dumped himself on the couch, yanking the licorice with his teeth. My father perched on the armchair, slurped his coffee, and then gestured with his mug at the pile of gifts. "Well?" he said. "Dig in."

I asked, "You're not going to pass them out?"

He rubbed his forehead, as if I had conferred upon him an impossible task. "Do you need me to?"

"It might make it feel a little more like Christmas."

"If you wanted decorations, Ed, you could have put them up yourself. Nobody was stopping you."

"You always put them up before."

"Your *mom* always put them up before," he said, and something in the room shifted. We sat with it for a moment, and then I lunged for the stack and tossed my gifts into each of their laps. "Merry Christmas," I said, but it didn't sound as mean as I'd wanted it to.

My father picked at the tape. Charlie grabbed a dirty steak knife from a dirty plate on the coffee table and stabbed the box, then sawed around the edges, not bothering to unwrap it. I went ahead and grabbed the gift from my mother, which turned out to be a raincoat. It would have been useful in Conrad Park except that the style was wrong, the kind a business executive or a flasher might wear.

My father opened his box, revealing two lowball glasses, their tops curved inward. He held them up and turned them over in the light, as if inspecting them for flaws.

"They're made specially for drinking whiskey," I said. "They're supposed to focus the aroma. I got you two in case you wanted to invite someone to join you."

"Oh." He looked embarrassed. "I don't think—I'm not quite ready for that yet, to be honest."

"I meant me."

Disapproval flattened his lips. "You're nineteen, Ed."

By then Charlie was putting down the knife and peeling back the box top. He gazed inside with disappointment. "I already have a Giants hat."

"Yeah but I molded a nice curve into the bill on this one. It took me a week."

"Great. So I can't take it back?" On his face was open hostility, which I returned.

"At least I got you something," I said.

"Yours is in my room. It's shaped too weird to wrap."

"So you gave up? Big surprise."

"Boys," my father said. "Please. It's Christmas. Be civil."

To invoke the holiday he had barely acknowledged, to claim authority after swearing off responsibility—it seemed even more absurd than prohibiting his college-aged son from having a drink while his eighth-grade son was stoned out of his skull and handling a knife. It was easy to turn my anger on him.

"Maybe I'll start being civil when you start being a parent," I said.

"Now wait a minute."

"No you wait a minute. You're not around any more than Mom is. At least she has the excuse of being three thousand miles away."

"Now just hold it right there. I'm here. Every damn day, I'm here."

"No, you're not. You're locked in your office."

"Well excuse me, but I do still have a full-time job, you know, not to mention my own life to worry about. You have no idea what this has been like for me, Ed. No idea."

"If you came out of your office once in a while, maybe you'd know why Charlie uses so much cologne."

When I glanced at Charlie, his face flashed a warning, then set-tled into cool hatred when I told our father, "It's to cover up the pot he's smoking."

My father glanced at Charlie, then leaned forward and pressed the heels of his palms against his eyes and drew them slowly out-ward. "Charlie," he said, with fatigue instead of outrage. "You can't smoke pot."

Charlie launched himself from the couch and stomped upstairs. After his door slammed, my father turned to me, lips folded in and eyebrows up, as though asking if I was happy, as though the news rather than the behavior was the problem. He rose, groaning, and followed Charlie up the stairs, bobbing on his bad leg. He knocked on the door, opened it, closed it behind him, and then talked a long time, though his tone sounded more like an academic summation than a reprimand. I couldn't make out the words until the end, when the door opened.

"It's only because he cares about you," he said, and Charlie's response was short and firm. "Yes, he does," my father said, and then, after another complaint I couldn't decipher, "He's still your brother."

***

The hospital was on a hill at the edge of town. I was directed all over its campus, through four separate buildings, before I was able to track Andrews down in a unit that reminded me of my dormi-tory. The waiting area had puffy armchairs, rich carpeting, and mauve walls lit by warm, incandescent sconces. The receptionist pointed me down a hallway, and as I approached the room I smelled spiced cider. The door was open, showing walls strung with colored lights and holly, a small tree decorated with tinsel and silver balls, a Crock-Pot steaming on the dresser.

Andrews's older sister was in an armchair, flipping through a mag-azine, a corgi asleep on her lap. Andrews was in the near corner, fac-ing the television, which played basketball highlights. His torso was propped against the headboard of a high bed with a crimson blanket.

His face looked puffed but otherwise the same. In slacks and gleaming black shoes his legs looked normal except for their perfect stillness. I stood in the doorway for several long moments, feeling out of place, uninvited, but then stepped into the room and lifted a hand in greeting.

"Garrison!" Andrews waved me over, then pulled me into a rough, back-slapping hug, and I drew so much comfort from it that I overdid it a little with the whacking and jostling. "Whoa," he said, wincing. "Easy does it. I'm broken, you know."

"Bruno probably needs to go out anyway," his sister said, clipping the corgi into a leash.

"Merry Christmas," I said when she was gone. "Where are your parents?"

"Getting Chinese food."

I gestured at the decorations. "Looks like you've got a pretty nice setup in here."

"It's not bad. All in all, I'd rather be at Berkeley."

I laughed. "Me too."

"Tough coming home?"

"No. Well, yes, but that's not what I mean. Things got kind of confused at the end of summer. I ended up going to a place called Sequoia College. I wanted to see if I could make the basketball team. It was pretty stupid."

"What was stupid about it?"

"I wasn't good enough. I don't know why I thought I would be. My parents got divorced," I added.

Andrews nodded, as if he understood the convolutions that connected my parents' divorce to basketball. "I've been meaning to call," he said. "I should've called."

"Shit, don't worry about that. How are *you*?"

He shrugged. "Still having a hard time believing it's real. But I'm glad not to be in so much pain anymore."

"You can still feel pain?"

"In my *back*, yeah. The legs are mostly numb. I can feel pressure in some places. There's also this weird electric sensation. It's hard to describe. And there's this thing where my leg muscles spasm and it does something to the dead nerves, but you don't know it's going on until you get this feeling like you're freaking out and going to die. You really can die from it, too. Your heart rate gets out of control and causes a stroke. That's pretty scary."

"It sounds terrifying."

"Otherwise I'm mostly just really bored. I watch TV and hang out with my parents. I keep going back to that day in my head and trying to cut my board the other way, or let the wave pass, or not go out at all. The counselor is trying to get me to work on acceptance, but I don't know." He gestured at his lower half. "This isn't me."

"That's kind of how I feel at Sequoia. It's like I keep waiting for my old life to come back."

He gave a laugh of recognition. "People keep telling me all these stories about disabled people doing amazing things but it only pisses me off. It's like you said, I keep wanting my old life back. Expecting it even. Like one day I'll wake up and everything will be back to normal."

We sat for a moment with this new understanding, nodding and smiling at each other.

"My parents should be back any minute," he said. "Want to stay for Chinese?"

I did, but it felt like too much of an intrusion. It was Christmas, after all, and they were a family. I said I should be going, then apologized for not visiting sooner. "I would have," I explained, "but I only just found out."

"Garrison." He clasped my hand like we were about to arm-wrestle. "You think I don't know that?"

***

I was on the couch that night watching the same old Christmas movie when the phone rang. Nobody else seemed willing to answer, so I did it myself. "Merry Christmas," my mother said, and then, after I'd said it back, "Would you like to talk?"

It was the first time I'd heard her voice since the day she'd admitted her affair, and I almost said no from force of habit before I caught myself. "Sure."

I thanked her for the raincoat, and we talked about the wet climate on the northern coast before slipping into our old routine. She interrogated me about my final exams, my drive to San Seguro, my other gifts, then delivered a long monologue about the discouragement of seeing voters pass measures like Proposition 22, especially in a state as progressive as California. It was as boring as ever, but the sound of her voice was like a hand on my back, massaging away the knotted muscles. When she was finished, I asked if she wanted to speak to Charlie. She said she'd already talked to him and to our father. I knew it had nothing to do with reconciliation, but still, I liked the idea of it—my parents talking on Christmas.

"Did he tell you about Charlie?" I asked.

"Yes."

"He's not doing well, Mom."

"I know."

"I think he feels abandoned."

"I think so too."

"It's mostly because of you."

"Yes," she said. "I know."

"It's partly because of me," I admitted.

"No. You've done nothing wrong."

I gripped the bridge of my nose, sinuses burning. I couldn't speak for a moment. Then I said it was probably getting late in Maryland, and she agreed that it was. Before hanging up, she said she loved me, and I said it back, as quick and casual as a touch pass.

***

I was on the back deck when Charlie found me. I had been standing out there a long time, just beyond the reach of light seeping from the sliding glass door, thinking about what I'd told Andrews about waiting for my old life to return. I hadn't realized it until the moment I'd said it, but it was true. I'd been under the impression that the strangeness was only temporary, that I would soon return to my old life as easily as I had returned to the old Christmas movie, and that it would be equally familiar and well preserved. It was the reason I kept doing such stupid things—turning down Berkeley, turning off my phone, turning into a bully on the basketball court. And I knew that I would continue to make these mistakes until I admitted what Andrews couldn't. My old life was gone. I had to build a new one.

"God," Charlie said, sliding the door shut. "I've been looking everywhere for you." He carried over a little plant in a clay pot. It had glossy leaves and thin wooden stems. "Here," he said, and handed it over. "I'm sorry I didn't know how to wrap it."

I was surprised by its weight and by the force of my gratitude. "Thank you."

"Thank Mom. She's the one who told me to get it for you."

He turned to leave, but I stopped him. "Hey, did anyone ever find out what happened to London?"

"Our dog?"

"Yeah."

"I'm pretty sure Mom and Dad took him back to the shelter."

"What? Who told you that?"

"Nobody. I just figured it out."

He went through the door and closed it behind him. I stood there holding the plant, breathing the night air, letting the chill wash over me as I peered at the black foothills that blotted out the bottom of the sky. I knew he was right, and I felt stupid that I hadn't seen it earlier, the reason for the adoption and the timing of the disappearance, but mostly I felt disappointed. I had gotten used to the idea of London out roaming these hills, living on whatever was available until he decided to come home.

PART II: PARIS

7

Arriving in Conrad Park was different this time. The days were short and the darkness long. When it wasn't raining, the sky was heavy, locked with clouds, and it saturated the days with gloom and stagnation and an awful sense of waiting. Whenever the sun broke through, students swarmed the lawns and courtyards to soak in the heat like reptiles but then scattered for shelter when another dark front blotted out the sky. An hour later it would pour again and be difficult to believe the sun had been anything other than a delusion.

But then a cloud break lasted two days, and another followed shortly after. Daffodils opened and baseball games began appearing on television. The air started to feel more temperate, and even when the clouds remained they were accompanied by a warm breath of wind and the fragrance of mulch. One day the cloud break simply didn't end. The skies were blue, and the sun gained strength, and the season made its imperceptible pivot.

By then I'd ditched English and declared a journalism major. I was also taking two journalism courses and covering the baseball team for the campus newspaper. At the end of the year, Patricia

Caldwell, the outgoing editor-in-chief, encouraged me to apply for a copy editor position. I did, but during my interview I showed issue after issue of the sports pages, which were filled with game previews, game recaps. Where, I asked, were the hard questions, the critical investigations, the lack of fear or favor I'd learned about in my courses? Had anyone ever wondered why A.C. Sullinger would give up the limelight of Division I basketball? Had anyone ever asked the last-place basketball coach if he was worried about his job? Had anyone ever considered whether fall "shoot-arounds" violated NCAA/NAIA season-limitation regulations? These were dark corners that needed illumination, I argued, but there was only so much you could do as a reporter—or as a copy editor. It required leadership.

The new hires were announced at the following editorial meeting. My invitation meant I would be on staff, but I didn't know which position I had been hired for until we were gathered in the Quonset hut. Patricia Caldwell started by introducing the new editor-in-chief, a chubby Black guy named Eli Duncan who had been the opinions editor. He had a habit of listening to people with his chin pushed back, eyes bulging, which is what he did as he read off the new hires. "I know we didn't advertise an opening for sports," he said after a short pause, and Gilbert Platt looked up from his magazine. I knew what would follow, and the quick succession of joy and guilt was like hitting a baseball off the pitcher's head. I didn't know whether to run the bases or go see if he was okay.

After the meeting, I approached Gilbert and told him how much I appreciated his guidance all year, that he was a big reason I was majoring in journalism, and that the football assignment next fall was his if he wanted it. He looked at me, wearing the deadpan that usually meant a joke was coming, and said. "Go fuck yourself, Garrison."

He walked out, refusing to train me. Patricia Caldwell had to do it, but I had so much anger and shame tumbling through me that I could barely focus. *Shit happens*, I kept wanting to tell Gilbert. *Deal with it.*

That pretty well summed up the attitude I'd developed since my conversation with Kyle Andrews last Christmas.

***

That summer I found work as a day-camp counselor. The pay was dirt but saved me living expenses, letting me stay for free in my dorm room, which meant I didn't have to return to San Seguro or visit my mother in Maryland. She wasn't happy to hear about it but stopped pleading to see me when I told her, "Then don't live in Maryland." I tried not to worry about Charlie there by himself. At least he'd have a parent present, unlike in San Seguro.

Another benefit of the job was that I got to eat all I wanted in the cafeteria at no charge, relieving me from a considerable financial burden, considering the bottomless appetite that had opened up in me since I'd decided to train for a marathon. I put in my miles as dawn turned to daylight, the air crisp and scented with grass clippings and dew, and by the time everyone else arrived at work, yawning and bleary, I was already alert and accomplished. As the heat deepened I set up kickball games and relay races for the children, cleaned up crafts tables and egg-drop experiments, supervised brown-bag lunches and swimming pool sessions. I led my campers from one event to another, walking backward, singing a callback to keep their attention:

Everywhere we goooo-OH!
People want to knoooow-OH!
Who we aaaa-ARE!
Soooo, we tell THEM!

After work, I was free to lift weights at the gym, watch baseball in the lounge, and spend many long hours reading novels on the front steps of the dorm building, enjoying the cool recess of shade and concrete while heat rose from the streets in shimmering corrugation.

That was what I was doing one afternoon when a three-legged cat came lurching up the walk. It was slender, its coat a glossy pastiche of grays and blacks. I closed my book over my finger and watched it, amused. When I made some clicking noises, it surprised me by trotting over to gum the handrail post and mewl. After scratching its head a little, I didn't know what else to do. It kept trying to climb onto my lap. It wouldn't leave me alone. Finally, I had to go inside to escape it.

That weekend, while I was digesting the tuna sandwiches and chocolate milk I'd wolfed down after a hard, hilly twelve-mile run, the cat came lurching up the walk again. This time I didn't call it over, but it came anyway, mewling, looking at me as if asking for something. "What?" I said. It sniffed its way to my tuna-scented fingers and began wailing with such desperation that I started to wonder if something was truly wrong. I jogged back to the cafeteria on deadened, aching legs, then came back with a fistful of tuna and let the little beast gobble it from my palm.

Monday morning, I caught one of the other counselors, Danielle Bisset, as she was punching her timecard. "Do you think you could help me with something?" I asked, and when she turned her attention on me, a tingle slid down my limbs and up my throat, as if my veins had suddenly opened and oxygen was spreading outward from my chest in pleasant saturation. Danielle was one of those rare girls who didn't seem to care about her beauty. She didn't sculpt her eyebrows or pump up her lashes or cover the small red pimples that sometimes appeared on her forehead or chin. She pulled her brown hair into a careless ponytail and wore slim eyeglasses that were always slipping down her nose. Even so, beauty lurked everywhere. She had lovely pale lips, dark eyes pooling kindness, a bright smile that always set me at ease.

When I explained that a three-legged cat had been visiting my dorm building, she gasped with pleasure, her eyebrows sloped in such intensity of tenderness and concern that I was reluctant to deliver the bad news. "I think it's a stray," I said as gently as I could. "I think it might be starving."

While I told her what had happened, she nodded, her face taking on a look of attentive focus, a look that promised to comprehend the problem and then solve it. "Can you feel its ribs when you pet it?" she asked.

"I didn't really pet it."

"And it doesn't have any collar or tags?"

"I guess I should've looked."

"Well then it's hard to say. Maybe I could come with you after work and take a look?"

"Fine with me," I said, then spent the rest of the day in a fog of anticipation.

The afternoon sun was hot and bright as we emerged from the cinderblock headquarters, forcing us to squint at the ground as we strolled toward my dorm building. We talked about work, which helped ease the transition to this unfamiliar space beyond it. I asked how she liked the job, and she said it was great, except that she always wanted to play games and make bracelets with the kids because she felt like she still was one. I asked what she thought of our coworkers, and she said they all seemed nice and she liked getting to know them. I asked if she minded spending the summer away from home, and she said she definitely did. "My two brothers are a lot older than me," she said, "so my parents had to wait a long time for me to graduate before they could retire to Arkansas. I guess the cost of living there is really low. But I don't have any friends in Arkansas, and now I don't have a home anymore in my hometown. So here I am. What about you?"

"I'm glad to be on my own," was all I said.

At my dorm we sat on the concrete steps and kept talking, and the air cooled pleasantly as the shadow of the building tilted into the street. Danielle speculated about how the cat had lost its leg, and I played the role of the astute and reasonable judge, allowing that her theories were indeed possible. Then she talked for a long time about horse dressage, a subject I never would have guessed could be so interesting. Sometimes I lost track of what she was saying because I was taking in the curve of her chin and jaw, the contours of her lips and nose, and the way all these features seemed to funnel attention toward her eyes, which I tried to think of anatomically, round marbles buried in flesh, to take away the sting of their beauty. Now and then loud cars passed in the street—souped-up trucks or clunkers missing their mufflers—and she stopped talking, smiling straight into my face while she waited for the noise to pass. It was almost too much to bear.

When she asked what I did with my spare time, I told her about my newspaper work, my afternoons reading novels, my running. She asked if I went very far, and I admitted I did. "I'm training for a marathon," I said.

"How far is that?"

"Twenty-six-point-two miles."

Her mouth hung open. She shook her head and laughed. "That's crazy!"

"If you love it, why not keep going as long as you can?"

"What do you love about it?"

"I don't know. It just feels good. When I'm running I feel okay about everything."

She nodded. "It helps you focus on the good things."

"Or at least not carry around so much of the bad."

"Happiness is a choice we make every day," she said, as if in agreement.

That wasn't it either, not exactly, but I didn't mind. It was enough just to be there with her, to have those big kind eyes pointed at me while she asked about my life.

"So where's this cat?" she asked.

"You probably think I'm making it up just to hang out with you."

She ventured a mischievous smile down her shoulder.

"It doesn't come every day," I said. "We could try again tomorrow."

"Tomorrow I have to work at the Humane Society but I could come back the day after."

"Well then I think you'd better come back the day after," I said.

"Well then I guess I'd better."

She was giving me a playful look—one that was close to fondness, even affection—and I wondered how I would make it through forty-six hours without her.

***

The next day at work we kept bumping into each other between activities. We stuffed our coats into the headquarter cubbies at the same time, passed each other going into and out of the equipment room, set up lunch for our campers on adjacent patches of grass. Sometimes we offered brief comments: "Hot already, huh?" or "That's cool that you volunteer at the Humane Society." Sometimes we threw each other teasing expressions: *You again!* Sometimes we traded pleased and intimate smiles.

After work, I sat on the dorm steps with a book but couldn't focus. My eyes kept sliding over the type without picking anything up. For weeks I had been perfectly content to haunt these steps alone, but now I felt nothing besides boredom and restlessness and deprivation. I watched the street, where nothing happened, and missed Danielle.

The next day, after we had strolled to my dorm, chatting and laughing and stealing glances at each other, ready to spend the whole afternoon together, I was disappointed to see the cat come lurching up the sidewalk. Danielle gasped and rushed down to meet it. She heaped affection onto it, cooing and stroking its throat as it rolled in her arms, pawing the air. "This cat gets plenty to eat," she said, looking at me with happy eyes. "It's a healthy size."

"Really? Because the other day it was acting like it hadn't eaten in—I don't even know how long."

"I'm pretty sure this guy's from a good home."

She tried passing him to me, but I told her I was more of a dog person.

"Well then why don't you come to the Humane Society with me some time?" she said. "I'll show you lots of great dogs."

After work the next day I followed her up the hill in my Corolla, then followed her into the raucous kennel on the pretext of seeing the dogs, though pretext and reason quickly became muddled. As I moved from pen to pen, listening to her describe each animal while it barked and wagged its tail, my heart lifted.

"If you want to take one out to play," she said, "we've got a yard in back."

"I want to play with them all."

"Then I guess you'd better come back," she said, offering that same affectionate smile.

"Then I guess I'd better," I said, returning it.

I was there every time Danielle worked a shift. I loved visiting her, but I also loved those dogs. I took a different one out each day to a little yard where dried weeds were beaten into the dirt, and I spent an hour or two throwing the ball and playing tug-of-war and wrestling, scratching their bellies and whomping their sides, joy strung between us like a tight wire. I was there so often that if Danielle and the other attendants were busy, I helped visitors myself, setting them up with toys and leashes, returning dogs to their pens, explaining their needs and personalities and quirks, getting people started with adoption forms and preparing myself for bittersweet goodbyes.

The only thing I couldn't handle was the defecation. The first day I turned a baggie over my hand and gripped a warm turd was my last. After that I notified Danielle, and she teased me affectionately as she did the job herself.

But it wasn't long before she asked me, turning a baggie inside out and twisting its top, "Why do you keep coming here, Ed?" She said it like an accusation. She seemed bent out of shape about something.

"What do you mean? Do you want me to stop?"

"I mean you keep coming and coming, but it's not for any purpose. All you ever do is play. It never leads to anything."

"What's it supposed to lead to?"

She shrugged and looked away, and I understood she was talking about something other than dogs. She was asking why I never made an advance on her. The answer was that making an advance wasn't easy at a Humane Society, but maybe that was her point.

"At the moment I'm living in a dorm room," I said.

"So?"

"So dogs aren't allowed, and anyway, it doesn't seem like the best environment for one."

"A dog could be very happy in a dorm room. I bet any of these dogs would love to go to your dorm room with you. You could find a way if you really wanted to."

"I also don't think I could handle the poop."

"But don't I always help you with that?"

She stood there holding the weighted bag, sweat pebbled on her upper lip, face as intense as Russo's when he demonstrated proper defensive technique. She was right, of course. I did want a dog. I'd always wanted one, since I could remember, and she seemed to calm down when I told her that.

I started evaluating the dogs with a cold eye, measuring their attractiveness and personality and size, weighing pros against cons. I found a tool that would allow me to scoop turds from the far end of a long handle. I also did a little research and discovered that a poodle would make the best choice, since poodles were hypoallergenic and didn't shed. But I had a hard time picturing myself with a poodle, and anyway, the shelter didn't have one.

I also started to see Danielle outside our normal routine of the day camp and the Humane Society. That week she began carrying a novel of her own to my dorm's front steps after work. Its glossy cover showed a stallion rearing on hind legs, looking elegant and indomitable. I liked having her long body there beside me, her legs crossed at the ankle, her finger rasping the corner of each page before she turned it. When I asked how she had become interested in animals, she said she didn't know, she'd always just loved them.

When she asked about my book, I showed her the cover. "I think his name is pronounced *Camoo*," I said. "I think it's French."

That Saturday we escaped the afternoon heat at the movie theater and then went for ice cream. Afterward she walked with me to my dorm building, and our parting was a scribble of awkward smiles and half-gestures. Neither of us seemed to know if we'd just had a date, or whether to expect a kiss, or how to initiate it. The next Saturday we made a day trip to the Redwoods and did one of the hikes my parents hadn't been able to, all those years ago. The trees were as shocking as ever—unbelievable trunks, distant canopies—and it felt good to be there with Danielle instead of my family, like living in my future instead of my past. But the parting was even worse. We hugged, then stood there, letting the goodbye grow stale while we waited for something to happen.

The Saturday after that I drove her to Lake Shasta, where we rented an aluminum rowboat. I loaded in the picnic I'd packed and then heaved us out into the sun, enjoying the smell of the lake water and baking canyon rock, the plush noise of the oars in the water, the way Danielle reached up to braid her ponytail. When I brought the oars in, she pushed down her shorts and peeled off her T-shirt, and I was enchanted by the blandness of her one-piece swimsuit. I liked her modesty, her long pale legs, the way she plugged her nose before stepping off the prow.

When she was done swimming we ate cheese and grapes. I gazed out at the long expanse of water that rippled and flashed in the sun, taking pleasure from the warmth and the movement of the boat.

"My dad used to have a little skiff like this," she said, reclining in the prow, "except with a motor in back."

"Yeah?"

"He kept it in the garage. He had to park his car in the driveway. Then one day he took my mom's spot in the garage because it was raining and he had something to bring in. My mom got home and had to park in the driveway. She came in all wet, and my dad looked at her like, *what have I done.* Sold the boat the very next day."

She laughed, remembering it, and then continued to talk about her parents. She said she hadn't forgiven them for moving to Arkansas, but overall, they were the best people she knew. The smartest person she knew was her brother, who had started some kind of tech company that had made him rich. Her other brother had become a youth pastor, and now he and his wife were trying to conceive, and she couldn't believe she was going to be an aunt. She was traveling to Arkansas to visit her parents for a week before fall classes started, she said, but she wouldn't see her brothers until Christmas, and she could hardly stand the idea of so much waiting.

She propped herself on an elbow and looked at me. "What about you? I haven't heard much about your family."

"What do you want to know?"

She brought her other arm around and cupped her hand over her eyes. "For starters, what do your parents do?"

"They're literature professors," I said, though that was no longer true. A few months earlier, my father had suffered, as he termed it, "a possible minor cardiac event" while shouting at a student during class. "The twerp had been rolling his eyes at me all semester," he'd explained from a hospital phone after giving me the news and assuring me he was fine. "Enough was enough." It was hard to picture my father shouting at anyone, and it concerned me almost as much as the medical issue. He'd finished the term on sick leave, and it was during this time that he'd decided to move into an administrative position. He was tired of the performance of teaching, he said, tired of working in front of an audience. "I just want to sit behind a desk and not have anybody look at me."

My mother had changed jobs too. She'd been doing heavy volunteer work for an advocacy group in Annapolis, but as they'd made their big push for an anti-discrimination law, more resources had started coming in, so they'd hired her. The pay wasn't great, she said, but it was important work and she loved doing it. "We're behind some of the other states out here," she told me during one of our phone conversations. "In Massachusetts and Vermont, they're already putting together lawsuits against the marriage exclusion. We aren't there quite yet, but this anti-discrimination legislation is the first step. It would be huge for us, just huge."

To tell Danielle that my parents were an administrator and a gay rights advocate, however, seemed like a misrepresentation of where I came from, who I was. My whole life, my parents had been literature professors.

"My parents were teachers, too," she said. "Elementary school. Did I already tell you that?"

I nodded.

"Four teachers. Imagine that." She blinked at the sky a moment, pleased by this symmetry, then looked at me again. "What are they like?"

"My mom stands behind a podium and lectures while everyone takes notes. My dad sits on the desk and asks questions to get people talking. That's what they're like outside the classroom too. My mom's very straightforward and determined. My dad's kind of dreamy."

"Which one cooks?"

"Cooks?"

"You know—food, heat. That kind of thing."

The answer was that my father had always cooked because his bad leg kept him from doing other chores around the house and yard. After my mother left, though, he mostly relied on frozen burritos and other microwavable food. I didn't know who did the cooking at Jane's house, and it wasn't pleasant to imagine my mother stirring a pot of something fragrant for someone else's children. "It varies," I said finally.

"Mine take turns," Danielle said. "But the one who's not cooking always tries to help and gets shooed out of the kitchen. It's cute. That's the kind of marriage I want someday. Don't you?"

"It's the kind of marriage everyone *wants*," I told her.

Later, Danielle spotted something big and ashen lodged in a shaded crevice of the rimrock. We couldn't understand what it was and decided to find out. I took up the oars and pulled us over.

"Do you have brothers or sisters?" she asked, squeezing sunscreen onto her legs.

The vigor of the exercise had already given way to tedium and difficulty, and I considered saying no just to save myself the breath. It also wouldn't have been far from the truth. Charlie had become so different from the boy I knew, so withdrawn and insolent, so contemptuous of sports and school and any form of hard work, that I really did feel like I had no brother except in a technical sense.

"Younger," I said, and after the next stroke, "brother."

Danielle rubbed the sunscreen down her thighs. "What's his name?"

"Charlie."

"What's he like?"

I swung the oars back and heaved again. There was no way I could fit it all into the gaps between my labored breaths.

"Want me to row for a while?" Danielle asked, as if reading my mind.

"That's okay."

But she insisted that I was hoarding all the fun for myself, so I let her take a turn. She wielded the paddles awkwardly, getting the hang of the oarlocks that reversed the forces she applied. The muscles in her chest stood up when she pulled.

"Your brother," she said, dipping the paddles back into the water. "Spill it."

I rubbed a tired shoulder, trying to find a place to begin. "Well, he's fourteen. He'll be a freshman in high school next year. He's already taller than me, though, and he's an amazing basketball player. If he plays his cards right he could probably get a full ride to college. He's been going through a rough patch lately, though."

"Rough how?"

I gazed out at the shoreline, not sure I wanted to get into it, though the reports had been rolling in at regular intervals. First, it was a case of mono that had knocked him out of basketball last winter. By the time he'd recovered there was only one game left, which he hadn't bothered to attend. When baseball season opened, he'd gone to two practices before quitting. At a birthday party a few weeks later, some kid's dad had pulled him out of the tool shed, where he'd been drinking from a stolen bottle of schnapps. A police officer delivered him home a few weeks later after he'd been caught passing around a joint with a group of older kids at the park, in full view of the children and parents at the nearby playground. At his eighth-grade graduation dance he was denied entry for showing up drunk, and a week later, our father found psychedelic mushrooms in his backpack.

"He's been getting in trouble," was all I told Danielle. "He's not focused on the right things. But if you try to help him, he thinks—I don't know what he thinks. He thinks you're against him."

She wasn't rowing anymore. She was sitting with the oar handles in her lap, looking concerned. "What are your parents doing about it?"

"I'm not sure. I've been away."

"You don't call?"

"Not really."

"Why not?"

I looked past her at the lake. I wasn't in the mood to hear her clichés about choosing happiness. "I'm trying to see if I can make it on my own."

"Sometimes all you need from a brother," she said, "is support."

"You can't support someone who won't let you."

"But you can still let him know you're there."

"That's a two-way street."

"Just go easy on him," she said. "It's hard being the youngest."

"Yeah, well, it's hard being the oldest too."

She smiled, as though we had reached an agreement, and I suppressed the urge to argue further, remembering what she'd just said about wanting support.

"Had your fill with the rowing?" I said.

She nodded. "I don't know how you went so long."

The sun disappeared behind the canyon bank as I pushed us into the cove, where we discovered a bobbing tangle of driftwood, the logs as big and smooth as dinosaur bones. I sidled the boat up and Danielle docked us with a long arm, her slender muscles tense until I twisted a rope around a log. I climbed onto the wobbling structure and Danielle followed, flailing her arms for balance. We set up a little camp for the rest of our picnic, chewing fruit and looking into the distance as the water lapped and sloshed in the many crevices beneath us. Two diagonal logs forced us to sit so close that our shoulders and thighs touched, and the contact wiped my mind clean of any possible conversation topics. I could think of nothing but the warm tingle of skin touching skin.

Finally, the silence grew awkward, and I said, "Did I ever tell you that my family used to have a dog that looked like a golden retriever but black?"

An elation of discovery broke over her face. "No!"

"We only had it for a few weeks." I offered her the watermelon, and she lifted out a slice.

"I bet it was a lab-retriever mix," she said. "That's how they turn out sometimes."

"He was a good dog, old London. I still miss him."

She took a bite. "Why did you only have him for a few weeks?"

I popped a few cherries into my mouth and worked them toward the front, where my incisors stripped their flesh as I collected the pits in my palm. She bit the watermelon again, waiting for my answer. "My parents got rid of the dog when they split up," I said, then flung the pits out over the lake. They arced into the sunshine and came down clicking onto the boat, which was drifting slowly away, the rope snaking behind it.

"Your parents are divorced?" she said.

"Yeah. They divorced about a year ago. They were together the whole time I was growing up, though."

"And neither one wanted the dog?"

I brushed off my palms and turned to her. "Look, I know what you're probably thinking, but the reason I haven't told you is because I was practically out of the house when it happened, so it didn't really have much impact on me. If anything, it was good to see that everything isn't always a perfect fairytale, because if you think everything is always going to be—I mean, if you think that nothing bad can ever—what?"

She had been shaking her head with increasing vigor. "That's not what I was thinking. I was thinking it's sad you had to give away your dog."

"Yeah but that's exactly what I mean. That's life."

"Is that why you didn't go home this summer?"

"I guess so. There isn't much of a home to go to."

She set her watermelon rind back into the dish. "I got in a big fight with my parents when they told me they were selling our house and moving. But that doesn't mean I don't want to see them. That would just make it worse."

"What makes it worse is pretending like everything's the same as it always was."

"Everything happens for a reason, Ed. You know that, right?"

"I know everything has a cause. But I don't think that means everything always works out."

"In the end it does. If it hasn't worked out, that just means it isn't the end yet. Who knows? Maybe your parents are happier. Maybe giving your dog away saved it from getting hit by a car or something."

"But dogs do get hit by cars. Something doesn't always save them."

She gave me a patient smile, as if we both knew I didn't really mean that. "If your parents didn't give away your other dog, then you wouldn't have a chance to adopt a new one, right?"

"I still could."

"Or if all that didn't happen, maybe you and I wouldn't be here together right now."

That much was true, and it brought me back to the pile of logs, the lake smell, the sloshing water. She put her hand on my wrist and moved it down to my palm, squeezing, as if to comfort me, and it made me aware of our bodies again—the contact, the closeness, the nakedness of her shoulder and leg. Something was on her face that made the distance between us collapse, and suddenly her lips were on mine, soft and cool and tasting of sugar.

I'd been imagining a moment like this all summer, but our disagreement was still playing the wrong chords inside me, and her touch seemed to further dismiss what I'd been trying to tell her—asking me not only to admit that I was wrong but also to please shut up about it. It made the kiss feel like a concession I wasn't ready to make, and all I could think about, as I moved my mouth against hers, was her insistence on the world's benevolence, her belief that it contained nothing but day camps and rescued dogs and big-hearted volunteers. It dropped a curtain between us, and kissing through a curtain was like kissing a stranger.

I couldn't bear it any longer. I sprang from my seat, took one running step, and launched myself at the water, cutting it with a hard dive, propelling myself through its cool embrace as long as possible before I finally pumped myself to the surface, lungs burning, and gave chase to the slow, empty boat.

It was a long row back.

8

Our summer work was nearly finished when one of the other counselors, Trisha, with her thick eyeliner and messy ponytail, her stout thighs and revealing shorts, asked me what was going on between me and Danielle. It was a question I'd been trying to avoid, especially in the new awkwardness that had emerged between us in the week since our kiss. Trisha must have seen my embarrassment because she snapped her gum against her teeth and smiled with such intimations of knowledge that I felt naked. We were in the equipment room, gathering rubber four-square balls into a wire cage, and I returned to this task as I responded, "Nothing. Why?"

Trisha gave a coy smile. "Someone wants to know."

The next morning I was loading milk and apples into brown lunch sacks when I got the same inquiry from Michael, who was loading the crackers and tiny tubs of peanut butter. He looked about twelve years old with his ash-blond hair parted on the side, comb grooves shellacked wetly into place. He was wearing a gentle, earnest smile until I answered with irritation, "Nothing. Nothing's going on."

"Then would you mind," he said, "if I asked her out? I wanted to make sure it was okay. Just give the word and I'll back off."

For a moment I couldn't speak. I stood there holding two cold milk cartons over their open bags, panic flapping in my chest, a feeling I recognized from the day I'd walked out of basketball try-outs. "Why do you want to do that?" I said.

"I like her. I think she's cute."

"You think she's cute."

"Yeah. You don't?"

I dropped the milk cartons into their sacks. "She's all right."

The rest of the day I was jumpy and agitated. My brow kept knitting up and I had trouble concentrating when people talked to me. At times I neglected the children I was supervising to watch doorways and peer around corners, not knowing what I was looking for. At the end of the day, while the other counselors lounged around, exchanging driver's licenses to see who had the worst photo, I gathered my things in a preoccupation of haste and evasion. Danielle touched my shoulder and asked me if I was okay. I felt the others grow quiet, straining to hear my answer.

"I'm fine," I said, though my heart was so full of fear and baf-flement that I could hardly look at her. "I have to go," I said, and rushed away.

The next day I called in sick, then felt so sick at the thought of staying home that I showed up on time, ready to work. I kept seeking Danielle out and then, in her presence, avoiding her. I didn't know what to say. I wanted to ask questions but I was afraid of the answers.

And then all at once it came to me, the way I would snuff out this silly conflict with Michael.

Late in the day I caught her alone at the drinking fountain. She slurped for a long time, hair gathered in her fist—a sight so lovely it pained me. When she straightened up and saw me, it was her eyes, this time, that wouldn't meet mine. "Oh," she said. "Hi."

"I was wondering if you had any plans this weekend."

She looked at my throat. "Why?"

"I thought I might finally pick out a dog, and I was hoping you could help me."

I had imagined her melting into happy relief, but her face only darkened. "What day?" she asked.

"I don't know. Saturday?"

Her eyes came up, big and round and sorrowful—a look that told me everything I didn't want to know. "How about Sunday?" she offered.

"How about Saturday?" I insisted, but from the tightening of her brow as her eyes dropped, I saw that she wasn't going to cancel her other plans. "Morning," I added. "Are you free Saturday morning?"

***

I picked her up at her dormitory and drove with the radio off, holding a computer printout against the wheel. The air was cool and pleasant but already carried the dry, sunbaked smell of deep afternoon, which meant it would be hot later. When I passed the street to the Humane Society, she asked where I was going.

"To get a dog."

"Where?"

"It's a surprise. I've been doing some research."

"What about the Humane Society?"

"They don't have the kind I want."

"You've been visiting those dogs all summer, Ed. Those dogs love you."

I tried giving her a reassuring smile, but she had already turned to the window. This wasn't shaping up the way I'd intended. I considered turning around, and I might have done it except that I really did want a dog.

I took one highway and then another. Before long we were in the pine forests. A pack of gleaming Harleys shot by going the other direction. Otherwise the road was deserted. We passed a pile of trash in the ditch that included a disintegrating mattress and mint-green dishwasher, its mouth hanging open. Creeping along, I found the dirt road mentioned on the printout and took it, slowing further, my tires bouncing over the ruts, green-needled branches clawing at the windows. We came upon a clapboard house with a tin roof. It was set behind a small orchard where red apples hung in the trees like clustered ornaments. A din of barking rose from behind the house.

"This place is weird," Danielle said.

"They're dog breeders, not millionaires."

"You have to be careful what kind of breeders you deal with, you know."

I didn't know, but I wasn't eager to have her begin explaining again how the world worked. There was nothing to do but get out and climb the sagging porch. Danielle reluctantly followed.

I knocked on the door and a woman in a flowered blouse opened it. Somewhere inside a TV blared. She had a tidy wave of gray hair and a blotchy face that seemed accustomed to irritation. She took a moment to run her eyes over us, as if to decide whether we were worth the bother. "Here for a pup?" she asked.

I showed the printout. "The ad said you had poodles."

"I was about to make breakfast. I've also got this sinus thing."

"Sorry," I said.

"You looking to buy, or just looking?"

"To buy," I said, and Danielle added, "Depending on what we see."

The woman stepped out, letting the screen door slap shut. "Come on then."

Danielle gave me an uneasy look, but we followed the woman around the side of the house. In back, four low sheds were outlined by dingy wood shavings leaking from the bottoms where the walls didn't quite meet the earth. Further down the trail was a high wooden fence and the sound of dogs barking, but the woman stopped us at the second shed. She popped the padlock and opened the door. A slab of light fell over half a dozen pink aliens huddled together in dirty shavings. They had a few thin wisps of fur and were capable only of crawling over each other with closed eyes, whimpering. The air that escaped was hot and muggy and ripe with animal stench. Danielle gripped my forearm, conveying her disapproval.

"Whoops," the woman said. She closed the door, clasped the padlock, and led us to the third shed.

Everything in it was the same except the animals, which looked more like puppies. Their eyes were bright and excited. They had fur corkscrewing from their backs, most beige, one black. They stumbled in happy confusion toward the door, tails flailing. The woman plucked up the first to arrive, a beige one, and closed the door on the others, setting off a chorus of yips and howls. She held the animal by the scruff of its neck, turning it back and forth for me while she explained the purity of its breed and the health of its parents. The puppy didn't seem to mind hanging there. It panted and blinked, its mouth curled like a grin, tongue lolling. It was a boy.

She tried to hand it to me, but I recoiled. "What's all this?" I said, gesturing at the brown smears on its hind legs and tail.

"What do you think?" she said, but then carried the puppy toward the house, where a crusty rag had molded itself over a spigot. She held the yowling puppy between her knees while she wet the rag and scrubbed its hindquarters.

Danielle said in a low voice, "Ed, I don't think this is a good place to get a dog."

"Why not?"

"What do you mean why not? Look around."

I did. What was a dog-breeding operation supposed to look like?

The woman came back and offered me the puppy again, and this time I took its jumping, fragile body in my arms. I let it climb up my shoulder and deliver its many exuberant kisses to my cheek and ear while Danielle asked the woman, "What do you feed them? Have they been checked for worms and parasites? How much time do they spend in that chicken coop every day? Can we see their mother? Their sire? Why not?"

The woman's answers sounded practiced and indifferent. I had trouble caring about them. I knuckled the puppy's ears and let it take my finger between its teeth, something warm spreading through me that eased away the tension and disappointment that had already crept into the day. Its drying hair was standing up in silly tufts that made me smile. "How much?" I asked, interrupting them.

The woman looked at me and named her price.

"That's a little steep, isn't it?"

"Go to the pet store and it'll be twice as much."

Danielle said, "Let us talk it over."

I was reluctant to give the puppy back, but I did, and then went to the car with Danielle. As soon as the doors were closed, she turned a look of injury and anger on me. "I think it's pretty crappy of you to bring me here," she said. "I don't know what you're trying to accomplish."

"They have the kind of dog I want."

"This is a puppy mill, Ed."

"A what?"

She explained in passionate and angry tones, at times close to tears, the suffering puppy mills created as they mass-produced animals for pet stores. Conditions were squalid, operators abusive or neglectful, mothers bred to death, offspring drowned if they didn't sell. To me, this seemed to build an argument for buying the puppy, to save it from such evils, and I said so.

"You can't reward these people by buying from them, or it just makes the problem worse," Danielle said. "Why don't you adopt one of the dogs you visited all summer? Didn't you like Lenny?"

"Poodles don't shed."

"All dogs shed."

"Not poodles."

"There's no such thing as a dog that doesn't shed. Besides, you're missing the point. You're not looking at the big picture."

"Maybe that's because when I look at the big picture, I see Michael in it."

I was surprised at my boldness, and I could tell Danielle was surprised too. She looked caught, then ashamed. She turned her eyes down and her face folded up, and I wished I hadn't said it.

"He said he asked if you minded," she said.

"That's true."

She was looking at her lap, where she twisted her slim fingers. "He said you told him it was all right."

"I guess I did."

"What else was I supposed to do, hearing that?"

"You did what you had to."

She looked over with a grimace, as if she still wanted to believe the best about me, and it struck me freshly how beautiful she was—not just in her features, but also in the spirit that arranged them into these expressions.

"Can I ask you something?" she said.

"Sure."

"What do you need to be happy in life?"

"Well, what do you mean by 'happy'?"

She blinked at me. "Happy. You know, happy. What do you mean what do I mean?"

"I mean things aren't always as simple as happy or not happy. Take someone like Gandhi. You think he was happy during his hunger strike? Happiness isn't always the most important thing."

"What I need," she said, "is love."

"But what do you mean by 'love'?"

"I mean love, you idiot. Love."

I was going to tell her that love was just a bonding instinct, a chemical in the brain, a concept invented to promote conjugal loyalty, but it was only to make a point. I knew what love was. I also knew the heartache of carrying around too many expectations for love, of wanting what wasn't available and believing it would arrive at every moment. I remembered standing on the deck last

Christmas after visiting Andrews, deciding to leave that version of myself behind, and how much better I'd been doing since then. I recognized a lot of that past version of myself in Michael, actually. It was easy to imagine Danielle with him—two people who saw the world as a sanctuary of purpose and fulfillment, who didn't want it to contain things like puppy mills, or lost dogs, or brothers who did anything other than support each other.

Danielle was gazing solemnly at the orchard.

"What are you thinking about?" I asked.

"I'm thinking that Michael probably wouldn't ask what love means."

"Probably not."

"And that Michael probably wouldn't send mixed signals all the time."

"No, I don't think he would."

"Dammit, Ed. I don't understand what you want."

"One thing I want is for you to keep being happy."

"I'm not happy," she answered.

"Then I'm not either."

"You don't want to be."

"That's not true," I said. "I just have a different way of approaching it."

"If you think things aren't going to work out, that makes them not work out."

"No. Some things just aren't possible."

"Anything is possible, but you have to think positively."

I shook my head. "That's just denial."

"Not letting yourself have something you want—that's denial."

"It's denial to think that you can have everything you want."

She turned, and with a look of despair said, "Do you want me?"

"I want you to understand what I'm saying."

"Then kiss me."

I didn't see what that had to do with understanding, but there was nothing to do except send my face toward hers. The kiss that followed was filled with a sense of expiration, of paying off debt. We kissed with detachment, observing the kiss from a cold and impartial distance. We could both feel it and feel the other one feeling it. It was miserable, but we kept kissing because we knew the feeling when it ended would be worse. And it was. We wiped our lips, cleared our throats, smoothed our laps. We looked out the windows, where the sun came down hard and white on the pines. The air was so stuffy I could hardly breathe.

"Maybe I'll go see about that puppy," I said.

She didn't object. She wouldn't even look at me.

I walked toward the fruit trees with my hand clasped above my head. I wandered out there a while, stepping on last year's rotten fruit.

The woman was waiting for me behind the screen door when I returned. "Ready to buy?" she said.

I asked to see the puppy again, the same one. The woman produced it, and having the dog in my arms was a salve. For a moment I didn't care where it came from if it would help me make it through the long car ride home with Danielle, the coming weeks and years without her. "How much did you say it cost?"

The woman named the same figure as before. I thought about what Danielle had said about supporting an operation like this, and when I looked at it objectively, I knew she was right. What I didn't understand was how she could look at it objectively. The puppy was trembling and whining, trying to burrow into my armpit. I imagined the woman locking it up in the pen after I gave it back. I imagined her holding it underwater.

"I'll give you twenty dollars less than that," I said.

"Sold."

***

The long-handled scooper didn't do much good. For one thing, the puppy didn't produce the same shapely waste as the dogs at the Humane Society, and for another, it wasn't housebroken. I had to buy yellow dishwashing gloves and carpet soap and a stiff-bristled brush. As I cleaned, my regret about Danielle was at its worst. I would remember the teasing smiles she used to give me as she carried out the task I hated most, and it made me understand how much she had offered me. The knowledge left me bereft, my longing like a hole in my chest that counteracted gravity, allowing my unmoored organs to rearrange themselves with weightless stupidity while I choked on the stench of my chore.

Work was difficult, too. To everyone's great delight but Danielle's, I brought the puppy with me, though most often I used him to avoid the other counselors. I was always walking him or finding him water or teaching him tricks, because to see Danielle and Michael even talking together, even standing in the same room together, was like a kick to the sternum—it left me aching, unable to draw a breath, concerned about my survival.

But that was the final week of camp, and afterward I no longer had to worry about running into them. By the end of the following week I had trained the puppy to do his business outside, where I could use my long-handled tool on the standard messes and walk away from the problematic ones. When I bumped into Trisha at the gym, squatting an impressive stack of weight, she told me that nothing had ever materialized between Danielle and Michael anyway. They'd gone on one date and decided to be friends. Then I had to worry even less. I wondered why that possibility had never occurred to me—being friends—but I also started to feel as if I had accomplished something worthwhile with Danielle, as if I had developed myself in some fresh and rewarding way.

9

I had agreed to share an apartment the following year with Knute Buhner, the sweet-shooting lefty who never played defense and cracked me up during interviews. I'd dropped by a few times after the season ended, and even without my notepad, he seemed to enjoy fielding questions, having an audience, getting me laughing. Then one day, as I was on my way out, he surprised me by asking if I'd be interested in taking over a teammate's lease with him. He was pulling a sweatshirt off, and I waited for him to emerge from the tangle of fabric with a shining smile and a punch line, but he only smoothed his staticky hair and said, "Interested?"

"Don't you want to room with a teammate?" I asked.

"Hell no. I get enough of those guys during the season."

The lease we were taking over belonged to Kenyon Cook, the former team captain. He'd spent the summer preparing for his law enforcement exams and wrapping up an advanced cadet program, and he looked sharp in his blue shirt and black tie the day Knute got back into town. He was excited to show us around the complex, a series of four-story buildings with white-slatted siding, tasteful verandas, roof shingles that looked like squares of smooth black sand. The indoor spaces still smelled of new construction—lumber, drywall, and carpeting. The landscaping was tidy and professional. It had a workout room and a Jacuzzi.

It was also within walking distance of campus and populated almost entirely by students. Kenyon Cook kept giving fist bumps to the other residents and then introducing us. A couple guys in an adjacent building were crouched on their third-story landing tending a little hibachi, filling the air with aromas of charcoal and teriyaki. They held up their fists at us, thumbs and pinkies splayed like they were miming telephones for a game of charades. It was a gesture of easy camaraderie, and we returned it.

When I showed up two days later with the puppy, however, Kenyon Cook winced and said, "Nope. No pets." I laughed, but he wasn't kidding. Knute crouched, wheeling his hands, dive-bombing the excited puppy, but when I tried to convince him to let me sneak the dog in, as I'd been sneaking it into the dorm, he stood and assured me he'd have no trouble finding a new roommate, as though my concern was a selfless one. For a moment I considered abandoning the animal, but when I looked down at him wagging his little stump of a tail, I knew I couldn't do it. Knute recruited a guy from the golf team to replace me, and I had to scramble for housing that allowed pets and didn't require a roommate, a tall order so late in the summer.

The only option I could find was a room for rent in a little bungalow in town. It had mildew-stained siding and roof shingles barely visible under beds of moss. The front door was turquoise, and the woman who opened it was incredibly short. She looked to be in her early thirties, her face hard and shiny with sweat, pretty except for her eyes, which were recessed in dark sockets, her expression hovering somewhere between cynical humor and depression. Her hair was copper-colored from a bad bleach job, chopped at the neck, swirled and cowlicked as if she'd just gotten out of bed. She had bruised arms and a butterfly tattoo smudged on her ankle. She said her name was Tanya Schmidt.

She asked my name and then the puppy's, and by now I had said it so many times to the women who stopped me on the street, and the women had heaped such affection onto the word as they repeated it, that I'd lost my reservations about choosing a name as feminine and pretentious as Paris. It was apt for a poodle, I thought, and went nicely with the name London. Besides, Paris was the guy who'd eloped with Helen of Troy, the archer who'd put the arrow in Achilles's achilles. It was a cool name, a masculine name—or so I'd convinced myself until I said it to this prospective landlord.

"Are you gay?" she responded.

The word felt barbed, but I worried that struggling too much against it would only tangle me up more. I made myself smile. "No. Why?"

She shrugged, yawning, and started the tour.

The place had a certain charm despite its age. There were two small bedrooms, the walls and trim and doors all painted bright white. The windows held heavy glass panes rippled with age. Crystal doorknobs were set into tarnished brass plates with old-fashioned keyholes, the kind good for spying. The phone was a heavy black unit with a rotary dial. In the bathroom there was a pedestal sink stained with rust, a claw-foot tub. She invited me to step through the shower curtain, and when I did, examining the old fixtures, she told me, "No jerking off in there. Anywhere else is fine, but I don't want to step in it."

I nodded, turning down the corners of my mouth, the expression of a reasonable man settling upon a reasonable compromise.

I was further shocked when I sat down with her to sign the paperwork and deliver my check, and she told me over an enormous mug of coffee that she actually didn't give a shit, I could jerk it wherever I liked. "I just wanted to see how you'd react," she said. "If you're the kind of guy who gets his panties in a bunch, you probably shouldn't live here."

The floor sloped. Doors stuck. The kitchen window was painted shut. It was small and cramped and hot and had only one bathroom, and I'd never lived in such close proximity to a woman. But there was a fenced backyard, the rent was reasonable, and I didn't have any other options. I signed the forms, tore off a check.

Without looking, she tossed it all onto a counter piled with bills and junk mail and receipts, then searched the house a few minutes, opening drawers and shoving around their contents before finally admitting she couldn't find the extra key. She peeled the one from her own ring.

I asked, "Do you mind if I leave Paris in the yard while I get settled?"

"Leave him anywhere you want. I like dogs. I used to have one but my ex-husband took him. Well, soon-to-be-ex-husband. He just moved out. He was the kind of guy who got his panties in a bunch. You wouldn't know it from looking at him but it's true. He freaked out if he saw my tampon in the garbage and never took off his shirt so I wouldn't see his keloid scars."

She was sitting across the kitchen table, elbows on its surface, both hands holding the coffee above a slab of afternoon sunlight, her face as easy and comfortable as if she was telling me about the idiosyncrasies of the water pressure.

***

I spent the afternoon ferrying over my few possessions, then shopping for the things I hadn't needed in the dorms—a secondhand mattress and chair, milk crates and particleboard for a makeshift desk. As I was carrying in the last of these items, a beat-up brown Datsun pulled to the curb and honked. Tanya came out wearing a collared white shirt and black slacks, an apron bunched in her fist. She said the restaurant where she worked was called Sammy's and that the number was in the phone book.

While she was gone I went to the supermarket and then organized the refrigerator, consolidating her scattered takeout cartons, liquefying zucchinis, and impressive assortment of pickled products on the bottom two shelves, alongside a torn carton of Hamm's and a half-finished bottle of pink wine. Afterward I went back to work in the room, hanging my clothes in the closet, stacking my books along the baseboards, unrolling my posters before deciding I liked the clean white blankness of the walls. The only thing on them was a window, which showed blackberry brambles clawing down a rotten fence.

It didn't seem dark out until I turned on the lights. I stopped what I was doing, grabbed the leash and scooper, and took Paris through the neighborhood as the shadows deepened. Scarlet spilled like wine across the western sky. The sidewalk dropped into a drainage ditch cluttered with sun-faded cigarette packages and Fritos bags. The neighbors' lawns were desiccated, overrun with weeds, here and there holding a collapsed wading pool, a gutted car, a grubby child holding a stick. Across the street were decrepit little businesses, their heating units hidden poorly behind cheap plywood housings. Behind them rose a long warehouse painted blue, unlit strings of Christmas lights plastered across the side in nearly invisible shapes.

Paris kept casting guilty looks at me, as if to show his reluctance to do his business in this environment. "Go ahead," I kept saying, but it made my chest ache to think about giving up Knute's apartment.

Back at the bungalow, while Paris lapped at his water dish, I picked up the rotary phone and took out the long-distance calling card my mother had sent me. For each digit, I had to crank the rotary and wait for it to slide back into place. It took a long time, and when my call finally went through, I was already irritated and impatient. "I moved today," I told my mother as soon as she'd said hello. "I just wanted to give you my new contact information. Ready?"

"No, hold on." On the other end drawers opened and papers rustled, and she took this opportunity to quiz me about my summer. I said the weather was hot, the job was fine, I had read most of Camus. Yes. Yes. San Francisco Marathon in October. No. Yes. I was living with a woman in town.

"A woman?" my mother said. "Are you dating her?"

"I'm just renting a room. I got a dog, so I had to find another place."

"A dog? What possessed you to get a dog?"

"I'm almost twenty, Mom. If I want a dog, I don't have to justify it."

"I didn't realize you wanted one."

"I've *always* wanted one," I said, and might have made an accusation about London except that it would have led to exactly the kind of conversation I was trying to avoid. "Do you have a pen yet?"

"I do, but actually, Ed, since I've got you on the phone, I should tell you that I have some news. Do you have a minute?"

"I'm right in the middle of unpacking. Is it about Charlie?"

"No, although—when was the last time you talked to your father?"

I gazed into the bridge of my palm as I massaged my temples with my middle finger and thumb. This was why I called so rarely. The smallest exchange always led to some big, inevitable discussion. "A while ago."

"Well then you should probably call him when you get off the phone with me, because there *is* a new development with Charlie. Should I just tell you?"

"What's your news, Mom?"

"Okay, well, it has to do with civil unions. Do you know what those are?"

"Not really."

After a moment, she said, "You should probably pay more attention to the news if you want to be a reporter, Ed."

"I'm a sports reporter. I pay attention to sports."

She sighed, then explained a court case in Vermont while I studied an empty jar of peanut butter Tanya had left on the coffee table. "Civil unions aren't perfect," she concluded, "but they allow us to make a strong public show of commitment and begin chipping away at the marriage restriction, especially when they go to out-of-state couples."

"I don't see why this is anything I need to know about."

"Well, because it's not just a political matter. When you get older, you get better at recognizing when things are right, and when they are, there doesn't seem to be much point in delaying them. I know it probably seems like this is all happening very quickly, but it's something Jane and I have put a lot of thought into, and we're very proud and excited to have an opportunity that couples like us have never had before."

"I don't get why you care about it."

She paused a moment, and I knew she was frowning down at a notepad as her pen inscribed crosshatches into its margins. "I guess I'm not expressing myself very well. What I'm trying to say is that Jane and I are planning a trip to Vermont."

"I get what you're saying but I don't get why you *care* about it. If you cared about commitment, you wouldn't have cheated on Dad."

This resulted in silence on her end and impatience on mine. I was only stating facts, and I didn't see why it had to throw us into this old routine of pain and guilt.

"I thought you had forgiven me for that," she said.

I wanted to tell her it was a matter of hypocrisy, not forgiveness, but it made me feel childish to continue objecting. Without further argument, I recited my new address and phone number, going slowly so she would be sure to get it all down.

"I didn't mean to upset you," she said when I was finished.

"I'm not upset. Have fun in Vermont."

After hanging up, I fixed a peanut butter sandwich and chewed it in front of the mind-numbing television, trying to blot the conversation from my mind. Afterward I returned to the phone to undertake the laborious task of calling my father, again with the card. When the call went through, I gave him my new address and phone number, then said, "Mom mentioned something about Charlie."

He released a heavy sigh. I heard his chair creak, and I imagined him ripping his attention from whatever document was spread across his computer monitor. "I don't know why I always have to be the bearer of bad news. I would think I'd have earned some credit by dealing with it all as it arrives on my doorstep."

"What happened?"

The chair creaked again. "The first thing I should say is that nobody got hurt. But last week Charlie was in a car accident. He was riding in some older girl's Jeep, and she came into a curve too fast, and the thing was so top-heavy it went tumbling into a field of lettuce. He was wearing a seatbelt and so was the girl, thank God. They were fine. But the police found them a mile away, hitchhiking. Turns out she had a lot of alcohol in her system. They both did."

I was hunched forward on the futon, concern and relief colliding in me like the air masses that spawned dangerous weather. I wagged my head at this dangerous new low point even as I pulsed with gratitude that it hadn't been worse, that it hadn't been a real tragedy. "And how are *you* feeling?" I asked.

"I would say I'm at the end of my rope, but I've said it too many times before. There always seems to be more rope."

"I mean the other thing. Have you had any more pains?"

"Not a one."

"Isn't that a bad sign? If it was indigestion, wouldn't it keep happening?"

"I don't know what you want me to do about it. Sit here worrying?"

"Isn't taking aspirin supposed to help?"

"I *am* taking it, and I'm eating so much oatmeal I could vomit." He released another deep breath, this one heavy with restraint, the sound of a man regaining his composure, and I wondered what had happened to the smiling, quizzical, self-assured man I'd grown up with, who could field questions endlessly without defensiveness or irritation. "He's here—Charlie," he said. "Would you like to talk to him?"

"Oh, I don't want to bother Charlie."

But my father insisted it would be no bother, and then there was the muffling sound of a palm pressing the receiver. I stood and walked to the window. Across the street, a man with a Mohawk was working his key through a vertical row of deadbolts beneath a porch light. When my father's hand lifted, the sounds of digitized gunfire and squealing tires drifted over the line behind the frantic tapping of buttons.

"What do you want?" Charlie said.

I wanted the same thing I did every time this kind of news came in—for him to tell me that he was all right, that he'd learned his lesson, that from now on he would do better. Instead I asked how our father was doing.

"How should I know?" he said. "He isn't grabbing his chest or anything."

"Is he eating a ton of oatmeal?"

"Oh yeah. I measure it every morning to see exactly how much is gone."

I found myself frowning at the crosshatches I was drawing into the margins of a phone bill. I put down the pen. "How was Maryland?"

"Fine."

"What's Jane like?"

"Pretty nice. Kind of serious."

"What are her kids like?"

"Funny. Hard to get rid of sometimes."

"Did you hear that she and Mom are getting a civil union?"

"Yeah."

"What do you think about it?"

"I don't care."

"They're practically getting married. You don't think it's weird?"

"It's weird but what am I supposed to do? Stop talking to her?"

Paris was whining at the back door. I crossed over and let him into the yard. "Have you changed your mind about going out for basketball?" I asked.

"Oh yeah. I've been practicing jump shots every day."

"You have?"

"Oh yeah. Right after my violin lessons."

"You're playing violin?" I asked, excited and astonished, before I realized Charlie was making a fool of me.

***

That night I eased out of sleep to steady, rhythmic banging. Someone was banging on a door. I rolled over, wishing whoever owned the door would answer it, then came to my senses and sprang out of bed, knocking Paris to the floor. I stumbled through the strange room, whacking my knee on a milk crate before I found the light switch. I stepped into old basketball shorts, then jogged down the hall, threw the deadbolt, and opened the door on Tanya in her collared shirt and slacks. Her fist was cocked by her ear as if wielding an invisible knife. She gave me an exasperated look that asked what had taken so long, her gaze unsteady, her big pupils having trouble finding a point of convergence. She slurred something I couldn't make sense of. She was clearly hammered.

She came inside, trailing the odor of slop water and whiskey, and mumbled her way into the bathroom, leaving the door wide open. I heard the click of the toilet seat and then toilet paper tearing along the perforations. She emerged still trying to button her pants, shirt pinched under her chin, showing her pale abdomen.

"Are you okay?" I asked. "Do you need some help?"

"Goff," she seemed to say, irritated, then gave up on fastening her pants and pushed past me. "A goff!"

She lurched into the living room, where she turned on the TV, flopped to the futon, and right away started to snore.

By morning her snores came from the bedroom. The TV was still on, tuned to a program where a panel of women debated whether Ellen DeGeneres deserved another shot at network television. I turned it off, then let Paris out and went hunting for his mess with the long-handled scooper, a difficult chore in the overgrown wilderness of the lawn. Afterward I put on my running shorts, tightened my shoelaces, and covered the three miles to campus at an easy pace. I used the track for a speed workout, and the three miles home were a slow burn. I took Paris for a walk, my sweat drying in the morning sun. I filled his food and water dishes, washed my hands, made eggs, showered, shaved, and then set myself up on the futon with a mug of coffee, plucking my bookmark from the Jane Austen I'd picked up, having grown suddenly tired of Camus. I looked up whenever Tanya's snoring caught, hesitated, and resumed.

It was almost noon, hot sun pouring through the windows, when she finally stirred. After thumping around in the bathroom she lurched into the kitchen, muttering obscenities as she ground her coffee. I heard cereal cascade, milk slosh—both mine, I realized—and then she came into the living room and turned on the TV by pressing the button with her big toe. She was holding a bowl and spoon and wasn't wearing any pants, just nubby beige underwear. I gaped over the top of my book at the contours nestled beneath the thin fabric. Her thighs were as muscular as a gymnast's. Her throat was a sculpture of tendon and clavicle. Mouth munching cereal, eyes glued to the television, she looked raw and fearless. Even her rumpled hair was sexy.

That afternoon, dressed in her waitress uniform again, apron bunched in her fist, she called from the front door that she needed her key. I set about peeling it from my ring as I crossed to her, but she wouldn't take it.

"Are you stupid?" she said. "I told you to make me a copy."

"When?"

"When I couldn't get in last night!"

I recalled the slurring and mumbling as she had come inside. I hadn't thought she'd been lucid. "You remember all that?"

"Fucking-A right."

"Isn't it your job to have keys copied? You're the landlord."

"Yeah, I'm the landlord, so I make the rules."

The Datsun pulled to the curb and honked. I offered her the key from my ring once more, but she refused it. "Just let me in tonight when I knock," she said. I was going to argue that I would be asleep, but I got the sense that it made little difference to her.

"Locked out of my own fucking house," she muttered as she left. "Un-fucking-believable."

She returned early that night, while the last traces of sun still dirtied the darkening sky. I hadn't even locked up yet, and she stormed in scolding me about security. What if she had been some psycho? What if she had been a jealous husband?

"He's jealous?" I responded.

She held out her palm and asked for the extra key.

"I was planning to do that tomorrow."

She lifted her face toward the ceiling, as if she might find some serenity there. Then she said, "Have you seen *Poltergeist?*"

"What?"

She repeated herself, enunciating the words with slow and infuriated precision. I thought she was referencing the movie to make some point about the danger I'd put us in, but she had apparently moved on from all that. "You'll love it," she said, and began searching through stacks of VHS tapes. When the credits were rolling she offered me a Hamm's, already heading for the kitchen, and then shouted, "You're taking over my fridge too?" We watched the movie with the lights off, sipping beer, her bare feet wedged under my leg. I stiffened when she put them there, startled that she would breach my personal space so casually and so soon, but I liked the physical contact. I was surprised that so little of it could set my blood pumping.

A few nights later, the muggy heat didn't back off after the sun went down. Unable to sleep, I went to the kitchen for ice water when I noticed Tanya face-up on her bed, nude, her limbs splayed like a starfish, her face shoved under a pillow, her body lit from the hallway. I stood frozen in her doorway, drinking in the sight, my nerves buzzing, until she raised her head, squinting, and said, "Turn off the light, Ed."

I did, then headed to the shower to do what she had given me permission to.

In the following weeks, I toyed with the idea that Tanya was coming on to me, but it was fairly obvious that she just had no notion of boundaries. She left the door wide open while she changed her clothes, while she showered, while she sat on the toilet, leaning over smooth white haunches. She wiped her hands on my bath towel, borrowed my socks, popped pimples on my neck. Without asking, she speared morsels from my dinner plate and poured pink wine into my empty water glass. When I was showering she often barged in to brush her teeth or put on makeup or blow her nose, her outline blurred and fractured behind the steamy, water-streaked plastic, talking to me so casually that I sometimes wondered if she realized her husband had left.

I learned that she was from Reno, where her father was variously and intermittently employed, often semi-legally, and mostly lived off of her mother, who cleaned hotel rooms and went mute when Tanya was twelve. She'd been a normal person, Tanya said, but then one day just kind of went away. Her father came home less and less after that. The last time she saw him, he opened his wallet and gave her thirty-seven dollars, then said, "If things get bad, tell someone at your school." He didn't know she'd already been expelled for truancy and misbehavior. Finally the state stepped in, and she cycled through several foster homes and alternative schools before running away and eventually landing in Conrad Park, where she'd been happily performing service jobs ever since.

What was wrong with your mom?" I asked.

"Hell if I know. She's still like that."

Then school was upon me, and I saw Tanya less often. I ran in the early morning, then spent all day going to class, doing homework, fulfilling my new responsibilities as sports editor. Tanya was usually at work by the time I came home to walk Paris in the late afternoon or evening. Some nights she came home early, while I was studying or reading, and tried to compel me to the living room with zombie movies or Twizzlers or beer, and usually I succumbed. Most nights, however, she came home long after I'd gone to bed.

She yelled back at the Datsun sputtering at the curb and then cursed her way through the house and turned on the television. Now and then she barged into my room to rub Paris's ears and give us both a detailed account of her awful night, her voice pitched between comedy and complaint, while I lounged nude beneath the covers, making wishes.

These accounts often featured an appearance by Derek, her soon-to-be-ex-husband, who apparently wasn't keen on signing the divorce papers. He kept trying to negotiate about the house, she said, although he mostly seemed to be holding out hope for reconciliation, which resulted in the shouting matches that Tanya detailed for me. Mostly they seemed to accuse each other of not caring enough, and one night Tanya got so worked up defending herself against the charge that her voice quivered. She put on a bitter smile while her eyes filled up, and to see it was as unreal and embarrassing as when my father's sob had escaped at the family meeting. The only thing I could think to do was put my hand on hers, and the moment I did, she hunkered down with us, curling around Paris, pulling my arm over her like a blanket. "You're a good listener," she said.

I didn't know if I was allowed to touch her further, but I didn't want to risk losing the comfort of her body against mine, so I just lay there, trying to keep my erection off her, enjoying the warmth and solidity of her body from the other side of the blanket. A few moments later she was breathing heavily and twitching. I knew I wouldn't be able to sleep like that, but I didn't move.

10

My favorite course that term was called Principles of Reporting, taught by a woman who shaved the sides of her head and looked too young to be a professor. She was passionate and articulate, and her syllabus was filled with provocative lesson titles. In class she approached them from both philosophical and practical standpoints, explaining the abstractions that informed the profession and the real-world techniques for carrying them out. It often left my head swimming with sensations of virtue and purpose that were a lot like the feeling I used to get sitting in the locker room after practice, sweat dripping from my chin while Russo talked about what it meant to be a team.

"As a reporter," she instructed one day, stalking back and forth behind the lectern, "you have to cultivate sympathy for every viewpoint you encounter, even the ones that seem absurd. At the same time, you have to retain a healthy level of skepticism for those viewpoints, even the ones that seem self-evident. That's a difficult balance to strike, and the only way to do it is by relinquishing your preconceived notions and approaching every subject with genuine curiosity and openness. That starts with the language you use, which is what I'd like you to work on today—"

I partnered up, as always, with Myra Devlin, a diligent student with eyeglasses that darkened in the sun and a puff of brown hair that smelled of Pert. The exercise was about choosing neutral wording during interviews, and when we'd finished, I asked Myra, "Don't you think some questions can't be neutral, no matter how you word them?"

"You shouldn't say, 'don't you think.' It's leading."

"Like what if someone is going on and on about how important commitment is, but they weren't committed enough in their own marriage to stay faithful. How are you supposed question them about that *neutrally?*"

She thought about it, then raised her hand.

"Well," the professor responded, crouching between our desks after Myra had explained our question, "maybe you could reference the marriage rather than the unfaithfulness: 'How has your own marriage influenced your opinion on commitment?'"

"But wouldn't that just let the person avoid the cheating?" I asked. "Wouldn't it be more productive to ask something pointed like, 'How can you claim to care about anybody else's marriage when you didn't care about your own?'"

"The short answer is yes, absolutely—sometimes you have to stray from one ideal to better fulfill another. Even so, it would be more productive to phrase your question, even that kind of question, with a little more sympathy. That goes beyond the language you use. It requires real compassion. Can you think of a more compassionate way of asking it?"

Myra cleared her throat. "Maybe, 'what *caused* you to cheat?'"

"Maybe. Ed?"

I looked at my hands and didn't answer. I was trying to figure out how to offer sympathy without also offering a pardon, and nothing was coming to mind.

Finally the professor said, "How about, 'do you think marriage is a worthwhile pursuit even when it's imperfect?' Or even, 'is the ideal of commitment valuable even when we fall short of it?' Do you think that might earn an equally productive response?"

She was looking at me with such kindness and sympathy that my resistance softened, which helped me see her point about the usefulness of compassion.

"Yes," I admitted. "More productive, probably."

***

I carried the inspiration from this class to my editorial work, where I found the purpose and camaraderie that had been missing from my freshman year. At the newspaper I had a team, and I liked my new teammates: the copy editor, Jessa Crain, a music major shaped like the cello she played, who often tipped her head back to let loose the kind of boisterous, unselfconscious laughter that nobody could help but join; the opinions editor, Kim Marzen, with her tiny face behind her enormous glasses, who in person was a pushover but in print was a monster; the news editor, Yusef Alrahmani, with his tight shirts and distressed denim jacket, who always delivered objections in the form of a question, a habit I admired and began to mimic.

But there was one new teammate who especially interested me: the photo editor, Lucienne Close. She was tall and gaunt, her face haunted with the gritty, sensual look of hunger. She wore exciting clothes, pieces more formal and daring than anyone else on campus. Her expression was by turn contemptuous and sedate. She had a habit of avoiding eye contact. She rarely smiled. It was impossible to imagine her telling me to think positively, or that happiness was a choice we made every day. She seemed to be sheltering some kind of pain or fear that had darkened her opinion of the world. All these things and more made my heart race.

Lucienne worked at the computer next to mine, close enough to swaddle me in the heady smell of her perfume while we labored through Sunday night to assemble the weekly issue, each of us pausing to eat pizza, take out contact lenses, change into pajamas and slippers, and then finally sliding away, one by one, into the muffled light of a new day. Lucienne was the only one who wore her day clothes straight through the night, who didn't ponytail her hair or wash away her makeup or hide in a hooded sweatshirt. I asked her about everything I could think of as we worked—her weekend, her classes, her background and tastes. She answered without elaboration, her voice somber, as if she was afraid of exposing her secrets.

I did manage to pick up a few tidbits. She was from the East Coast—where, exactly, I could never pin down. She referenced four or five different cities and seemed to have gone to school at all of them. After the 9/11 terrorist attacks, she wore all black for two weeks, but when I asked with compassion and deference if she'd known any of the victims, her only response was, "I must have." Her parents had apparently shipped her to "a woods" every summer for an all-girls camp, where the dirt and insects and older campers had inflicted various traumas upon her. She'd been allowed to sip red wine since grade school but had been prohibited from dating until her eighteenth birthday. When I asked how much she'd dated since then, she responded quickly, "Plenty." Then she glanced at me and let her eyes drop to the keyboard. "It's only been a year," she said.

She'd come to the West Coast to escape her parents. When I asked if they were still married, her response was, "Ostensibly." When I asked why she'd selected Sequoia College, she was quiet a moment. "Admissions are rigged," she said. "They don't look at the right things."

Her photos were adequate, not sensational. Some were weird— empty bleachers, road kill, a giant nipple. She liked to pitch these to the section editors, explaining their tangential relation to whatever stories they were running that week, her voice flat and hopeless, already resigned to a refusal. One week she wanted me to run the football story with a photo of a mannequin lying in a ditch. She said it expressed the deindividuation that team sports inflicted on athletes. "Personally I love the idea," I said, not wanting to insult her, "but do you think our readers will be smart enough to get it?"

She didn't argue. She converted the photo to grayscale, printed it, and taped it to the wall alongside her many other disturbing shots. I made a point to compliment the strangest of them, explaining the abstractions I saw, and she furrowed her brow thoughtfully, in a way that seemed to hide her pleasure.

***

The weather started to turn, a chill creeping in through the open windows at night, the plum-colored trees around the bungalow's neighborhood acquiring little red embers near their crowns. By then Tanya was staying in my bed a couple nights a week. I wore shorts and a T-shirt for her but no longer bothered to hide my erection, which she either couldn't feel or understood was beyond my control. Either way, it wasn't an issue. I usually had trouble sleeping, and the next day I was groggy and irritable, especially if I had to wake up early for a run, but I didn't ask her to stop. It was a comfort to have someone to hold.

Then one Monday she prodded me awake. The window blinds glowed with the buttery light of morning, which meant I'd been in bed only a few hours after a long night at the newspaper, and it irritated me that she would wake me. She was dressed strangely, wearing a blue blazer that was too big for her. She also had on makeup and earrings, and her hair was brushed soft. "Grab a condom," she said, and rattled a sheaf of papers at me. "I just got divorced."

After a moment of disbelief, I fished a condom from beneath the mattress and checked the its expiration date, my vision foggy and my head heavy from sleep. She was already kicking off her shoes and peeling away her pants and underwear, her back stooped in the plain morning light. When she tugged down my shorts, I tensed, feeling exposed and embarrassed. I was no virgin, thanks to

Brittany Mercer, but that seemed little more than a technicality as Tanya rolled the condom on.

My head felt stuffed with cotton, my left nostril clogged, my mouth syrupy and rank. Hers, when she climbed on top of me, smelled of cigarettes. We averted our faces, not kissing, trying not to even breathe on each other, while Paris sat in the doorway panting. I couldn't feel much through the condom, and we bucked at each other clumsily, without synchronization. She kept instructing me, "Stop moving your hips," and, "Your elbow's in my ribs." Finally she found a rhythm, then gasped, shuddering. After that something built behind my numbness and broke.

She smiled down at me, hair curtained around her face. She was naked below the waist but still wearing the ridiculous blazer. Before uncoupling us, she squeezed me a couple times down there—without hands—and said thanks.

"Thank *you*," I answered.

We had sex a few times a week after that. Tanya turned out to be surprisingly conventional. She usually liked to kiss a long time before starting. Sometimes she put me on top and other times claimed the top for herself. That was our only variation. I made the mistake once of asking if she wanted to try some other position, and she shot back, "Like what, doggy style?" I could tell she found it ridiculous, and the name of it, spoken aloud, inclined me to agree.

Besides, I enjoyed it fine the normal way, and I enjoyed her enjoyment. She was loud and fast and generous, easily satisfied and eager to satisfy me. I would only have preferred the sessions more often, and in the beginning I tried to initiate them. "Are you stroking my hair?" she said, as if only a pervert would try such a thing. "Less fondling, more back-rubbing," she said during my massages. One time I leaned over and kissed her hard on the mouth, then peeked up and saw her eyes looking past me, watching the television. I sat back. "Gum?" she said, and produced a crushed package from her pocket.

So I waited, and invariably she came to me, shaking me awake late at night after the Datsun had roared away, or walking over and straddling me while I studied the libel trial of John Peter Zenger, or just snapping her fingers as she got up from the futon and telling me, "Pants. Off." I felt none of the impatience or anxiety that had always descended upon me before at the idea of sex. There was something so comfortable and ordinary about ours that it took away the desperation in my desire, the romantic majesty I had always invested into physical intimacy. It was casual and uncomplicated, just an ordinary part of living with a woman like Tanya, it seemed—no different, really, from peeing with the door open or sharing food or breaking into tears over your ex.

***

Lucienne, meanwhile, had started taking the seat next to mine at our Wednesday editorial meetings, and if she had a question, she whispered it to me rather than addressing Eli Duncan. After prowling the sidelines at football games, she scanned the crowd until she found me, then came over to ask for consultation about her shots. While we worked Sunday nights, she piped up at random times to ask why the Winter Olympics were no longer held the same year as the Summer Olympics or to debate the relative genius of John Galliano and Alexander McQueen. Some Sundays, in those vague hours between nighttime and morning, when everyone ached from the long hours of sitting, I stood behind her chair and squeezed her shoulders. Getting no objection, I moved up her sinewy neck and worked down her back, thrilled by the delicacy of her muscles, the hard scapula and vertebrae knuckled just below the skin.

She also started to answer my questions less reluctantly. She told me about the options she was considering after college—a year or two of travel through Europe, maybe a series of artist colonies, but ultimately a move to New York for an internship at a major fashion magazine to launch her career shooting models, she didn't care how long she had to do it for free. When I asked why she didn't want to stay out West, she said, "You never know where you stand with people here. They'll smile at you while you talk but then won't say hello the next time you see them. I guess it's a West Coast thing, but I don't know what you're supposed to do with that. How do you make any friends? That's why I joined the newspaper—well, that and building my portfolio. But you're the only one who seems to take me seriously."

When I asked about her parents, she called them a painter and a sculptor "with day jobs," though the jobs turned out to be fairly serious—her father was an executive at a graphic design firm and her mother was a state legislator. In many ways she admired them, she said, although they were, in her estimation, terrible parents. Her father preferred golf and sailing to his wife and daughter, and her mother was a hawk presiding over Lucienne's dinner plate. They both drank too much and fought constantly when her mother was home, though they had a talent for making it sound like casual banter and pretending that nothing ever upset them. They were both waiting eagerly for Lucienne's grandmother to die so that her mother could inherit the estate in Nantucket and move in permanently to "oversee its restoration." Lucienne was quite sure that they would never divorce, though, even if they lived apart.

"We're Catholic," she explained.

It sounded like what I'd been arguing my mother should have done—stay married, no matter what. I'd imagined that everything would have continued on as it always had, but now I reconsidered, imagining my mother at home against her will, faking a smile, filling everything with bristling innuendo, while my father drank and looked away. It would have stolen the comfort and wholeness from the house as surely as her absence had, tightening every moment with pressure, worry, and anger.

"Do you think they'd be happier apart?" I asked.

"It's not about happiness. It's about keeping up appearances."

"My parents got divorced a little over a year ago."

"Parents suck," she said. "The only reason I put up with mine is because they're very supportive of my photography."

Our conversations were usually one-sided like this, which suited me fine. I wasn't eager to answer questions about my family, or my reason for choosing Sequoia, or especially my living situation. And so I was grateful Lucienne never asked.

***

Tanya, on the other hand, had no trouble offering up her darkest secrets or asking about mine. "In sixth grade," she told me once, tying off the condom and dropping it in the wastebasket, "all I ever thought about was sucking off my science teacher. He was this young guy with long hair. I could never get up the guts to try it, though. I sucked off Jason Wozniak instead and was totally happy."

I listened with horrified fascination. I couldn't begin to think of how to respond. "Were you abused?" I asked.

"Come on. It was nothing like that. You never stole panties from one of your sister's friends or something?"

"I don't have a sister. I have a brother."

"Yeah? What's he like?"

And that was how she drew information from me. "Tall," I answered.

"Taller than you?"

"Yeah. Not that it matters. Not to him. He's not really making much of himself. He kind of lost his way."

"How old is he?"

"Almost fifteen. He's a freshman in high school. But he's turned into one of those kids who skips class to smoke. He shows up to school dances drunk."

"That's the kind of kid I was."

"He used to be a great basketball player. I mean great. He could have played in college, easy. His grades have gotten terrible too. I'm not sure how he'll get into college at all, at this rate. I don't know what he's going to do."

"He'll get by. I did."

"It's not just about getting by. It's that he doesn't care about anything anymore. When we were kids, he was always tagging along and asking me for advice. It drove me crazy, but I always tried to steer him in the right direction because he's my brother—especially when it came to basketball. Now anything I say, he does the opposite, just to show he doesn't give a shit about me or basketball or anything."

"If someone's going out of their way to make you feel like shit," she said, "usually it's because you made them feel like shit first."

"Try telling that to him," I said, thinking of all the times he'd hurt or belittled me—ignoring my attempt to rescue him from the family meeting, refusing to help me work on a new move for Sequoia, getting high before the pickup game. "I used to have this dream of us playing on the same team in college, him coming in and making it as a freshman, me keeping my eligibility for a fifth year. I always thought that would be so cool."

"I didn't know you played basketball."

"I don't, really. Not anymore."

"So then why does he have to? Let the kid figure things out for himself."

That wasn't the point, but I didn't know how to explain it any better. "It's just this dream I've always had," I told her.

After these conversations Tanya liked calling me by my last name. "You're all right, Garrison," she might say, or, "You crack me up, Garrison," or, "Deep down you're just as fucked up as the rest of us, Garrison," as if this was some kind of compliment.

It made me feel a throb of warmth and connection with her, especially when it happened after sex. I described this feeling to myself as really intense friendship. At times I wondered if we were developing something more, but I was happy with things the way they were, and I was pretty sure Tanya slept with me just because

I was there. I imagined she probably would've done the same no matter who had rented from her. I saw myself as the first in a succession of very satisfied tenants. It was hard to believe she had been married once—and recently.

***

I was running in the afternoons now that the weather was cool, and as I tapered off my mileage for the race, I started bringing Paris on my short runs, at first for his sake, but then for mine. It was a hassle to have him there, but it also made the time pass more quickly. He carried a length of leash in his mouth like a dead duck and trotted dutifully beside me, glancing up now and then as if to ask if he was doing a good job. His little tufts of fur had become curling beige locks that looked almost human. They were especially dense and fluffy at the crown of his head, so that it looked like he was wearing a ridiculous toupee that flopped over his eyes. If I asked him a question, he would cock his head, looking up from beneath his toupee while he trotted, as though he might understand if I would only repeat myself once more. It made me laugh, and sometimes I had to stop running and wrestle him affectionately to the ground.

The weekend before my marathon, there was a knock at the door, and I opened it on a skinny guy in baggy jeans and dirty white sneakers. He looked to be in his mid-thirties, his hair parted down the middle and swept into two clean arches that swooped toward his ears. His nose was like a blade and his glasses were a decade out of style. "You must be the tenant," he said. "How do you like living in my house?" He looked down at Paris, who was trying to wriggle past my shin, his whole body quivering with the excitement of a visitor, and asked, "Where's Tanya?"

"I don't know."

"Mind if I come in?"

I was too surprised to prevent him from pushing past me. I waited by the door, as if I were the visitor, while he stalked through the house, checking rooms. When he was satisfied with his search, he threw himself onto the futon and pushed his chin at the TV, where the Giants were playing the Dodgers with the sound muted. "How can you watch this crap?"

"Bonds has sixty-seven homers. He's three short of the record."

"Me? I like action. Boxing. Football. Basketball was all right until Jordan retired."

"He's not retired anymore. He's coming back."

"What, again?"

"Yeah. For the Wizards this time. He just announced it."

"Where's Dennis Rodman playing these days? I love that guy."

"I think he's out of the league."

He nodded ruefully, as if this confirmed the sorry state of the sport, then picked up the remote and crossed his feet on the coffee table, perfectly at home. I sat down and went back to my astronomy worksheet. I didn't know what else to do.

When Tanya came in twenty minutes later, she stared daggers at me before turning the look on Derek. "You two nice and comfy?"

"It's getting cold at night," he said, eyes on the TV. "I need some blankets."

"Then go buy some fucking blankets."

"Why should I? The ones here are half mine. Other stuff is too."

"Forget that I paid for it all."

"Take it up with the judge."

Ten minutes later he was carrying a grocery sack of kitchen utensils with two blankets tucked into his armpit, his other hand gripping a plunger. At the door he turned and said, "Oh, I forgot to tell you," and pointed the plunger at me. "Touch my wife and I'll fucking kill you. Understand?"

My face went hot. Derek was just a skinny guy who needed a haircut, not the burly type I'd been picturing, and he had no claim on Tanya, especially now that they were divorced. But until that moment he had always just been a figure from Tanya's stories, and his jealousy seemed to exist only as an inconvenience to us. I'd never thought about what the jealousy felt like, or what was beneath it. He offered a smile but it came out crooked, and when his eyes slid to Tanya, I could see the grief and humiliation he was trying to conceal.

He came back a couple days later in the evening, when Tanya was at work. I pretended I wasn't home. He rang the bell relentlessly, as if to annoy someone into letting him in, then began to move around the house, trying doors and windows while Paris ran from room to room, barking. I started to feel sorry for him. I knew what it was like to return to your old life only to find locked doors, closed windows. Finally his truck rumbled to life. The engine revved, the tires chirped, and he was gone. Ten minutes later the phone rang. I didn't pick up, and the guilt in my chest felt as hot and swollen as a sprain.

When I told Tanya about his attempted break-in that night, she dropped her purse and apron on the carpet and shook her head. "Can you believe I used to find that kind of thing romantic?"

"Romantic? Why?"

She kicked off her shoes and began unbuttoning her shirt. "I used to think the most important thing about a guy was how much effort he was willing to make. I thought that was how you could tell whether you meant something to him or not." She peeled off the shirt, then pushed down her pants and stepped out of them. "But then the effort dries up, and what are you left with? Don't be with someone who feels like it's a chore. That's what I learned. Next time I'll look for a guy who doesn't have to make an effort."

She was right. I thought of how much effort I'd made with Brittany and Danielle, and it was suddenly clear how much better it would have gone if I'd been casual about it, like Tanya was. Caring too much had sabotaged me, and the same thing was happening now with Lucienne.

"That's always been my problem," I said. "Trying too hard."

She crawled into bed and embraced me. "You keep hoping people will grow up, but some can't. It took me a while to realize that. You will, though. I can tell. You just need some experience. Have you ever even had a real girlfriend?"

I thought of Brittany, Danielle, Lucienne. "No," I said. "Not yet."

11

That Wednesday I went straight from class to the newspaper office and found Lucienne sitting at the conference table in a black pea-coat. Nobody else was there yet. I moved to her slowly, casually, like someone who didn't care too much about the conversation he was about to initiate. But her head was in her hands, her elbows propped on either side of a manila folder, and when she glanced over with red, watery eyes, I could see the conversation would have to wait a moment. "What's the matter?" I asked.

She withdrew a letter from the folder, handed it to me, then put her head back in her hands. It read, *Thank you for submitting the photo collection "Risk" to Reinhardt's gallery. Unfortunately, we are unable to . . .*

"It's not even a real gallery," she said. "It's just that dumb café on Third Street."

She slid the folder over, so I opened it, and inside were glossy, oversized portraits of naked young men and women, their genitalia exposed, their postures protective, their nervous eyes trained just past the camera, as if receiving orders from someone who held them there against their will.

"Who are these people?" I asked.

"Friends from home."

"Your friends posed naked for you?"

"I paid them to. That's generally how it works."

When I came to the last one, it took me a moment to recognize the subject as Lucienne. Without her clothes she looked as frail and vulnerable as a cancer patient, her body pale and scrawny, breasts small, pubic hair clinging between her legs like a frightened pet. Her face was drawn, her eyes so frank and embarrassed that I wanted to wrap her in a blanket and lead her out of the frame. Instead I touched her shoulder through the thick wool of her coat and said, "These are good."

She looked up, a glimmer of hope piercing her expression. "Really?"

"Yeah. You can feel how nervous everyone is."

"That's exactly what I was going for. That's why it's called Risk."

"You should send it to a real gallery, one that isn't trying to sell people coffee."

"You think so?" She took the folder from me and began looking through the photos again. "I thought a real gallery would want something more commercial since they're actually trying to sell it."

My hand was still on her shoulder, and I took it away before saying, "Hey, what would you think of coming to San Francisco with me for my marathon?"

"What, to watch?" She kept flipping through the photos. I could tell the idea didn't thrill her.

"And to shoot the finish," I said. "I've heard you see some crazy stuff."

"Like what?"

"I don't know. If you want to find out then you should come with me on Sunday."

"Sunday? What about newspaper?"

"It's in the morning. We'll be back in plenty of time."

She thought about it a moment. "How far is San Francisco?"

It was three hours, so we left long before sunrise. I was giddy about the race, full of nervous energy and excitement, though that was nothing compared to my nervousness and excitement about having Lucienne in my car, filling it with the smell of her perfume, absconding with me from the tight boundaries of our professional relationship. As we twisted east through the dark pine forests and then cut south through pastureland, I took care to still myself, to swallow the reckless comments crashing through my mind, while Lucienne sipped coffee from a paper cup and groaned. She seemed to be coming awake in small increments. It was very early.

It was raining as we came into San Francisco, daybreak easing in slow and uniform like stage lights coming on. The bay was gray and empty, the Golden Gate's towers hazy in the graphite-colored mist, though the roadbed was alive with brake lights. On the other side the blocky white city came into view, and I aimed for the dark huddle of skyscrapers in the financial district, dominated by the elongated pyramid of the Transamerica building. The Corolla's old engine worked hard to propel us up a steep hill, tires slipping on the wet asphalt. Big drops plunked from the crisscrossed power lines overhead, linking the flat-fronted dwellings crammed on either side. On the way down my brakes squealed. Near the Embarcadero I seized an open parking spot, and when I set the parking brake and killed the engine, my shoulders relaxed. We were here. There was plenty of time.

The rain was loud on the windows and roof. Wind gusts buffeted the car and tossed the palm fronds on the waterfront, where the piers jutted into the bay's gray chop.

"Are they going to cancel it?" Lucienne asked.

"I don't think so."

"You're going to run in this?"

"I guess."

A chill crept in, so I turned on the engine, and as the dry heat bloomed from the floor, I thought about how pleasant it would be to stay in the car with Lucienne. I looked at her. Seams of light lay like ribbons on her face, bending and shifting as they slid. When I closed my hand over hers, she looked at me with curiosity, then turned her palm up and interlaced her fingers with mine. I squared my shoulders and leaned in, reminding myself that this didn't have to be a big deal. Lucienne leaned in as well, almost imperceptibly, and her eyes moved down to my lips.

Her mouth tasted bitter from the coffee but it was soft and warm. Her kisses seemed to ask polite questions, then answer them with other questions, and I restricted myself to this pleasant and mysterious dialogue, though I was surprised at how tentative she was, having grown used to Tanya, who poured herself into my mouth.

Eventually I had to pull away. I gave her my keys and said, "Wish me luck."

She regarded me with a placid, satisfied expression, but as I climbed out, she said, "You're not really my type, you know." I looked back to find a smile turning up the corners of her mouth. I returned it, then closed the door.

In the starting gates I huddled in the crowd of runners wearing a cheesy grin, wanting to tell them all what had just happened. Techno beats thumped from big speakers and a man with a loudspeaker made garbled announcements. Then the gun went off, and the crowd surged forward, and it was here.

We went north along the Embarcadero, the surf sloshing noisily beneath the piers, the marina a thicket of wildly pitching masts. From there we turned onto the Golden Gate Bridge, which looked different on foot—an impossible hill. On one side Alcatraz sat on its lonely rock and on the other a barge was headed out to sea. The elite runners were already coming back the other direction, led by a small brown man with a shaven head and a white man with a thick, rain-soaked beard. They ran side-by-side, motoring along at an easy, incredible pace. The trickle of runners after them slowly became a flood, and the flood became my flood. I followed it around an orange barrel and headed back over the bridge.

By then water was sloshing in my shoes, my sodden socks bunching at the toe. Droplets crawled down my arms and face like fat ticks. The rain had soaked my shirt, plastering it to my body and weighting the fabric so that it chafed my armpits and nipples. Volunteers in hooded jackets offered tongue depressors gobbed with Vaseline, and I smeared the greasy stuff on, repulsed. Still, when I thought of Lucienne, I smiled.

We dropped into a park, traversing the byzantine trails, looping between massive evergreens, circling ponds choked with floating vegetation. We emerged onto Haight Street, running between its colorful storefronts—smoke shops and record stores and pizza joints and big urban murals. My stride by then was choppy, my knees stiff, my shoulders sore from holding up my hands, but after mile twenty there came new depths of fatigue, every step sending bone-deep reverberations of pain all the way up to my hips.

At mile twenty-five we were pinched between the baseball stadium and McCovey Cove, into which Barry Bonds had hit many of his seventy-three home runs that year. I imagined them plopping into the gray water, chased down by kayakers, and I wondered if Charlie knew about his record.

At mile twenty-six the crowds thickened. Spectators in slickers and heavy coats cheered and rang cowbells and held soggy signs. It was impossible to spot Lucienne, but I imagined her eyes on me and hoped she was impressed by my determination, my commitment, my ability to endure. When the finish line came into view I tried to speed up but my legs didn't listen, and I was surprised to cross it without elation, just the relief of a hard task being over. A woman dropped a medal around my neck, and then I was being herded beneath a big white awning, where I wandered among bowls of banana halves and hot, plated pancakes and peanut butter sandwiches, surrounded by other runners wearing medals. Their faces were dazed and glistening, like mine. That was the part that filled me up most—the knowledge that I was one of them, that we had all done this impossible thing together.

I'd just accepted a cup of tomato soup, piping hot, when I heard Lucienne holler my name. She was at the side gate, enclosed in a clear plastic umbrella that fit over her shoulders like a lid, her smile fractured and distorted behind the rain-streaked plastic. I staggered to her, feeling stunned, stupefied with exhaustion, until she lifted the umbrella to receive me. Her mouth tasted now of cinnamon, and it moved me in a way the finish line hadn't. The marathon would always be something between us, I realized, and it was as if all my training, without my even knowing it, had been for her.

I hobbled with her to the car, my knees stiff, my feet smashed. She gripped my arm as if to hold up my weight and offered solicitous little comments as she navigated me: "Careful now, here's another curb." Otherwise she chattered happily about the great shots she'd gotten. "People were making all kinds of crazy faces," she said. "I'm going to blow some of them up so the whole frame is just a huge close-up of one part of their face—like, how much misery can you get from just a mouth or an eye?" As she said this, she turned her eyes on me, then, a moment later, her camera. "Jesus," she said, shooting. "You look like a corpse. Are you okay?"

On the way home I blasted the heater. Lucienne took off her scarf and coat and sweater, all the time talking. "I don't know what would possess someone to run a marathon. I bet a lot of runners have body image issues, actually. It's like an exercise disorder, basically. Some of them probably have eating disorders too. It's a wonder more models don't take up marathons. Is that why you're so thin?"

"No. I eat as much as I can."

"You're lucky."

"You're thinner than I am."

"Yeah but I work at it. I used to want to be a model, but I don't have the face for it. Plus I'm not tall enough."

"You look like a model to me."

"Have you ever been to New York?"

"No."

"You wouldn't say that if you had been to New York. Those girls are fabulous. I could look at them all day long. But if I want to shoot them I need to figure out how to make people more comfortable around me—especially when they're naked. That's what I was trying for with my friends, but then everyone looked so terrified that I just said fine, it'll be about that instead. I'm basically a very uncomfortable person and I think it rubs off on people when I'm shooting them. That's one reason I like you. I feel all right around you. You seem okay with everything."

It was exactly how Tanya seemed to me, and I silently thanked her for showing me how to do it.

Lucienne lived in one of the cookie-cutter townhouses near the DMV. The complex was a bland assembly of cheap construction, row after row of identical carports and concrete staircases sandwiched between squared shrubs. Signposts directed me through an array of five-digit numbers, speed bumps jostling my tires. When I pulled to the curb outside her apartment, she smiled and leaned across the seat for another kiss. "Your lips are freezing," she said. "See you at the newspaper?"

I waited until she was inside, then drove away thinking about what she'd said. I doubted Lucienne would ever get the hang of making people feel comfortable, but I admired the tenacity with which she applied herself to the pursuit. It took the same kind of determination and endurance as running, which would have made it easy to fantasize about a future together if I wasn't trying as hard as I could to keep it casual.

At home Paris was sprawled on the futon next to Tanya, who was pinching green olives from a jar. When I opened the door, Paris raised his head, then scrambled to his feet and rushed over. Tanya put down the jar, sucked her fingers, and hurried to apply a lighter to the candles adorning a pink, lopsided cake, saying, "Shit, shit." Beside it was a banner, three notebook pages taped together, onto which she had scrawled in black Sharpie GOOD JOB ED. Paris was dancing on his hind legs, pawing my thigh. Tanya finished with the candles and lifted the banner over her head. "Well?" she asked. "How was it?"

I relaxed into the heat and the familiar smells. I grinned at Tanya and gave Paris a good hard rub behind both ears. "Hi, everyone," I said.

***

I had no idea how long I'd been asleep that afternoon when I became aware of movement in the bedroom. There was a rustle of clothes, a double-thump as one shoe and then another hit the floor, and then a shift in the mattress, a burst of cool air beneath the blankets, a warm body sidling up beside me. When I opened my eyes, Tanya's face was inches from mine, filling my vision, a swath of bronze hair across her cheekbone. Her bare toes twiddled my shins and her pubic stubble rasped my hipbone. Her breath smelled of frosting when she said, "Are you all worn out?"

I was so tired my eyeballs and teeth and organs ached, but that wasn't the reason I hesitated. I'd meant to end these sessions if things with Lucienne ever turned romantic.

"I'm pretty worn out," I told her.

"I'd better let you sleep then." Her head dipped under the covers.

"Yes," I said.

When she came back up, I rolled toward her. "Just lie back," she said, pushing me down, then tore a condom wrapper with her teeth, rolled it on, and we began our sensitive choreography, having learned, through these many weeks, how to read each other, please each other, move together as one.

12

When basketball season rolled around in early November, I kept the assignment for myself, and my first call was to Knute Buhner. I'd realized by then that it would have been improper to room with a source, so I mostly felt like I'd dodged a bullet, at least until I explained that I was working on a preview article for the basketball team, and Knute answered, "Then you'll probably want to talk to someone on the basketball team."

"I thought that's what I was doing."

"Sorry. I quit."

"What? Why?"

"It takes up too much time, and what do you even get out of it? It's not like I'm on scholarship like Sully and those guys."

I was confused. From what I understood, athletic scholarships were against the rules in Division III sports, and academic scholarships went to students who were even more proficient in the classroom than I was. I'd applied for all of them the previous spring but won only the two hundred dollars that came with the Honor Society's GPA award. The more substantial scholarships, some covering more than half a year's tuition, had gone elsewhere.

"Won't you miss it?" I asked.

"Not really. I'll light it up in intramurals. *That'll* be fun."

Next I called the coach. The domestic noise of his family was in the background as he answered my questions about new player rotations and offensive strategies. When I asked about athletic scholarships, he confirmed that they weren't allowed in Division III. "We do offer a few merit-based awards," he added.

That week I filed two public information requests, one for the academic scholarships awarded by the college and another for eligibility reports for the men's basketball team. It turned out that A.C. Sullinger, the Division-I transfer, was receiving a number of academic scholarships at Sequoia despite his 2.8 grade point average—respectable, certainly, but not worthy of the high prizes he'd taken away from students like me. Other players were receiving lesser amounts.

It had the makings of a scandal and a big story, but I sat on it, trying to figure out what to do. I'd gotten to know Sully from our interviews. He was from a rough area and was the first in his family to attend college. He was also humble and kind, quick to celebrate his teammates but reluctant to accept praise for himself, even though he made plays that nobody else on the court was capable of. An article about improper benefits probably meant he would never play basketball again. It might also mean an end to his education. I didn't know if I wanted to be responsible for something like that.

***

My mother started calling about Christmas. She said she was making plans for Charlie and me to come to Maryland, and not just for the holiday. She and Jane—"the woman I'm with," she always added, as if I had trouble keeping track of all the Janes in her life—had everything in order for their civil union and they thought it would be nice if everyone was there to attend.

"I don't know," I said. "I'm pretty busy."

"Even over the break?"

"I'm also seeing someone. She'll probably want me to spend Christmas with her."

It took my mother a moment to respond. "Is that true?"

"Is it really so hard to believe?"

"Of course not. I thought maybe the real issue was that you felt uncomfortable about coming. You never mentioned a girl before."

"I never mentioned her because it never came up."

"What's her name?"

I hesitated for a split second, caught in a tumble of confusion that was becoming familiar to me. "Lucienne," I said, even as it occurred to me I would probably spend the holiday at the bungalow with Tanya.

"Well, I think it's terrific that you're seeing someone. In fact, I'd love to meet her. Would she be interested in coming with you?"

"I can ask," I said, in a tone that meant she was certain to refuse, and that the refusal would be hers, not mine.

After hanging up, my mind kept snagging on my hesitation, and I hated that I'd had to hesitate at all. I kept meaning to break it off with Tanya. Every time I spread a cloth napkin in my lap at the restaurants Lucienne chose, every time I settled in to watch unintelligible foreign films with her, every time I kissed her with slow propriety while yellow candlelight flickered in her bedroom, I made new resolutions. It seemed simple enough in those moments. I would simply tell Tanya I'd met someone my own age and that I could therefore no longer continue to—I didn't know which term to use for our bedroom activities, but I knew that before I found it, Tanya would shrug or belch or turn up the TV, saying "suit yourself" or "your loss" or some other short quip that would demonstrate her indifference to such conventions and how easy it was to replace me.

The problem was that drawing boundaries didn't seem terribly urgent until I was in danger of crossing them, and when that danger arrived, a hot pulse of desire shattered my resolutions. I kept deciding that one last time would be okay.

But the next afternoon, while taking Paris for a long, frigid walk around the neighborhood, skirting pools from the blocked storm drains, I decided I couldn't put it off any longer. When we returned, Tanya was sitting on the futon in a hooded sweatshirt and no pants, her feet propped on the coffee table while she painted her toenails black. Paris lapped at his water dish, then curled up by the wall heater, chin on the ground, watching me move to the futon. I sat down next to Tanya, summoning my courage, and during this small opening, she said, "Guess what today is."

I shook my head, distracted. The windows were already darkening with early nightfall.

"My anniversary. Today would have been nine years."

I looked at her. "*Nine?*"

She glanced at me to confirm it, then reloaded her brush and went back to work.

"How'd you meet Derek anyway?"

"He was a line cook where I was waiting tables, and we started messing around. He didn't have anywhere to live, so I let him crash at my place. We went to the courthouse like four months later and got married. His idea, obviously."

"Why'd you take him up on it?"

"Like I'm supposed to know he'd turn out to be a bastard after only four months."

"Why'd you stay with him so long?"

She dabbed at her microscopic pinkie nail. "Why do you *think?*"

"I asked because I don't know."

"Well that's too bad because I'm not going to say it."

She was speaking as though we both understood what she meant, but I was genuinely confused. "Say what?" I asked.

"That word."

"What word?"

"You know what word. It's got four fucking letters, but it's cheesy and makes me feel like a moron, and I'm not going to say it."

"Love?"

She cut her eyes at me, then put the brush in the jar and used a cotton swab to wipe away the polish rimming the nails she'd just done.

I couldn't picture Tanya in love. She seemed too tough for it, too independent, too casual with intimacy. Then again, nine years was a long time. She would have been about the age I was now, and maybe less jaded than the Tanya I had come to know. I told her, "I used to have some pretty naïve ideas about love myself."

"Oh yeah?"

"These days I'm more realistic about it, like you."

She laughed, not kindly. "Like me."

"My parents got divorced too, you know."

"Yeah. You keep mentioning that."

"Have you ever had an affair?"

"I didn't fuck you until the divorce went through, I made sure of that."

"What about before?"

"It was just cuddling. Me and Derek were already finished anyway. He just hadn't signed the papers yet."

"I mean before me."

She put down the cotton swab and pulled another dollop of black polish from the jar, starting on her other foot. "One thing I remember about my dad before he left was how he used to bring me over to other women's houses and make them pretend to be my mom for an hour before they went into the bedroom together. I hated it, and I hated my mom for making him do it. That's why I don't cheat and I don't put up with cheaters."

I had no reason to feel guilty about this. Tanya and I weren't in a relationship; Lucienne and I weren't sleeping together yet.

"Did Derek cheat?" I asked.

"He tried."

"How'd you know?"

"I could just tell. He denied it for a while but finally he was like, 'Okay, okay, I *tried*, but nothing happened.' Like he thought that would get him off the hook. But I threw his ass out."

"It was the same with my mom. Things didn't add up. You could just tell. Then I called her out on it one day and she admitted it."

"She cheated?"

"Yeah, but the most frustrating part is that she wouldn't admit it was cheating. She still won't, even though she was still married to my dad when she started seeing this—other person."

"What do you mean 'other person'? Was it a chick?"

I hadn't been prepared to share that, but it was too late to take it back. The amusement on Tanya's face was intensifying at the same rate as my discomfort.

"Your mom's a lesbian?" she said.

"That's not the point."

"That's hilarious. That explains a lot, actually."

"What does it explain?"

"How you are."

I looked at her skeptically. "How am I?"

She leaned back, cupping her elbow in her palm and twirling the tiny brush like a philosopher might twirl a cigarette. "Let's just say you like to take things slow. I thought it was because you were young but this makes more sense."

"Did I do something wrong?"

"No. You just always act so—what's the word? Like you keep stopping yourself. Like you think I'm doing you some big favor." She bent to her nails again. "You shouldn't worry so much. You might enjoy yourself more if you weren't so bottled up."

This was Tanya speaking. Was there anyone, by comparison, who didn't seem bottled up? "I enjoy myself just fine," I said.

"Look, I don't mind. Obviously. I'm just saying, you want to fuck me from behind, fuck me from behind. I don't mind. I'm not gay."

I didn't like the criticism, or the way she was speaking about my mother, or the implication that my sexual behavior had anything to do with my mother. "The point is," I said, "getting married means deciding not to be with anyone else. It doesn't matter whether it's a man or a woman. You want someone else, you shouldn't get married."

"So I should've stayed with Derek?"

"That's different. My dad didn't do anything wrong."

"Who cares? Why should he be married to a lesbian? Who does that help?"

"It's not about who it helps. It's about the principle."

"So you want people to stick to their mistakes for the principle of it instead of going out and fixing them."

I shook my head. What I was saying was very simple and didn't need a lot of unnecessary complication. "You didn't like it when Derek went after another woman, right? Well, my mom did exactly the same thing."

"And it blackened your tender little heart, didn't it?"

"No. The one it really damaged was my brother."

She rolled her eyes as she returned her attention to her nails, and it made me uncomfortable in precisely the way I used to feel uncomfortable every time she walked into the bathroom during my showers, leaving me to wonder, as I angled myself away behind the steamed, soap-scummed shower curtain, what she could see.

She put one final dab on her pinkie, then fanned out her toes and wiggled them with the dexterity of a circus performer. "That's too bad. I kind of like blackened hearts." She wielded the little brush in my direction. "Want to do yours next?"

I knew she meant my toenails, but I wasn't interested in blackening those either. I grabbed my jacket and said I was going to see a friend. I was halfway to Lucienne's before I remembered why I'd sat down with Tanya in the first place.

***

Dating Lucienne was expensive. She wanted French, she wanted seafood, she wanted glamorous eight-dollar mocktails. She had long ago staked out the finer establishments in Conrad Park—all of which would be woefully inadequate in any real metropolis, she informed me. When I asked why, she gave me a disbelieving look. "That mural?"

I squinted at it. A few bright swaths cut a background of dim blotches. "Yeah?"

"It looks like it came off a rack at Target. And the plants?"

I examined the one on the partition behind us. It had dark glossy leaves. "What about them?"

"Come on, Ed. They're *fake*."

I ran one of the leaves between my fingers and still couldn't tell.

Lucienne always managed to outspend me at these places, though she barely ate. I knew because the check was always mine. She didn't even bother to excuse herself to the bathroom or rummage through her purse when it came. She just thanked the server and waited for me to pay. In this age of gender equality it didn't seem fair, but I didn't know how to object, and I didn't want to embarrass myself with a complaint.

Then we spent Thanksgiving together in San Francisco. For dinner we had sushi, a tradition in her family, and by the time we emerged it was after nine. Lucienne suggested we stay in a hotel, and when she offered to let her father pay, flashing his credit card, it was such a novelty and relief that I accepted before the implications dawned on me.

The hotel she chose was an upscale place with doormen and an elevated glass atrium. The room was sleek and modern, all bare surfaces and straight edges and the biggest white bed I'd ever seen. Lucienne headed straight for it, and the sheets rustled behind me as I examined the miniature percolator and the well-hidden ironing board and the tiny bottles of liquor, as if I was curious about their brands and varieties rather than their very existence. I tested the ballpoint pen on the stationary, reviewed the binder that listed room service and television options, nudged away the curtain, and looked down on the street, where cars were stacking up at a light.

"Ed."

I turned. Lucienne's bare shoulders were propped on a pillow, everything else a long lump under the blankets. Her dress lay rumpled on the floor under a lacy black bra. I nodded, and she tracked me with apprehensive eyes as I walked around the bed and set about removing my clothes. My mind scrambled for excuses, but they all amounted to the same thing—rejecting her, which I could afford even less than the hotel room. I would simply have to put an end to things with Tanya—for real this time. It was the only way to avoid any overlap and keep myself from crossing a terrible boundary.

Still, when I was down to my boxers I felt shy, so I slipped into the sheets still wearing them. A bad feeling, something like thievery, crawled on my skin, and it grew worse as we began to kiss. Lucienne lay beside me, impossibly long, her cold toes all the way down by mine, her hips narrow and knobby and motionless as a statue's while my hands moved over them. She didn't push into my touch, didn't arch her back or writhe her legs or screw up her face or reach for me. She just reclined against the pillows as if lounging on a poolside chaise, as if at any moment she might pull away and ask me to bring her a piña colada.

"Are you okay?" I asked.

She looked worried. "Why? Am I doing something wrong?"

"I just want to make sure you're okay."

"I'm fine," she said, tugging at my boxers. "I'm ready."

She felt different around me than Tanya did. That there could be any variation in this was an interesting discovery, and I made a mental note about it. It was good to learn new things. Eventually her body started to move beneath mine, but she was always a half step late, as if reasoning through her responses instead of succumbing to them, as if she was more concerned with getting things right than getting what she wanted, or wanting anything at all. I wondered if that was how I seemed with Tanya, if that was what she'd meant about me being bottled up. The thought left me nervous and distracted, but that didn't mean I wasn't enjoying myself. I liked it fine.

"Do you want to try getting on top?" I asked.

"Do you want me to?"

"I'm asking if *you* want to."

She stared into my face, as if trying to divine the right answer, so I took the initiative and flopped onto my back. She climbed on, propping herself up on locked elbows, looking down at me as if awaiting further instruction. "Whenever you're ready," she said, offering an awkward smile, and something occurred to me.

"Lucienne, have you done this before?"

Her eyebrows rose and her expression became very earnest. "This position?"

"Any of it."

Her eyes slid away. "I've done enough."

I didn't know what that meant except evasion, which seemed like answer enough.

I arranged her hips on me the way Tanya liked to arrange hers, then moved them with my hands the way Tanya moved her own. "Close your eyes," I said. "Don't worry about me. Just do what feels good."

Her hips began to rock and squeeze on their own. Her eyes clenched in concentration. Her breathing quickened, and she started to sweat. But no pleasure came into her face. She wore the kind of expression you saw on people at the gym as they worked through a set of bicep curls.

"Lucienne."

She opened her eyes, and her attention was right there on the surface, awaiting further communication.

"Are you enjoying this?"

She nodded quickly, as if I had asked whether she was enjoying her soup. "Just getting a little tired."

I nudged her, and she slid off me. We lay there a moment next to each other, looking at the ceiling, arms pinned to our sides. When she sat up to reach for the sheet, her spine protruded like a knotted rope. "I know I'm weird," she said, tugging it over her shoulders. "I'm sorry. I just wanted to try it."

"It's fine. It was nice."

When she went to the shower, I lay in bed imagining Tanya, but after finishing I only felt worse.

***

I'd told Tanya I was volunteering at a soup kitchen and then crashing with a friend, but I came home resolved to tell her the truth. Three times that weekend I steeled myself, walked into the room she was in, and said her name firmly, like someone who needed to talk. But when she turned her attention on me, it was full of warmth and amusement and intimacy, and something strangled me. I broke into a sweat, my heart kicking. Twice I changed the subject, and the other time I couldn't manage to say anything at all. Tanya watched me and laughed.

It became clear I needed a push, so I stayed away from Lucienne and waited for her to call, which made the ringing phone feel like a near-death simulation. I let Tanya answer, praying it was Lucienne, praying it wasn't.

Then on Sunday morning I emerged from the shower to find Tanya holding the receiver to her mattress-creased face, her hair rumpled and eyes sleepy, though that didn't prevent her from turning a look of inquiry on me as she said, "Yeah, he's right here."

I tightened my towel and took the receiver, my heart kicking so hard that I looked at my chest to see if it showed.

"Hey," Charlie said.

It was so unexpected and disorienting that for several long moments I wasn't sure how to respond. "Charlie? Hey. Sorry. I thought you were—someone else."

"How's college?"

"Better, actually. Why?"

"You've got a little house or something there, right?"

"I rent a room, but yeah, it's in a little house."

"Do you think I could stay with you for a night?"

Scenes unfurled in my mind—Charlie touring campus with me, meeting Lucienne, unrolling a sleeping bag on my bedroom floor, sitting at the kitchen table while I made eggs. "Sure."

"And could I bring some friends?"

The scenes changed, then dissolved. "Friends? How many?"

"Five. There's a concert in Eureka, but we need a place to crash."

"Eureka's like ninety minutes from here."

"Well that's where it is. You can come with us if you want."

"Can't you come by yourself?"

"No. How am I supposed to get there?"

"Have Dad drive you or something."

"Right. Maybe he can come see The Dwarves too."

"There isn't room for five people here, Charlie."

"We don't mind the floor."

"It also isn't my place. I'm just renting a room. It's not my call."

"Then could you at least ask your landlord or whatever?"

"She's going to say no."

"Okay, great," he said. "Thanks a lot, bro."

"Is there any other—" I started, but he had already hung up.

Tanya watched me replace the receiver, her arms folded. "No," she said. "Feel better?"

"He's just using me for a roof. If he comes for a visit, I want him to actually hang out with me."

"Then why didn't you tell him that?"

"I did, basically."

"Yeah, well, you should try saying what you mean and see if it works out any better for you."

I steeled myself, and my voice sounded strange when I said, "It's funny you should mention that, Tanya. Because you're right, certain things are hard for me to say." I looked at her, and she gave me a goofy expression, mocking me with so much glee and tenderness that all I could do was stand there, gripping the towel at my waist, gagging on everything I couldn't say.

"No shit," she said, and patted me twice on the chest.

***

My mother called again about Christmas that evening. "I can't wait any longer to buy plane tickets," she said. "They're almost gone. Have you had a chance to talk to—what's her name again?"

I nudged the curtain aside. Tanya was at work, and I waited for the approaching headlights to pass—not the Datsun's—before responding, "Actually, that's something I wanted to talk to you about."

"What is?"

Very little appealed to me less than discussing my love life with my mother, but since she was something of an expert in navigating infidelity, I thought she might have some handy advice. I looked down at Paris, who seemed to take this as some kind of affirmation and barked. "Well," I said, "there's Lucienne—"

"That was the name. Such an interesting name."

"And then there's Tanya."

"You mean—?" She paused, and when she began again, the uncertainty in her voice was replaced by hard-toned interrogation. "You're dating two women, Ed?"

"It's not like that."

After a moment she said, "It's none of my business, I suppose. But whatever you think about me and my decisions, please don't take it out on those girls. They had nothing to do with it."

"I know that. I'm not. I'm just not sure what to *do* about it." But I already regretted bringing it up.

"As in how to end it with one of them?" my mother asked.

"Yeah."

"Have you chosen which one?"

I surprised myself by responding, "How do you choose?"

"Well, it's going to sound trite, but the best policy really is to follow your heart. Worrying about people's feelings can lead you away from what you really want, and in the end that's not good for anyone. You have to do what's best for you."

"That's a pretty selfish policy."

"Ed, I was confused, just like you're probably confused now. That's what happens if you aren't honest with yourself. That's exactly what I mean. That's why it was so difficult."

"I should go. This was a bad idea."

"All right. Just think about what I said, okay? And I do need to know if you're coming for Christmas. There are only a few seats left out of San Seguro."

"San Seguro? Why not SFO?"

"I thought you'd prefer flying with Charlie."

I felt a pang of sympathy for him, having to face the holiday with my mother and Jane by himself. For a moment I even reconsidered my plans. My mother, perhaps sensing my hesitation, said, "He'll miss you."

I laughed. "It's nice of you to say so, anyway."

"It's true," she said. "We'll all miss you."

***

I arrived early for the next editorial meeting and was happy to find Lucienne already there, as usual, seated at her computer, feeding brown celluloid strips into the negative scanner. I hadn't seen her since our long, silent drive home the morning after Thanksgiving. She hadn't called once.

"Hey," I said, crossing to her. "What are you doing for Christmas?"

"Going home."

Images from the negatives flashed across the screen—basketball players in various mid-flight poses, cradling or corralling or reaching for the ball. I took a seat and swiveled to face her, hoping my face showed the goodwill and optimism I would've been feeling if I'd been able to resolve my dilemma. Attaching myself more firmly to Lucienne, I'd decided, would give me the security I needed to finally break free from Tanya. "Well," I said, "what would you think about spending Christmas together?"

She took her hand from the mouse and moved her eyes over my face. She looked like she wanted to tell me something difficult but didn't know how. "I already have a plane ticket," she said.

"What if I got one too?"

"Don't you think it's a little early to spend holidays together?"

"We just spent Thanksgiving together. Plus I'd love to meet your parents, see where you're from, all that stuff. Remind me where you're from again?"

"Usually I fly into Boston because that's where my dad's company is based, even though he does most of his work in New York. But my mom's going to be in Hartford for a few days after her session adjourns, so he's picking me up at the airport there."

From this information I could glean no answer to my question.

"The flight's probably full by now," she added.

"So I'll take a different flight."

She gave me an expression of reluctance. She seemed to be measuring something in me. "My parents aren't expecting company."

"There's plenty of time to tell them."

She winced.

"What?"

"I don't know if I *want* to tell them," she said.

"Why not?"

"Because they're expecting me to bring home someone a little more—a different kind of guy. Didn't I tell you you're not my type?"

When I failed to answer, she gave a pained little smile that acknowledged the harshness of her words but stopped short of apologizing for them. Questions banged through my head, but before any of them could find an exit, Lucienne's eyes shifted up. I followed them over my shoulder and found Eli Duncan, his chin pushed into his neck, waiting for us to acknowledge his presence. "Ed, we need to talk."

I carried my disappointment and confusion to the corner behind the old light table, where he told me in a low voice that

Gilbert Platt had just turned in an application to be the sports editor spring term. "I told him the position wasn't open, but it wasn't open when you took it from him. You convinced me with all your talk about those big exposés you were planning. I don't know what happened to all that, but you've got two issues left before winter break, so now would probably be a good time to follow through."

While the other editors arrived, I looked over my information on A.C. Sullinger, trying to figure out what to do, still distracted by the exchange with Lucienne. The documents I had about his scholarships and GPA were probably enough on their own, but pursuing an article responsibly would mean confronting the coach, who had been so nice to me, and confronting Sully himself, who had done nothing worse than let the college cover his tuition, and manipulating Knute Buhner into betraying his old team, which happened to be the team I'd come to Sequoia to join. The other option, however, was to lose the team I'd found to replace it.

When the editorial meeting began, I announced what I had, hoping we could dissect the ethical implications, but Eli Duncan broke into a big grin, and Kim Marzen announced that she would reconfigure the opinion pages around the article. Yusef Alrahmani began to argue that it belonged in his section, news. I fought to keep control over it in sports, but Eli Duncan ruled that, yes, it was most certainly news, probably the best news story we'd had all year. He held forth about the reporting it would require from me and then about appropriate photography for such a sensitive subject while Lucienne folded herself over a notepad, scowling with concentration as she scribbled.

When the meeting was over, she glanced at me, and the scowl changed to a conciliatory smile. It made me feel a little less sick over the A.C. Sullinger article, and I gave a forgiving smile back. Maybe there was more to what she'd said. Or maybe I only had to find out what kind of guy her parents were expecting and then show her that guy was me.

She came over as the meeting dispersed. "I'm sorry about what I said. I was angry. I shouldn't have said it."

"Thank you."

"Let me make it up to you?"

She offered to take me to dinner, and all at once it came to me—a way to force a resolution to my dilemma between her and Tanya and at the same time show her I wasn't someone to be taken for granted.

"All right," I said. "How about Sammy's?"

"I thought you never wanted to go there."

"Well now I do."

13

The weathered hardwood floors, the stark wooden furniture, the white tablecloths and low votive candles, the wine barrels standing on end, topped with clustered bottles or sprays of flowers—they gave the place a look of spartan elegance. The uniform I'd seen so many times at home, black slacks and collared white shirt, which had always seemed to speak of grease and exertion, looked trim and tasteful on the bustling employees. It was nothing like the dive bar or diner at which I'd imagined Tanya working, and as I tried to recalibrate my picture of her, I felt a flash of disorientation.

The hostess's bulging mouth parted to reveal her braces. I asked if we could sit in Tanya's section, then glanced at Lucienne, ready to make some leery deflection, but she just spun and followed the hostess, who had flashed another metal-filled smile and then set off at a brisk pace, menus cradled in her arm. At the table Lucienne read her menu while I watched over her shoulder. I had to keep taking slow breaths and reminding myself that this was necessary, that I'd put it off too many times already.

When Tanya finally appeared from the kitchen, she had two plates in each hand, her hair pulled into a paintbrush stub, her uniform as trim and tasteful as everyone else's, except for the apron, which hung to her ankles. It flapped and kicked as her short legs motored her across the dining room. Then she met my eyes. Her gaze slid to Lucienne, and she stopped. For a long moment she stood there in the middle of the dining room, taking us in.

Then she spun and charged the hostess stand, where the girl with braces made a few fearful, uncertain replies, showing her palms. She looked like someone trying to reason with a mugger. Tanya made a beeline back to the kitchen, plates still in her hands, her face a mask of grim determination. I didn't like seeing her like that, but at least things were out in the open. The hard part was over.

"Maybe you could get your landlord to bring us a bottle of wine or something," Lucienne said, closing her menu.

"Maybe."

Lucienne picked up the menu and put it back down. The other customers twisted in their seats, chewed ice cubes from their empty water glasses, nudged credit cards into precarious outcroppings over the edge of the table. When Tanya finally came bursting from the kitchen again, a couple men nearby beckoned, as if trying to hail a cab. She ignored them to come stand beside our table and stare down at me, her face calm except for a mouth cinched like a drawstring and eyes that looked like they could knock a man from a galloping horse.

I began a panicked mental scramble, searching for a phrase or gesture that would undo the wrong I'd just committed before remembering that it had to be done, that doing it was the whole purpose of coming, and that it corrected a greater wrong.

"Excuse me, miss?" said a man at the next table.

Tanya kept her eyes locked on mine. They were demanding and outraged, but I could think of nothing to say. The silence went on and on.

"Well, you finally did it," she said. She tilted her head at Lucienne. "Who's your friend?"

"She's photo editor at the newspaper."

"Oh, so you're just out doing a little *journalism*."

She made the word sound like an obscenity. I glanced at Lucienne, wondering how much was obvious to her already, and she gave me an expression that straddled amusement and confusion. I took a breath and let it out. "Actually we're on a date."

Lucienne added, "We're celebrating Ed's big break."

"And you asked to sit in my section," Tanya said, ignoring her.

I cast my eyes toward the hostess stand, as if to confirm some impossible species of bird that had alighted there. "Yes."

"Because you were dying to have this little interaction right here? Because you thought I'd behave myself in a public place? In my place of employment?"

I glanced again at Lucienne. Her expression asked whether Tanya was crazy and whether I was going to stand up for myself. "I thought it was the polite thing to do if you knew a server," I said.

Tanya held a smile on me that looked genuinely mirthful except that it lasted too long and she didn't blink. "Polite," she repeated, then turned the smile on Lucienne, as if maybe she would appreciate the humor. "Here's the thing," she said, squinting in false acknowledgement of the delicacy of the matter. "When you have to wait on people you know, it kind of makes you feel like shit. Because this? Right here? This is you putting yourself on a pedestal and expecting me to stand around like a fucking servant asking what I can get you."

"I guess I didn't really think it through."

Tanya broke into another smile, which she aimed again at Lucienne. "He didn't think it through," she reported.

"It's not a big deal," Lucienne said. "Why are you being so weird?"

Tanya ignored this and turned back to me, her face suddenly full of bitter wisdom. "How would you like it if I came home and ordered *you* around—go do this, go get that."

"You do," I said.

"Well that's because I'm your fucking landlord. And anyway I never heard you complaining. If you didn't like it then I'd expect you to say so rather than coming in here and asking me to nod and smile while you tell me how you want your fucking steak cooked."

"We can eat here if we want to," Lucienne said. "Why are you making such a big deal out of it?"

Tanya turned to consider her, and it seemed almost friendly when she said, "Has anyone ever told you that you look like Shelley Duvall?"

"Who's that?"

"Have you seen *The Shining*?"

"No."

"She's in lots of other stuff too. All pop-eyed and weird-looking with her long face and fucked-up teeth. Body like a skeleton. Do you have some kind of disease?"

"Excuse me?"

Tanya shrugged. "You look like you have some kind of disease."

"What's your problem?"

Tanya paused, face twisted between a smile and grimace, and I waited for her to say what the problem was—a brief, accurate statement about our relationship that would cut Lucienne and ruin me. I accepted this as the price for my inability to end things with Tanya on my own. I just wanted it to be over.

But she only said, "Ask Ed," then spun and motored back to the kitchen while protests erupted around us. As I watched her recede, I felt my relief rise into admiration. I hadn't thought Tanya capable of such diplomacy, especially toward someone who'd just slighted her.

When she disappeared behind the swinging doors, however, all of this was washed away by a great wave of liberation. It was over. I was officially a one-woman man, and with this came a feeling that made me want to twirl around a lamppost, dance a merengue, road-trip across the country to wherever Lucienne was from.

"Well she looks like an Oompa-Loompa," Lucienne said, watching the kitchen doors. "A trashy one."

"Let's get out of here," I said.

"No." She unfolded her napkin and spread it in her lap. "She doesn't get to decide where we eat."

So we waited, and finally two water glasses arrived, borne to us by a sandy-haired guy wearing a puka shell necklace. He told us that Tanya had asked him to cover our table, then offered a halfhearted smile that revealed what he knew of me.

After he was gone, I reached across for Lucienne's hand. It had occurred to me that I could take her to bed again tonight. Without all the worry from last time, maybe it would go better. I could do all sorts of things with her—like clear up the messy conversation that had landed us here.

"Listen," I said. "I know that stuff about Christmas probably seemed to come from nowhere, but let me tell you what's going on. The reason I'm looking for somewhere to spend Christmas is because they have this new thing in Vermont called a civil union. Have you heard of it?"

"Who hasn't?"

"Well, my mom's going to Vermont with—with the person she left my dad for. Another woman."

"Your mom's a lesbian?"

"Yeah. And she's doing it around Christmastime so we can all be there for it. But I don't want to go."

Lucienne widened her eyes and blew a stream of air, as if to say, *Wow, tough one.* I pursed my lips in mute confirmation.

"Which one wears the dress?" she said. "Or do they both?"

"I don't know. I don't really want to find out. That's why I need somewhere else to go for Christmas. And the place I'd like to go most is wherever you're going."

"Can't you go to your dad's?" she asked.

I pictured him locked in his office, drinking whiskey, the big empty house echoing around him, and I knew it would be no better there, maybe worse. "That's not really an option. Not by myself, anyway. Not unless you wanted to come with me."

"I can't."

"Why not?"

She enunciated her words carefully, as if to keep them under control. "I just can't."

And my own question became less about divining her reasons than making her state them explicitly. "Why not?"

"My parents are expecting me."

"And a different kind of guy."

She pressed her lips together and looked away.

"I'm not good enough?"

There was warning in her face. "I told you, we're Catholic."

"So what?"

"We do things a certain way. There are certain expectations."

"And what's wrong with me?"

"It's not a matter of that. You don't understand what it's like where I'm from. There are certain things you're judged on."

"Okay, then what will people judge me on?"

"Well for starters, your parents are divorced and your mom's a lesbian."

I was going to say, "Who cares about any of that?" but caring about it was the basis of my whole argument for coming with her. *I* cared about it, and I wanted to avoid it just like she did. But not because Jane was a woman. Why couldn't anyone see past that?

"That's not the world I come from," Lucienne continued. "And it doesn't help that she's getting a civil union. That's the kind of issue my mother would call 'toxic sludge.' She'd kill me if I dragged her into it. I don't think I have to tell you that there's a very delicate balance in our household right now. Can you imagine if my mother didn't get reelected?"

"You're talking about our parents," I said. "That has nothing to do with you and me. Besides, I thought you wanted to get away from all that. I thought that was the whole reason you came to Sequoia."

"Yeah, but there's my life here, and there's my life there." She pretended to grip one in each hand, then moved them apart.

"So if my parents were still married, it would all be fine?"

"No. I said that's just for starters."

"So then what's wrong with *me*?"

"You didn't call me for a week after we slept together, for one thing."

"*You* didn't call *me*. Is that what this is about?"

"For another thing," she continued, struggling to keep her volume in check, "you're not my type. How many times do you want me to say it?"

Tanya had by now resumed her duties with graceful efficiency, delivering checks and refilling water glasses, chatting and laughing with everybody in a way that earned their instant forgiveness. She whisked by our table several times, close enough that I could smell her powdery deodorant. I suddenly wished that she had gone ahead and said why she was upset, so that Lucienne could see that not everyone found me so inadequate, that I was actually very much in demand.

When Tanya finally glided back to the kitchen, I asked Lucienne, "Do you think it's weird for me to be living with another woman?"

"Why? Should I?"

"I guess it depends what you're comfortable with."

She put her elbows on the table, and it sounded more like a protest than a question when she said, "Why shouldn't I be comfortable with it?"

"I think Tanya might have—well, *feelings* for me."

"I got that. Are you into thirty-year-old townies?"

"Maybe I don't think about people in categories like that."

I'd meant it as a criticism of Lucienne's small-mindedness, but it came out sounding like a confession. Lucienne pulled her chin back, her eyebrows riding high on her forehead. "Did something happen between you and her?"

I wondered how an innocent person would react to such a question. Would he laugh it off or take offense? I ended up doing a little of each, blending them into an expression that must have come across as pure culpability. The disgust on Lucienne's face deepened. "Oh my god, Ed."

"It's over now."

"*Now?*"

"It's . . . been over."

"And what, you brought me here to rub my face in it?"

I didn't deny it. "At least it's in my past. You're talking about our future."

She didn't deny it either.

The waiter delivered our food wordlessly, as if he could sense the tension at our table, and we ate in silence. The only exception was when Lucienne complained that the stems hadn't been removed from the spinach in her salad, her voice pitched in a register of injustice that reminded me of the way she complained about her parents, and the editors who wouldn't run her photos of headless Barbies, and now me, as if we were all pieces of a story she was telling herself about how the world was slighting her.

It dawned on me that she had a bleak view of the world only because she expected it to treat her perfectly. In that regard she was a lot like Danielle. The difference was that she would rather complain about the world's flaws than fix them. She would rather look good in a bad world than look bad in a good one.

Tanya had managed to disappear after cashing out the customers around us. I was relieved. By the time the waiter laid down our check, it was clear that the whole evening had been a terrible idea, and I was eager to end it without any further catastrophe. Lucienne reached for the check, and I let her. She paid with cash, then stood and headed across the dining room. I followed in the wake of her perfume, trying not to feel impatient when she angled toward the restrooms. The moment she reached for the handle, however, the door flew open, and Tanya came barreling out. They nearly collided but caught themselves in time, stopped, rocked back on their heels, and then stood there, face to face, their wide-eyed surprise shifting into gentle, smirking hostility.

Lucienne spoke first. "You're a bad waitress."

Tanya replied, "You're an anorexic cunt."

After a moment of shock, her mouth molding itself into shapes of speech that never arrived, Lucienne turned, marched past me, and pushed herself out to the dark parking lot. Tanya stormed over and glared up at my face so hard that a forked vein stood up in her forehead.

"How long?" she demanded under her breath. The glass door was sweeping shut, and it occurred to me that I should let it.

"I don't know," I said. "A little while."

"You fuck her?" Tanya hissed.

"Jesus." I glanced around. The customers were oblivious, loaded forks continuing the journey from plate to mouth.

"*Did—you—fuck—her?*" Tanya repeated, pronouncing each word at well-spaced intervals, as if I were a child or foreigner or someone else with comprehension problems.

"Why? Am I not allowed to?"

"*Allowed* to?"

"It's not like you're my girlfriend."

Nothing in her expression changed but it was suddenly full of contempt. "What am I then? Your fuck buddy?"

That seemed an accurate term, but I knew better than to say so. "How about my friend? My roommate?"

"No, how about your long-term fuck buddy who lives with you, and listens to you talk about your day, and then talks about her own day, and then you fuck and sleep together cuddling and shit, but definitely *not* your girlfriend. Is that a little clearer?"

"I didn't realize you saw me that way."

"How did you *think* I saw you?"

"Just as, you know—a tenant."

"A tenant."

"Yeah."

"A tenant I happened to be fucking."

"I didn't think it was a big deal."

"You didn't think it was a big deal to fuck the same person for three months."

"I didn't think you'd get your panties in a bunch about it."

Whatever measure of restraint was left in Tanya's face dropped away, and she smiled at me in a craze of pain and anger that was hard to believe I could have caused. Then she blinked, and blinked again, and turned to look through the restaurant doors, where halogen lights swam on the wet windshields in the parking lot. Her expression faded, as if it had burned out all its fuel.

Two other waitresses were approaching. One laid a gentle hand on Tanya's shoulder and asked, "You all right?"

Tanya looked at me in resignation, as if she should have known better than to put any measure of faith in me. She looked at the other waitresses with the same expression, as if they were sure to appreciate her situation. Then she looked up, and her eyes filled with tears, just as they had the night she'd sat on my bed, defending herself against Derek's accusations about not caring enough. It was as shocking now as it had been then, and I felt the same hot blast of repugnance for myself that I'd once felt for him. I could only watch, paralyzed and speechless, as the other waitresses led Tanya away, one on each side, propping her between them like an athlete who'd just blown out a knee.

14

We rode home in silence. Lucienne sat with stiff, wounded hauteur, wearing a look of bravery and pain. "Will you please stop up here?" she asked with ice-cold courtesy. I bumped my car into the lot of a convenience store with plate glass windows and a bright, shadowless interior. Lucienne went in and spoke to the clerk and then waited at the counter, looking like someone formerly glamorous, down on her luck.

The clerk handed her something and she paid for it. As she got into the car she tore the cellophane from a package of cigarettes. She depressed the lighter on the dashboard, then met my eyes, as if waiting for me to object. I put my arm over the seat and backed out.

The rest of the way home she blew smoke at the cracked window, where it was vacuumed into the slipstream. The odor disgusted me, and so did the sight of her lips on the moist filter, her cheeks going hollow as she dragged, but I wasn't in a position to complain.

When we arrived at Lucienne's apartment, I pulled to the curb rather than parking. Lucienne pulled gloves from her purse and put them on but then sat there with her hands in her lap, staring out the windshield while the engine ran and the heaters blew.

"If I was anorexic," she said finally, "I wouldn't have eaten that salad."

"That's true."

She regarded me with narrowed eyes, as if giving me the opportunity to retract my answer before adding, "Then again, who knows?"

Any concern this aroused in me was extinguished by the memory of her cold disapproval. Apparently I wasn't good enough to worry about her health. Maybe it wasn't her type. "That's true too," I said.

"I might just go to bed."

"Okay."

"I might smoke a few more cigarettes first."

"Okay."

She scrutinized me for some sign of disapproval, which I couldn't muster. She got out and slammed the door, and I watched as she fumbled her keys in the entryway, having a harder time than usual with the lock. At one point she flung the keys down and crossed her arms, looking up in exasperation. When it became apparent I wasn't coming to help, she picked them up and opened the door with no further trouble.

For a while I drove the dark streets, turning randomly, trying to lose myself in an unfamiliar part of town, but after my marathon training, I recognized it all. I had run everywhere. I was having a hard time pinning down how I felt. I couldn't even tell whether it was a good or a bad feeling. When I passed a large brick building with a vertical BOWL sign lit yellow, I pulled in. It seemed as good a place as any to let my mind settle, and I thought it might feel good to fling a heavy ball, knock things down.

As I walked from my car I could hear the balls thundering down their lanes, the crash and clatter of pins, the muffled rock music. When I opened the door, the volume jumped, and I recognized the song. It was Nirvana, from an album Charlie used to play on a loop, and the music seemed to describe my feelings to me, wandering through depressive chords until it lifted to a rage of distorted guitars and shouting. I'd always found that part off-putting, though now it seemed a nice counterpoint to the sad melody, offering another shape for despair and a moment of relief from it.

I wondered if that was what Charlie got from his music, his Dwarves and Marilyn Manson and Nirvana. I was even disappointed when the song ended, giving way to the bouncy chords of Bob Marley.

The bowling alley floor was split, the bottom level devoted to the glossy lanes where adults and teenagers sat talking and laughing, the top level devoted to pool tables where bands of smoke drifted under cool green lamps suspended from the ceiling. Behind the pool tables was a bar with a cash register and a grid of cubbies stuffed with shoes. I went to the bar to ask about getting a lane, but the bartender, a short man with a cleanly shorn scalp and brown mustache waxed into two little curls, threw down a coaster and asked, "What'll it be, boss?"

On impulse, I let my eyes move to bottles behind him, searching for my father's brand.

***

I woke later in piercing light. It came pink and unpleasant through my eyelids. The front of my skull pounded and my mouth was a noxious blend of liquor fumes and toothpaste. The room seemed to spin around the fulcrum of my head. I wasn't sure where I was except that it was soft.

When I pried my eyes open, shading them with my palm, I saw Tanya standing over me in her waitress uniform, eyes sharp as broken glass. Her shirt was unbuttoned halfway down her chest, showing pearlescent bra cups. Her black shoes hung from two hooked fingers. "Wrong bed, asshole."

It started coming back then, the hours at the bowling alley, the whiskeys going down more easily as I told my troubles to the bartender, the obvious answer waiting for me: it had been difficult to end things with Tanya because I hadn't wanted them to end. I'd discounted her the same way Lucienne discounted me. I remembered repeating this to myself as I walked home through a misty drizzle, crawled into Tanya's bed, and waited for her, snuggling Paris, excited to tell her the truth.

But now I was groggy and disoriented and still half drunk, and the closest I could come to expressing myself was to lift the covers and mutter, "Get in."

"You should have gotten it from that goon you brought to the restaurant because you aren't getting jack shit from me."

That was when I heard the toilet flush. I looked to Tanya for information, but she only glared at me, her mouth small and eyes big, a look of anger and impatience that said I was to blame for the coming trouble and therefore deserved no pity.

"Jesus H.," Derek said as he came into the room, fumbling a bottle of ibuprofen that belonged to me, ratcheting its childproof cap the wrong direction. He hadn't bothered to fasten his jeans. "Who're they trying to keep out of these things?"

When he received no answer, he glanced at Tanya, then followed her eyes to me, and a new understanding sunk through his features. He took a moment to show Tanya the depth of his outrage before chucking the bottle at her feet. It skipped off the carpet and ricocheted from the closet door, rattling like a maraca.

"I think he's drunk," Tanya explained.

Derek closed his eyes and put all ten fingers to his forehead, as if summoning some psychic faculty.

"Don't freak out," she said.

"What's he doing in our bed?"

"Excuse me? Our?"

"Are you fucking him?"

"I'd rather not."

He turned, measuring me, looking ready to attack, and my mind was suddenly clear, my body tense and alert. "Are you fucking my wife?" he said.

"I don't think she's your wife."

Tanya took his wrist and pulled him toward the doorway. "Why don't we go to your place?"

"This is my place! Everything in here is mine!"

"Your new place."

"Why are you doing this to me?" he cried as Tanya led him from the room. "Where the hell did my life go?"

"You left it with that whore in Modesto."

They moved through the house yelling, slamming doors. They sounded like builders remodeling. Paris went after them, then yelped and came slinking back to the bedroom with his tail between his legs. I called him onto the bed, hoping that when all this blew over Tanya would come back and join us, and I could say the things I'd meant to.

Finally they went to the porch and shouted at each other there, and then a diesel engine was running. A truck door banged shut, then another, and the truck blasted its way into the distance. I imagined Tanya on the porch, showing both middle fingers to the taillights. I listened for her footsteps, for the creak and thump of the front door, but the silence went on and on until I understood that she'd gone with him.

I put on basketball shorts and a sweatshirt, then went through the house turning off lights, closing cupboards, straightening picture frames. I let Paris out. The bleariness and headache had returned, so I found the ibuprofen Derek had thrown, pried off the cap, and placed two tablets on my tongue before gulping a full glass of water. I shredded some cheese over a plate of tortilla chips and melted it in the microwave, then munched the nachos standing in blue light from the television. I let Paris in.

After that I started feeling better. I brushed my teeth a second time, and I was debating whether to floss again when the living room began to pulse with blue light. A few moments later the whole room swirled and pounded. Headlights raked the window. A door slammed. There were muffled voices, and a few moments later Tanya pushed through the front door, calling over her shoulder, "I will. I *will*." She closed the door and turned the deadbolt. "Christ."

She was dressed exactly the same as when she'd woken me earlier, shirt unbuttoned past her bra, a black shoe in each hand. Her hair was stringy and damp, her skin waxy, goose-bumped. She flung the shoes away, sat on the coffee table, and wrenched her foot up to examine its sole.

"What happened?" I asked.

She picked at something and said, "Neighbor called in a domestic disturbance. I needed a ride home anyway."

"I mean between you and Derek."

She looked at me, her expression hovering somewhere between anger and amusement. "As in whether or not we fucked?"

"Did you?"

"How is that any of your business, *tenant*?"

"Did you?"

The amusement in her expression evaporated. "You're a piece of work, you know that? You've got some real issues."

"Me?"

"Yeah you." She abandoned the excavation of her sole and limped across the room on her heel. I followed her to the bedroom, where she executed her customary search for clean clothing, lifting articles to her nose and letting them fall.

"Look," I said, trying to reset the conversation. "The reason I was in your bed is because I realized you're right. You *are* my girlfriend. It took me by surprise, but I'm okay with it, and I want to—"

"You think I care about that?" She tossed a pair of sweatpants on the bed and began unbuttoning her shirt. "If I cared about that, I would throw your ass out."

"I have a lease."

"So?"

"So you can't just throw me out."

"I'm the landlord. I can do whatever I want."

"Listen, I didn't think you were looking for a boyfriend right after your divorce. I didn't think you wanted something that serious. If I did, then I never would've—"

She was laughing.

"I'm serious," I said.

"I know. That's what makes it so hilarious." She let her shirt fall from her shoulders and pushed down her pants, revealing a skimpy black triangle of underwear. "You thought I was more of a slut, is what you're saying."

"That's not what I meant."

"Yes it is." She pushed her feet into the sweats and hoisted up the waistband. "You thought just because your mom got all slutty after her divorce, the same thing would happen to me."

"Excuse me?"

She cupped her hands over her mouth, as if calling from a great distance. "Your *mom's* the slut, not me."

"You don't know anything about my mom."

"I know you're so hung up on her you can't stand being with anyone else."

"I *can* stand it. That's what I'm trying to tell you."

"I know she cheated."

"That has nothing to do with me."

"Yes it does. It's what fucked you up, and whatever fucks you up is what you spend the rest of your life trying to re-create."

"I didn't re-create anything," I told her. "You weren't—we hadn't established what was between us. Besides, I'm not the one who's fucked up."

"Oh yeah?"

"*You're* the one who's fucked up."

"Oh yeah?"

She reached behind her back, and her bra went loose. It fell as she bent to push the sweatpants back down, and this time her underwear went with them. When she straightened up, her hips rolled around the dark feminine wedge of her pubic hair. I looked away and then looked back, trying half-heartedly to master the charge in my groin. She stepped toward me, and I felt her nakedness like warmth from a fire. When her hand touched me through the mesh of my basketball shorts, I chirped at the pleasure of it.

"What if I told you that Derek and me were getting back together?" she said.

"What?"

She slipped her hand under my waistband, and I gasped at the iciness of her nimble fingers. "What if I told you we never actually got a divorce?"

"Are you serious?"

"Why? You don't mind if I'm married, do you?"

I was already grabbing her wrist and hauling it from my shorts. "Knock it off."

She reached for me with her other hand, and I snatched it away with my other hand. She laughed and licked my neck, and when she pushed her naked body against me, my mouth found hers. Our tongues slid. Then she was pulling me across the room, flopping onto the bed, and I kicked the shorts from my ankles, peeled off my sweatshirt, and tucked my pelvis into the familiar, comforting groove between her thighs. She rolled a condom over me.

"My husband is going to be pissed," she said.

I decided to ignore it. Her purpose was only to hurt me, and I thought I might as well get some pleasure when it was available, especially when it came with a new understanding of what Tanya meant to me, a core of emotion much more powerful than the physical pleasure I'd always assumed I was seeking. It was the body influencing the heart, I finally understood, and the heart notifying the body where it stood.

Maybe that was why a sense of wrongness tumbled into my stomach the moment I slid into her. She was still talking about "her husband," and even through the physical pleasure, I became aware of the hostility and degradation in what we were doing. It seemed to defy some basic premise of the sexual act, and I understood that the pleasure wasn't worth it. This occurred to me not in words but in a sadness and reluctance that tightened the muscles around my eyes, churned up a hollow nausea in my gut, flexed my back into hard resistance. I struggled free from her arms.

"You're sick," I said, stepping into my shorts.

"So are you," she called after me. "So is everyone."

15

The predawn air smelled of cold, wetness, and wood. I headed up the trail at a jog, careful with the footing but stumbling occasionally over half-buried roots and rocks. Distinctions were dim between the black trunks and the dark gray spaces that separated them. As the light came up, I saw a white mist was laced through the branches, the sky edged silver around low purple clouds. I hoped they would hold their peace, though already I felt the cold air washing down and breathed the icy scent of precipitation.

Droplets tapped my face, bouncing from my cheeks. A few minutes later, the hail rattled in the trees and scattered itself along the trail like flung beads. I ran in a hunch, now and then shaking the ice out of my hair. Later it became rain and soaked my clothes, though I was warm from the rushing blood. My legs felt weak, already unaccustomed to running after six weeks without it, but I wanted to keep going and so I did. My headache eased as last night's alcohol seeped from my body and other toxins seeped from my mind, so that finally, coming off the mountain nearly two hours later, I felt light and loose, my mind clear, my insides scoured clean.

As I ran through campus, puddles along the sidewalks reflected blue seams where clouds were coming apart. Birds darted around, trilling. The air smelled clean and damp, and when I stopped at a drinking fountain outside the library, I noticed small green buds already lining the sticks of a naked shrub.

I finished my run at the bowling alley, where I convinced a janitor to see about my keys. I let the engine run until it had defogged the windshield, and then I went for a burrito and coffee, biding my time. I wasn't eager to arrive at the bungalow, or see Tanya, or face the future of awkwardness and mutual rebuke that surely awaited us.

But I expected nothing like what I found when I finally pulled up. Everything I owned was scattered over the front lawn—my mattress, computer, clothes, cereal boxes and broccoli, papers and notebooks and textbooks—darkened and dripping with rain. I sat there in the car, running my eyes over it, outrage and disbelief grappling for territory inside me. Then I shut off the ignition and stormed toward the bungalow. Heavy metal from the '80s blared inside. It made me remember the Nirvana song from the bowling alley, and before opening the door, I wondered what cocktail of sadness and rage Tanya was sipping inside.

She sat on the floor, back propped on the futon, pushing Cool Ranch Doritos past her stretched lips, her eyes fastened to the television, where silent images from a horror movie flashed. Paris sat beside her, watching the chips make their journey from bag to mouth. I jabbed my finger at the open doorway and yelled over the music, "What the hell?"

Tanya turned a stereo knob, and the noise vanished. "You're evicted," she said, eyes glued to the television. "Effective immediately."

Part of me knew this was inevitable. Part of me even preferred it. Still, I made claims about legal contracts, proper notice, discrimination, rent paid in advance, swinging from indignation to entreaty and back again.

Tanya wasn't impressed by any of it. "Effective immediately," she kept saying, crunching chips, eyes on the television. "If I can kick my husband out, I can kick your sorry ass out too."

Hearing myself compared with Derek did something to me, and my protests collapsed into a crater of regret. If she wanted me to leave, maybe I should. Dragging my possessions inside wouldn't save them anyway. I peeled her key from my ring, tossed it into her lap, and took down the leash. Paris was at my knees in an instant, wagging his hips and whining with excitement, thinking we were only going for a walk.

"Paris stays," Tanya said.

I clipped him in. "I don't think so."

"That dog is mine just as much as it is yours."

"I paid for him."

"That's not how it works." She stood and came across the room. "You abandon an animal, it stops being yours."

"I'm not abandoning him."

"You already did." She grabbed the leash. "Who do you think's been taking care of him while you're off banging other chicks?"

I tugged at the leash but she kept her grip, so I reached down, unclipped it from his collar, and called him to the open door, slapping my thigh. Paris came bounding after me until Tanya called, "Ah, ah! Stay." He looked back at her, tail slowing. Then we were both calling strings of commands to him, and he walked in a circle, trying to do all of them at once, until he finally cast one last glance at me, full of apology, it seemed, before ducking his head and trotting to Tanya.

It was just as well. I didn't know what to do with Paris anyway. I hardly knew what to do with myself. "Just till I find a place," I told her.

I spent a few minutes wandering among the wreckage in the yard, eventually grabbing my backpack and a wad of clothing, barely caring what I kept. I left the rest where it was. Walking back to my car I spotted my basketball, the leather dark with moisture and probably already ruined, but I stooped to retrieve it.

***

There was only one place I could think to go, and I was about as eager to arrive there as I was at the bungalow. After opening the door for me, Lucienne slouched against the doorframe, arms crossed, as if debating whether to let me enter. Her eyes looked dark and tired, as if she'd had as restful a night as I had. Otherwise she was as stylish as ever in her wool dress and black leggings and tall leather boots, and I remembered the thrill it used to give me to be in her company.

"Why are you all wet?" she asked.

I was still in my running clothes, soaked and grimy. I held my tepid coffee in both hands, trying to warm them. "I was out running during the storm."

"Why didn't you dry off?"

"That's what I'm here to talk to you about."

She left the door open as she retreated inside, not exactly an invitation. I had the urge to head straight for the shower, or at least grab a dish towel from the kitchen, but even that much seemed presumptuous after the way our night had ended. Instead I followed her into the spare room she used as a closet and sewing workshop. The walls were lined with clothing racks organized into rainbows of color. At its center was a table with a sewing machine shrouded in plastic. Her satin-lined sewing kit was open to reveal its mess of spools and pins and bobbins. She seated herself at the table, then took up a pincher tool and began to pry stitching from a dress's hem.

"I'm sorry about last night," I began.

She just kept ripping.

"I didn't know that's how Tanya was going to react," I said, "but if you didn't feel comfortable about me living with her anymore, I would understand. Actually, while I was out running this morning, I got to thinking that maybe I shouldn't even go back at all. The only hitch," I continued, "is that I don't have anywhere else to stay. Except here."

"You said something happened with her. You said she still had feelings for you."

"All the more reason, right?"

She glanced at me, and something new was in her eyes—an authentic version of the sorrow she'd always played at before. "I have to ask you something," she said, turning her eyes down and pulling a short length of fabric between her two fists. "It kept me up all night, and I'd appreciate an honest answer."

"All right."

"Did anything happen between you and her while we were dating?"

I couldn't bring myself to admit it, though I didn't want to lie either. The technical distinctions I'd invented seemed suddenly ridiculous.

Finally Lucienne glanced up, her face shifting from inquiry to knowledge.

"You don't understand," I explained. "I never meant for it to happen in the first place, but then one morning she barged into my room waving her divorce papers, and—"

Lucienne leaned away, glaring at me in disbelief, as if I had just offered her something rancid. "I don't want to *know* about it."

Then her eyes softened, drifting away, her gaze turning inward, her face closing into the same expression she had used to pitch her disturbing photos to the section editors, as if she was already resigned to disappointment, as if she was tired of harboring silly hopes and trying to kill them before someone else did. It hurt to see, and I decided to drop the charade.

"When was the last time you were with her?" she asked.

It took me a moment to admit, "Last night."

"Physically, you mean?"

"Yes."

"Did you have sex?"

I looked at the hand gripping the coffee cup. It was cold and red and blissfully unaware of what was going on in the room. "Yes."

She sat with that answer a moment, and then her eyes turned glassy. She tilted her head down and shielded it from view like she would shield her eyes from the sun. She reached up periodically to wipe her cheeks. It was hard to watch. I wanted to comfort her, but when I put a hand on her shoulder, she twisted away and looked at me, her face a wet mess of anguish that made me wish I could drop straight into the fiery abyss that surely awaited me.

She stood and carried her tears into the bathroom, shutting the door. I stayed where I was, hating myself, wondering how I could have ever believed it was okay to be involved with two women. I felt like a monster, and I wished the nausea in my stomach would open my throat and let me expel the hot shame clotted in my chest.

When Lucienne finally emerged, she looked raw and vulnerable, her face stripped of makeup, her skin puffy and red, especially around the eyes. She met my gaze, straightened her back, and donned an expression of dignity and purpose. "Ed," she said, voice firm, though I also detected a note of condolence, and it astonished me that she was capable of that small measure of kindness. I nodded, trying to make it easier for her, though it filled my lungs with needles to know what she was choosing. She had no other friends at Sequoia. She preferred loneliness to me.

"I'm breaking up with you," she said.

In a way I admired her for it, and in another way I was happy to be free from her—and from the version of myself I'd fashioned in her presence. But that didn't take away the disgrace, or the sting of rejection, or the sense of waste, or the feeling that something must be wrong with me, something important that I couldn't see, though it was stamped on my soul like a brand, so that wherever I went in life, other people would recognize it, and then they would abandon me, too.

***

In San Seguro, there would have been a dozen couches offered to me—although that probably wasn't true anymore either. In Conrad Park, I could think of only one, and it was a long shot.

"Whoa!" Knute Buhner said as he pulled the door open. He grinned at me while warm air billowed out, carrying the scent of air fresheners. "Nice *legs*, Garrison!"

I was still in my running clothes, grimy and wet, and I could see his laughter shift to reluctance when I asked to come inside. The decor was tidy and tasteful—floor lamps, glass tables, bamboo growing from a fishbowl filled with smooth white pebbles. The couch was black leather, and sitting on it were two women in tank tops and boxer shorts, hair rumpled, holding yellow highlighters above the textbooks spread in their laps. Reclining in front of them on the carpet, his head propped against the shins of the brunette, watching what looked like a basketball game until I realized it was just bloopers, was the guy who'd taken my place. He had a well-trimmed goatee and wore a baseball cap with the brim pushed up, and seeing his easy repose produced a stab of envy and remorse so painful that I almost left.

Instead I suffered through introductions and polite hellos before following Knute to the kitchen, where he resumed slicing a bell pepper. He chided me, laughing, when I explained what had happened with my landlord, but he sobered the moment I asked for a favor. He looked up from the bell pepper and asked, "What kind of favor?"

"I need a couch to crash on. Just for a few nights, until I find a new place."

He glanced toward the living room, then scratched the back of his neck. "I don't know, man. This place is pretty small, and it gets real cramped when there's company—as you can see." He grinned, giving me a moment to appreciate what he was saying. "Plus, the couch is a crucial part of the operation. Without the couch, the whole system falls apart. You get what I'm saying?"

There was nothing to do but tighten my face and nod.

"Look, if you *really* needed it, like really needed it, we could figure something out. If it's an emergency I'm not going to hang you out to dry, obviously. I wouldn't do that. But is that really what we're talking about here? An *emergency*?"

"I guess not."

He smacked my shoulder. "Don't worry. You keep flashing that much leg, you'll find a place in no time."

***

I snuck into my old dorm building with my wet bundle of clothes and a handful of quarters from the ashtray of my car. I stripped to my underwear in the laundry room and shivered while everything tumbled in the dryer. A couple girls passed by the doorway and called, "Woo *woo!*" but it didn't dent my misery.

I went to the gym for a hot shower and afterward put on dry pants, dry socks, a dry shirt and sweater. It made me feel a little bit more like myself. I considered who else I could stay with but had no other options. I'd betrayed everyone I cared about—the women, the basketball players, the editorial staff. I didn't realize the last one until right then. I wasn't going to write the article about A.C. Sullinger. It meant I was finished as sports editor, but I was finished with betrayal too.

I had a bowl of hot soup at the café next to the library, then went to the reading room, where the whiskey hangover and sleepless night and long morning run all caught up to me. Later someone shook me awake and said the library was closing.

I drove around town scouting places to park, my eyelids heavy, my wipers clearing the drizzle from the windshield. Finally I nosed into a dark alley on campus between two academic buildings, my headlights intensifying against the battered green paint of a dumpster until I stopped and cut the engine. I wanted the radio but I was afraid of nodding off and running the battery dead, so I locked the doors, reclined my seat, and listened to the rain.

A loud clacking startled me awake. It was very cold and it took me a moment to figure out where I was. The clacking came again, and I understood that someone was rapping on my window with a hard object. Outside was the bright disk of a tilted flashlight, raindrops zipping through the beam. Beside it were a blue shirt and a badge. I cranked down the window.

"Conrad Park PD," said a familiar voice, then: "Hey, ain't you that dude from the paper?"

I rubbed my eyes and looked past the flashlight. It was Kenyon Cook, Sequoia's former power forward and team captain, the one who'd come jogging down to kick me off the court the day I showed up for the shoot-around. He looked diminished in the police uniform but still imposing. "What're you doing here?" he asked.

"Napping."

"Had anything to drink?"

"No."

"You sure about that?"

"Yes."

He swung his light into my eyes, and I flinched at the glare. He studied me a moment longer, then turned off the light and slid it into its holster. "Go on home then," he said. "I won't write you up, but you can't sleep here."

I waited for his squad car to pull away, then backed out and drove aimlessly around town, not searching for anything, just driving, not knowing what else to do.

When I found myself on a highway I'd run during my marathon training, though, I had an idea. I followed it a couple miles out of town, peering at the dark shoulder for the fire road. I had to turn sharply when I spotted it. The gravel hissed beneath my tires, plunking the axle and chassis while I swerved to avoid ruts and potholes and skull-sized rocks. The road was barely wide enough for two cars to pass in opposite directions, and after a few miles it narrowed further, until it was barely wide enough for one.

I looked for a turnout where I could park for the night, not wanting to block the road, but no turnout appeared, so I pursued the puddle of my headlights more deeply into the forest. Black trees grabbed at each other above me. Pine boughs and naked limbs slapped the windshield, and in my rearview they waved angrily, smoldering red, before they sunk into the inky night. Finally I was unwilling to go farther. I didn't like blocking the road, but it seemed impossible that anyone else would find their way out so far.

When I turned off the engine and cut the lights, the darkness was astounding. I blinked a few times but couldn't tell the difference between having my eyes open and shut. The only sound was the rain, big drops from the trees that smacked the roof and hood in irregular rhythms. After I had reclined my seat, I found myself trying to anticipate them, and it gave me a jittery, nervous feeling. A chill reached up from the floor and pulled itself in. I considered blasting it away with the heater, but I had no concept of how long my gas would last in idle, and I could think of nothing worse, way out here, than waking to an empty tank. I put on the extra shirt and jeans and socks I had grabbed, wishing I'd been wiser about my choices. Instead of grabbing the basketball I should have grabbed something useful, like a blanket.

My mind reeled in the darkness. Tanya and Lucienne kept appearing before me, faces contorted with pain, and I could hardly believe I'd caused it. I'd been so focused on technical distinctions that I'd never considered the more basic question of how it would feel to be in their position. I'd thought only about how they fit into my life rather than how I fit into theirs. That was the real betrayal. The sex was just a symptom of it, and now I saw through it to the other symptoms. I thought of Tanya's troubled background and divorce, and it occurred to me to feel concern for her instead of amusement. I thought of Lucienne's emaciated body, her talk about models and disorders, and it occurred to me to feel alarmed instead of excited. I thought of the way I'd ignored every signal of their distress until now, when I'd lost the right to offer any worry or help.

I shifted onto my side and brought my knees to my chest, but this time sleep wouldn't come, and little by little the despair of insomnia overtook me. Still, I kept my eyes shut, pretending sleep was close, because otherwise the desolation might have swallowed me whole.

I woke shivering, my hands and feet like blocks of ice. The rain had stopped. I had no idea what time it was. I had the sense that morning was not far off, but I didn't know whether to trust it.

Before long, gray shapes of daylight perched like strange birds in the black foliage. By then I had made a decision. I put up my seat, ignited the engine, and then slowly, carefully, backed the whole way out of the forest.

PART III: HOME

16

The sun rose over the desert to the east, brightening great swaths of fallow cropland where hulking machines slowly combed the earth. Past Monterey, the landscape looked thirsty and overexposed, but it was good to see that the broader world still existed and to remember that my troubles in Conrad Park were just one small part of it. It was also a comfort to know I was headed somewhere on purpose rather than by accident, and that a shower and a bed would be waiting for me. When I came through the familiar streets of San Seguro, though, I remembered everything else that was waiting, and my anticipation soured into nervousness. I hadn't been home in almost a year, not since that last awful Christmas, and nobody was expecting me.

The feeling got worse when I saw the house. The yard was like a crop, heavy nodes swaying on tan stalks. Overgrown shrubs blocked the windows. The siding was covered with bird shit that converged at a mud dome hanging under the eave. The basketball hoop had been dragged around the side of the garage so that only the backboard was visible over the roof corner, but its frayed sandbags were still piled at the edge of the driveway, one split open, spilling sand. I parked beside them, got out, and made my way up the porch steps, where an old propane tank squatted like a goblin. It was strange to knock on the door, even stranger to clench my hands politely and wait for an invitation to enter the house I'd grown up in.

My father answered wearing a ratty bathrobe over pajamas. Wisps of steam uncurled from the porcelain mug he gripped. The shaggy wings over his ears were now more gray than brown. His beard was gone, and his face was swollen in a way that made his eyes look small. It made me worry about his health, and the same worry was reflected in his expression as he took in my disheveled state. "Ed? What are you doing here?"

"Can I come in?"

He swept his arm back in invitation, and the theatrical gesture, coupled with the loose sleeves hanging from his wrists, made him look like some kind of bankrupt wizard. "Don't you have school?"

"Not on Saturdays."

"You know what I mean. Is everything all right?"

"Is there more coffee?"

He shuffled toward the kitchen on his bad leg, and I followed. The sink was full, the counter cluttered with dishes and detritus, the trash overflowing. Old resentments began to creep up on me while my father banged the cupboards, searching for a clean mug. Finally he took down a teacup from the china cabinet, filled it with black coffee, and handed it to me wearing an expression of bewilderment and concern. "I think we're out of milk," he said. "Are you sure you're okay?"

"I don't need milk."

The dining table was lost under papers and torn envelopes, books and magazines, a cardboard box spilling foam peanuts. "Sorry," my father said, bulldozing the papers with his forearm. "I wasn't expecting company."

The term might have depressed me if I'd had any more room for depression. And he was right. I was a visitor, an outsider. I was company.

I sat where my father had cleared a space. He sat across the table, watching me sip the scalding coffee, his face flexed with inquiry.

"Is Charlie here?" I asked.

He shook his head. "He's doing community service." The surprise must have registered in my expression. "It's not what you think," he said. "It's mandatory."

"For what?"

He leaned forward, elbows on the trash-covered table, hands rigid, as if measuring the space between them. "Ed, tell me why you're here. Did something happen?"

"A lot of somethings happened."

He requested more information by lifting his eyebrows.

"The short version is that I got kicked out of my place," I said.

"Kicked out? Why?"

"Girl trouble."

He only stared at me with the same unnerving concentration.

"I got a little too close to my landlord, is the gist of it," I explained. "Landlady, I mean. Then she found out I was seeing someone else, and now all my stuff is in her front yard getting rained on."

He sat back, relieved, and it occurred to me how trivial these matters must have seemed to him after what he'd been through with my mother. "Well, romantic trouble is difficult no matter which side of it you're on," he said. "I know that as well as anyone. But I also know how easily it can get in the way of everything else. A little adversity can drag you down a long way if you let it."

He cast a significant look across the table, as if he was on the verge of confessing something, and I found myself nodding to encourage him.

"What I'm trying to say," he continued, "is that a little romantic trouble doesn't mean it's okay to abandon your obligations. Your top priority should be your education whether you're at Berkeley or anywhere else."

"I don't have anywhere to live, Dad. I don't know what I'm supposed to do."

"You could stay with a friend. You could get a motel room, at least until the end of the term. You could start looking for a new place. Besides, if you had a lease, you might be able to—"

The small territory of my patience was quickly constricting, and I interrupted him: "I don't *have* any friends. Okay? I know you have your own life to worry about, but I slept in my car in the forest last night. I don't have anywhere else to go. Can I just take a couple days to figure things out? It's Saturday."

He was still frowning at me but the disapproval in his face had shifted into something else, and it took me a moment to recognize it as sympathy. "That's not true, is it? You have friends."

I stared into the coffee mug, where rainbows floated on a thin sheen of oil. I shook my head. "I've been—it's been a hard couple of years."

A scowl had crept into his expression, but rather than looking dismissive or belittling, as it had last Christmas, it looked sorrowful, private—the expression of a man who doubted himself, who was tired of letting people down. It made him look as different to me as the physical changes I'd noticed before. "Okay," he said, and startled me by reaching across the table to pat my hand. "Stay as long as you like."

***

Charlie's community service, it turned out, was court-mandated. A month earlier he had walked out of a convenience store with two candy bars and a bottle of malt liquor. He needed forty hours of service to expunge the theft from his record, so on Saturday mornings and Sunday afternoons he picked up trash from the side of a highway with other juvenile delinquents.

"I'm just happy he agreed to do it," my father said. "I certainly couldn't have made him. He's in open mutiny these days."

And then my father launched all his other complaints against Charlie. He skipped school, stayed out all night, no longer made any pretense about hiding his marijuana use. "I take things away, he takes them back. I say he's grounded, he leaves anyway. I block the door, he pushes me aside. I've been looking into military schools. I'm hoping it doesn't come to that but I don't know what else to do. It's affecting my work, my sleep. I don't feel well lately." He massaged his chest, and then his eyes rose to meet mine. "Maybe you could talk to him."

"I've tried," I said, though that wasn't exactly true. I'd only dominated and ridiculed him in a pickup basketball game. "It didn't go well," I added.

"Could you try again? Your mother and I can talk until we're blue in the face but it only makes him more rebellious. It'll sound different coming from a brother."

"No it won't. It'll just make him resent me more."

"All I'm asking is that you try. Please, Ed. He needs it."

There was no denying that, but it was hard enough to hear about Charlie's conduct without also becoming instantly responsible for it. This was exactly what had driven me crazy about my father since the divorce, the way he abandoned his post as a parent and then charged me with parental responsibilities. But he had just shown me a kindness, and I felt obligated to reciprocate it. "Fine," I said, then corrected my tone and told him, "Okay. I'll try."

***

The rest of the house was as filthy as the kitchen and dining room. In Charlie's room the blinds were drawn, giving the space a dim subterranean look. The air was close and musty, tinged with a stench of scorched plastic and incense, the sheets twisted into a coil, the floor littered with clothing and food wrappers and CD cases. My father's office was a chaos of papers and books, as if it had been torn apart by thieves searching for valuables. The back lawn was another crop, and the foothills were as gray as old lumber, awaiting the rains that were still a few months away.

The only tidy space in the house was my bedroom, though a thick layer of dust had settled over everything, even the bed, which released a powdery cloud when I flopped onto it. I craved sleep, but being in the room was too strange, like trying to nap inside a shrine to the dead. The old hats and jackets hanging in the closet seemed to belong to someone else, an old friend I'd lost contact with. The childhood participation trophies lining the bureau looked shabby and cheap. They belonged to the skinny kid who gripped a basketball or shouldered a baseball bat in the old team photos, beaming innocently at the camera. The last time I'd seen the photos, that kid had been me. Now it was someone else, some version of myself I'd left behind, and I felt a surge of regret over the chain of bad decisions I'd made since then.

The bathtub was grimy and discolored, the shower curtain thick with mildew, but I was refreshed by the spray of hot water and foaming soap. The clean clothes my father lent me felt good on my skin. I cleared a spot at the dining room table to do schoolwork but then ignored it to carry away the rest of the wadded napkins and the calcium-stained water glasses and empty cereal boxes and junk mail and torn envelopes and food-flecked receipts. When the table was bare, I scoured the sticky patches, wiped the whole thing down, and applied a coat of polish I found under the sink, filling the air with the aroma of orange peel. I used the damp rag to rub great furry wads of dust from the chairs and then bumped the screaming vacuum against the table legs. Afterward the table looked like an animal restored to its natural habitat, and a feeling of peace settled through me.

I looked for lunch in the refrigerator but found only a mess of wilted produce, expired condiments, and questionable leftovers. I was unloading it all when my father left to pick up Charlie from the work crew. I waved goodbye, realizing I was excited to see my brother. He and I had been at odds recently, but it was hardly the first time. Our whole lives he had annoyed me, and I had demeaned him, and we had fought and tattled and suffered our punishments. And then we'd gone on being brothers.

I remembered one time in particular when I'd let him watch me glue seeds to a poster board for a science project. He stood on a chair right beside me, leaning over the project, and I grew so tired of his requests to glue one himself that I finally shoved him away. This was nothing unusual, except that this time his feet got tangled in the chair, and he cracked a front tooth on the tile floor. He wailed while I apologized desperately and called for our mother. When she came in to see what had happened, though, Charlie hesitated. He told her he'd been testing how strong the tile was, and then his sheepish eyes slid over to seek my approval. It was a preposterous lie, but I couldn't help feeling grateful, even impressed. Charlie was capable of forgiveness—and more.

I ended up throwing out half the contents of the fridge, which sent a cloud of fruit flies spiraling toward the ceiling. I rinsed and dried the remaining jars before returning them to a gleaming, sanitized interior. I was nearly finished when I heard the garage door rumble open, the car doors clap. The door to the laundry room swung open, and I had a moment of shock when Charlie ducked under the frame.

He was a giant. He must have been at least six-and-a-half feet tall, with hands I could hardly believe and an adult's face, the brow ridge and jaw prominent, though red boils were still clustered on his cheeks and throat. Even more shocking was his purple hair and the ring threaded through his septum like a bull's. He wore black jeans stuffed into heavy black boots, and his bony wrists protruded from the sleeves of a black bomber jacket covered with patches. Beneath it he wore a T-shirt with band names scrawled in wild, off-kilter seesaws around the outline of a fist. He crossed the room glowering at the floor, as if entering the house filled him with animosity, and when I said hello, the word landed like a torpedo.

"*God*," he said, face smeared with an ugly expression of fright and aggravation, as if I'd played a mean trick on him. "What are *you* doing here?"

I was so unnerved by the sight of him that I didn't know how to answer. I looked at the pickle jar and dishrag in my hands, but they produced no meaningful logic. "You grew," I said. "You look—" I gestured at his clothes—"different."

"You don't." He moved his eyes over my father's shirt and khakis to let me know this was an insult, then turned and stomped upstairs.

My father came through the door a moment later carrying a small paper sack.

"You didn't tell Charlie I was here?"

He shucked the sack from a whiskey bottle. "We don't say much to each other anymore," he explained.

***

I spent the afternoon dusting and vacuuming my room and washing my sheets and clothes. By the time I crawled into bed that evening, I was exhausted to the point of collapse. Every time I drifted to the precipice of sleep, though, a thought about Tanya or Lucienne broke over me, and I was jolted awake by the same feeling that might have come from the realization that I'd left the stove burning. At first, I thought it was just the pain and guilt of a double breakup, but eventually I understood it was also a feeling of deprivation. I missed them. Tanya and Lucienne were the only real friends I'd made in Conrad Park, and recognizing it produced such a sharp sense of loss that it sent my heart into a frenzy, and the possibility of sleep barreled into the distance like a train I had barely missed.

Waking up the next morning was like crawling out of a hole. Sunlight flooded the room and the house was silent. It was nearly eleven. I went to the kitchen, where my mood was immediately fouled by the mess and the stench. I wondered how my father and brother could stand it as I navigated the clutter for a mug of coffee and a frozen burrito. When I opened the refrigerator, looking for hot sauce, its tidy interior gleamed like an oasis of civilization in post-apocalyptic rubble. After breakfast I tried concentrating on my schoolwork, but I couldn't stop thinking about the little pocket of beauty I had created there.

Finally, I got up to examine the kitchen mess again. It felt hopeless, but I could at least get rid of the smell by taking out the trash. After flapping a fresh bag into the can, I filled it with the food scraps the fruit flies must have been living on, took it out, and shook another clean bag in. I set some crusty dishes to soak while I emptied mugs and glasses and loaded them into the dishwasher. Then I took on another small task, and then another, and as the counters gradually became visible, as the floor tiles were restored to their original color, as the stench of rot was replaced by the astringent odors of chlorine and lemon, the hopelessness I'd felt about the mess gradually dissipated. When I was finished, I stood there a long time admiring my work before wandering into other rooms, cataloguing their messes, planning my attack.

I was in the bathroom, bleach fumes searing my nostrils, when I heard the garage door rumble. My father appeared down the hallway holding a stack of books against his chest, breathing hard. "Holy moly," he said, eyes pointed at the kitchen. He limped out of view and said it again. He reappeared, still carrying the books, and gave me an astonished look from the far end of the hallway, as if he'd just witnessed a car accident. "You've been busy."

I wiped my hands, then went down to lift half the books from his chest.

"Just dump them with the others on that armchair," he said, bending to set his own stack on the study floor. After straightening up, he glanced around, and his voice was low and guilty when he said, "I guess I didn't realize how bad it had gotten in here."

An hour later I was back at the dining room table, backpack open, ungluing soaked papers from one another, though I wondered if it was really worth it to do the readings, complete the assignments, prepare for next week's final exams. It was also Sunday, which meant that in another couple hours the editorial team would begin assembling the newspaper—the one centered around my big exposé. All it inspired in me was the vague resolution to call later, and when the phone rang, my first thought was that Eli Duncan had found me.

My father came in with a hangdog look to offer me the receiver.

"Ed?" my mother said. "Thank God. I called your number on campus but your landlord told me you weren't living there anymore and made it sound like something awful had happened."

Tanya and my mother on the phone together was not a pleasant thought. "She's just angry at me, Mom."

"Why? What's going on?"

"She threw me out. Lucienne dumped me. The rest of it you can probably guess. I didn't have anywhere else to go, so I came here."

"Oh, Ed. I'm sorry to hear that. Are you okay?"

"I'm working on it."

"Is that what she meant about Paris? She kept saying something about trouble in Paris. She wanted me to tell you. It sounded like some kind of code."

"Paris is my dog."

"Oh. Well listen, does this mean you can come for Christmas? Because actually, the reason I was trying to get ahold of you is because I'm about to book Charlie's flight and I need to know whether to buy one plane ticket or two. I'm sorry to be so abrupt, but the tickets won't be available by tomorrow. I hope they're still available when I get off the phone with you."

My mind groped for a reason to refuse, and it occurred to me that maybe this was part of the problem—making myself appear at the mercy of forces beyond my control rather than admitting how I felt. I remembered Tanya advising me to say what I meant.

"I'm sorry," I said, "but I can't."

"This is important to me, Ed. I'm your mother and I'd like you to be here."

"I get why you had to leave. I get that it was probably for the best, rather than staying and pretending. But I can't be there while you marry the woman who wrecked our family."

It was the simple truth, and in the silence that followed, my mind stopped racing ahead for rebuttals and justifications.

"Thank you for your honesty," my mother finally said. "But I wish you wouldn't think of Jane that way. It wasn't her fault. It wasn't anybody's fault, really. It was just a set of circumstances."

"She knew you were married, didn't she?"

"That was one circumstance, yes."

"Then she knew she was wrecking a family. You can't say it was nobody's fault."

"The circumstances were there whether Jane was part of the equation or not, Ed, and it wouldn't have done any good to go on pretending—like you just said. Jane helped me with that."

"You *were* pretending, then? You weren't happy with us?"

"I was *always* happy with you. None of that was pretend."

"You can't have it both ways, Mom. You can't say you were pretending and also not pretending. Jane can't be the reason you left and then not the reason at the same time."

"That's the wrong way of looking at it."

"No, it's just not the way you want me to look at it. I've been thinking about how hard all this must have been for you. I really have. But that doesn't make the logic work, no matter how vaguely you word it."

"Some things are beyond logic." But she must have heard how flimsy that sounded, because she quickly added, "In any case, I guess I'll have to respect your decision, but that won't keep us from missing you. Do you think you might be able to visit some other time? Or maybe I could come see you in the spring. Do they have a Mom's Weekend at your college?"

I said I would look into it.

***

That evening my father came home with two bulging grocery bags after picking Charlie up from the work crew. He unpacked them onto the counter, looped a stained apron over his sweater, and began measuring ingredients with fussy concentration. A hearty aroma of beef and potatoes filled the house. It was a casserole with cream sauce accompanied by piles of steaming broccoli. We all sat down together to eat it, Charlie's eyes red and glassy, my father still wearing the apron. We didn't say anything, just cut and forked and chewed, sipping often from our water glasses, fixing our eyes on our plates or letting them drift to the place where a centerpiece might be if this weren't a household of men.

When his plate was clear, my father put down his fork, wiped the corners of his mouth with a finger and thumb, and broke the silence. "I take it you're staying again tonight, Ed?"

I'd been putting off the decision, but I saw now that the delay had become its own kind of decision. "If that's okay."

"How much school are you intending to miss, exactly?"

"I don't know."

"Have you at least made arrangements for your absence?"

"I meant to," I said, and thought of the newspaper staff congregating in the office, asking Lucienne where I was. "I will tomorrow."

"Good. Because I want you to know how seriously we take your education, your mother and I both. And I want you to know that students who fall too far behind, they often never catch up—especially at this point in the semester."

I plastered a bland smile onto my face and gave him a long stare. "I know."

"Good. Because I don't want to minimize the importance of those things. Also, as soon as you're ready, I think I have an idea for what to do about your living situation. But I also wanted to tell you," he said, and then he looked at me with a new expression, one filled with timidity and warmth, the look you might give a girl before asking her to a dance—"I also wanted to tell you how nice it is to have you around."

He looked like he meant to say more but only pressed his lips together and gave a firm, conclusive nod before scooping more casserole onto his plate.

"So I guess it's okay for *him* to skip school," Charlie said, looking at his plate, where his fork tines carved a pit into his food.

"It's a different situation entirely," our father said.

"It's always different for Ed, isn't it?"

"I've given you every opportunity," my father began calmly, but before he could finish, Charlie dropped his fork and stood, tipping over his chair. He went pounding up the stairs as if trying to destroy the risers. A door slammed. Music blared.

My father met my eyes. I could feel an alliance hanging between us, and I could sense my father feeling it, too. "You haven't had a chance to talk to him yet?" he asked.

"Not yet," I answered.

17

The talk was like a splinter in my mind. What could I possibly say to Charlie, and how could I say it without sounding like a Boy Scout or an asshole? The problem was that talking was so deliberate. It wasn't how we'd ever interacted before, and so it felt conspicuous and unnatural to try it now. It would have been better if we could *do* something together, like shooting hoops in the driveway—just passing and shooting, not talking about anything, like we used to.

On Monday, while Charlie was at school and my father at work, I dismantled the bird nest under the eave, washed the siding and windows, pruned the bushes, and pushed the rumbling mower over both yards, spiraling inward. I was raking up the clippings when a school bus squealed to a halt at the end of the drive. After it rumbled away, Charlie came trudging around the corner, a towering figure with a flannel shirt tied around his waist and headphones arched over his scraggly purple hair, holding his backpack like a clutch. He glanced at me, face sullen. I mouthed my question, and he dropped the headphones around his neck. "What?"

"Why are you taking the bus? Can't you catch a ride with Dad?"

He brought his shoulders to his earlobes and then let them sink.

"Want me to drive you tomorrow?"

"Not really," he said, but it came a little too quickly, and there was a hesitation before he clapped the headphones back over his ears and trudged away. He looked like he wanted to accept my help but didn't know how.

The next afternoon I swept the driveway with a push broom, a task that left me sweating and out of breath. I also duct-taped the split sandbag, then searched briefly for my cheap rubber ball before I remembered punting it the day I'd taken Charlie to the Mission court. So I grabbed my ruined leather ball, the one I'd taken from Tanya's lawn. The leather was coarse and discolored where it had been wet, so it didn't bother me to scar it on the asphalt, though for now I only sat with it on the porch steps, waiting.

Finally, the school bus squealed to a stop and then rumbled away. When Charlie came down the drive, headphones around his neck this time, I hopped up and jogged over. "Hey, will you help me with something?"

He looked hesitant but not unwilling. "What?"

"Dragging the hoop back into the driveway."

He eyed me with suspicion. "Why?"

"So I can use it. I haven't shot hoops since I don't know when."

"I thought shooting hoops was the whole reason you chose your college."

"It was. Turns out that's a really stupid way to choose."

His look of insolence relaxed. I thought he might even smile. He didn't, but with his guard down I could finally see my brother again.

"I didn't make the team," I explained. "I guess I didn't even really try out."

"Why not?"

"I could tell I was out of my league. I didn't want to embarrass myself."

He followed me around the house, where I walked the hoop's pole down with my hands, ending up at the backboard. Charlie lifted the base, the heavy end, so that he was carrying practically all the weight himself while I merely guided us across the drive. He put his side down, and I let it pull the hoop upright. We took turns heaving the sandbags onto the base. When we were finished, he dusted his hands and said, "You should've tried out."

"Why's that?"

He shrugged. "You were good. Remember your last game?"

"That stupid game." I lifted the ball and passed it to him, but he sent it right back, so I executed a drop-step and banked it in. "That game was what made me think I could keep playing."

"Maybe you could've."

I passed him the ball, and he passed it back again. I tried a mini-hook. "Maybe. I'm not the best judge of things anymore. Ever since I got to college, it's been one mistake after another. Since Mom left, basically. This time it got me thrown out of the house I was living in. That's why I'm here. I don't really have anywhere else to go."

I sent him the ball, and he sent it back. I faced up, stepped through, and banked it in, saying, "Are you still going to that concert?"

"Probably not. Why?"

"I heard a Nirvana song the other day and it reminded me of you. What are The Dwarves like?"

"More punk than grunge. Faster riffs, not so clean."

"What do you like about it?" I said, passing the ball.

He caught it, shrugged, then threw it back, but this time he surprised me by calling "double-team." I gave him a bounce pass, and he popped the jump shot. He looked surprised and satisfied, his wrist hooked, eyes on the hoop. A charge of joy lifted through me.

"Garrison to Garrison," I said. "Wish I had a shot like that at your age."

His arm fell, and he wilted, as if from a bully. His eyes slid away, his shoulders slumped, his hands found his pockets. And so before the opportunity was completely gone, I told him, "You know, Dad was hoping I'd have a little talk with you."

I said it dismissively, with a conspiratorial smirk, trying to imply that I thought it was as silly as he did, but Charlie didn't take it that way. He was already reaching for his backpack, looking wounded. He was acting as though I'd insulted him, as though the only one who'd ever made any mistakes was me, and I felt a hot pulse of frustration. Why did he think everything was always about him? Why was he so eager to murder any kind of camaraderie between us?

Ten minutes later, the cloying odors of incense and marijuana drifted through the house. They were still thick when my father came home. "Now you see what I mean," he said, setting his satchel on the counter, then giving me a long look of hopelessness and fatigue. "You want to see what happens when I ground him for it?"

There was a shouting match upstairs, and then Charlie rushed down in his patched bomber jacket while my father shouted threats and commands. He went to the phone and tried to dial, but my father yanked the cord from the receiver. Charlie pried it from his hand, then boxed him out, knees and elbows flung wide like a rebounder while he reconnected it and made his call. "Can you come get me?" he said. "I've got some. Hurry up."

And then Charlie was heading for the door, raising a glass pipe out of my father's reach like an adult withholding cookies from a child. He continued down the driveway while my father shouted after him, forbidding it. He came back into the living room afterward, breathing hard, massaging his sternum. A shock of hair stood straight up, and his face shone with sadness. "That's what happens," he said. "It isn't good for my heart."

I lost sleep that night listening for Charlie's return, and I knew I couldn't put off our talk any longer.

***

The next day I was in the garage using the vacuum's extension nozzle to suck up the drifts of dust that had collected behind the furnace and water heater when I thought I heard the front door close. It was just after lunch, and nobody should have been home for another few hours. I turned off the vacuum and heard footsteps, then voices.

When I entered through the laundry room, Charlie was standing at the pantry with a boy so much shorter and younger-looking that it took me a moment to realize they were probably the same age. The other boy's eyebrow was pierced, his ears peeking through a curtain of lank brown hair. He glanced over, looking sedated, as if nothing in the world could possibly surprise him, least of all me.

"What are you doing here?" I asked Charlie, who was studiously ignoring me.

"Getting a snack."

"Don't you have school?"

"Don't *you?*"

"I thought I explained that."

"So did I."

"Jackpot," the other kid said in a surprisingly deep voice. He pulled down a bag of Oreos, and they trudged upstairs, the pantry doors still hanging open.

For a moment I considered waiting for my father to come home and letting him handle it, but that felt like a double betrayal—I would betray Charlie by tattling and my father by adding another burden when I'd promised to shoulder some of it myself. I closed the pantry doors and headed upstairs.

Through the doorway I could see Charlie leaning over a bureau drawer, rummaging through the mess inside. The friend stood in the corner watching, hands in his pockets, back slumped. When I knocked to announce myself, Charlie slammed the drawer and faced me, raising himself to his full height. "Did you mess with my stuff?" he said.

"Just the laundry."

"Were you in my room?"

"Just for the laundry," I repeated, unable to keep the irritation out of my voice. His was the only room I'd stayed away from, not wanting to make things worse by invading his privacy. I'd been dying to pull the curtains, open a window, let fresh air and natural light flood the room. I thought he might have appreciated this restraint, along with the stacks of fresh laundry that had appeared in his closet.

I shot a quick glance at the friend, who gazed back with sleepy amusement. There would always be a reason to avoid our talk, I decided, and to delay it any longer felt the same as delaying it forever. "Like I told you yesterday," I said, trying to ignore the friend, "I'm here because I made some mistakes. What I've realized is that most of them have come from the same thing—not thinking about other people enough. Now I'm trying to do better and get my life back in order."

Charlie watched me warily, as if he knew the trick I was pulling.

"You should be doing the same," I told him. "If you think Dad treats you differently, it's only because he's worried about you, and I don't blame him. Do you have any idea what you're doing to his heart? What if he keeled over one day? How would you feel then? If you want him to treat you better, maybe you should try doing the same for him. Maybe you should try taking other people into consideration once in a while."

"Maybe I would if he didn't treat me like crap."

"He's trying to help you, Charlie. We both are."

"No you're not. All you ever do is criticize me, just like you're doing right now, and then you leave. You try to act like you're there for me, but you aren't. You never are."

"I'm here now."

"You're here because you don't have anywhere else to go. You just said that. You're here for *yourself*. Stop trying to act all high and mighty like you know what's best for me. You don't."

When I didn't respond, he exchanged glances with the friend, as if apologizing for the interruption. The friend gave a look that said it was okay but couldn't he wrap it up?

Charlie opened the bureau drawer again. "Get out of my room."

"What about you?" I said. "When have you ever been there for me?"

"I never left," he said, rummaging again. "You're the one who left."

"The day Mom told us she was leaving, I needed you to come look for London with me and you wouldn't do it. The day I told you about Sequoia College, I needed you to help me work on a new move, like I've done a thousand times for you, but you said you didn't feel like it. When I needed you to come play basketball with me and my friends, you had to go get high first."

"I don't have to play basketball if I don't want to."

"What about what I want? Have you ever taken that into account?"

He found what he'd been searching for in the drawer, palmed it, then turned to face me. "Why should I?"

"Because I'm your brother."

"Well then maybe you should try taking into account what *I* want. You're always trying to force me to play basketball, but I don't *like* basketball. I'm not like you. I don't *want* to be like you."

As if to illustrate the point, he revealed the small film canister he was palming, popped its lid, and extracted a slender white joint. One end was tapered, the other black with ash. Before I could say anything, he produced a lighter from his pocket, then offered both to me. But even if I wasn't already suspended in the thin fissure between anger and self-control, even if I wasn't already convinced he was only mocking me, even if I hadn't been laughed at the last time I'd accepted a joint, even if I wanted to try it, what did Charlie expect me to do? Take it from him, ask for instructions, and then sit there getting high in the middle of the day with my little brother and some kid I didn't know, both of whom should have been in school?

"Here," he said, jabbing the joint and lighter at me. "Here, Ed. Take it. Take it. Be like me. Be like me." The friend snickered, and that cleared up any remaining doubt about whether Charlie had meant the offer in earnest. "Annoying," he said, "isn't it?"

I reached for the joint, not to smoke but to confiscate it, and Charlie, recognizing my intentions, recoiled.

"Give it," I said, turning my palm up.

"No. You're going to take it."

"You're damn right I am. Someone needs to. It's disgusting. *You're* disgusting. Would you look at this place? What happened to you?"

He responded with a smile, then sat on the bed and calmly placed the joint between his lips. He gave me a long look of bitterness and hostility, as if daring me to do something about it, before spinning the flint and raising the flame. His eyes dipped briefly as he lit the tip, then came back up, and he kept them locked on mine as he took a long drag. Without thinking, I stepped forward and slapped it from his mouth. The joint flew sideways onto the carpet, and at first Charlie's face was only shocked. Then it sharpened into rage.

He bolted up and came at me. I caught one of his shoulders and one of his wrists, and we grappled, wagging our elbows, pushing and twisting, resetting our feet, straightening and reversing our-selves, stumbling around the room until we slammed the bureau and our hands flew apart. With jabs and deflections we reached for each other again. This time, Charlie got his arms inside mine, his big hands clenching my collar and pulling the fabric tight around my shoulders and neck, and I could only loop my arms around the outside and hold my brother's sleeves like handlebars as I backped-aled, being driven across the room. When I slammed the wall, the whole house seemed to shake.

Charlie's face was pointed down at mine, nostrils flaring, lips peeled from gritted teeth. It felt strange to look up at my little brother. I tried to struggle free, but he was too strong. He shook me and then slammed me into the wall again, and this time my head knocked the plaster. Something banged to the floor in another room and my vision swam. I could smell his sour breath as he hollered, "You think you get to waltz back in here whenever you want and tell me what to do?"

He drove me slipping and stumbling through the doorway and threw me to the hall floor. When I struggled up, he pressed a knee into my spine and drove me back down, twice, until I lay there on my stomach, no longer resisting.

"Okay," I said. "You win."

The weight of his knee released. I turned over and saw him in the doorway, legs splayed, arms flared, leaning forward as if to meet another collision. "You don't live here anymore," he shouted, jabbing his finger at me. "You don't have a say in anything."

I looked at the long finger, the ponderous hand, the adult's face furrowed with hostility. My shoulder hurt where it had slammed the wall. I was dizzy and my head throbbed. My collar was stretched halfway down my chest and a seam in my sleeve was torn. "I can't help you if you won't let me," I told him, standing up.

"I don't need your help."

"Oh yes you do."

"Just stay away from me."

He went to pick the joint off the carpet and stamp out the fibers it had singed. When he saw me standing there, he came back and kicked the door shut. On the other side, the friend said something and Charlie laughed. I stood there for several long moments, looking at the grain of the door's veneer until my eyes burned.

***

Charlie and his friend were long gone by the time my father got home. I was sitting over a tumbler of whiskey, trying to dull the awful feeling of the fight. I kept thinking about how big and powerful Charlie had become, and what a waste it was for him to squander those gifts bullying me and my father rather than putting them to use on a basketball court. I remembered what I'd said to him—when had he ever been there for me?—and I felt how true it was. I also thought about what Charlie had said—that I only ever criticized him—and I considered the possibility that my criticism had the same effect on him that my father's had on me. It had only made me resentful and defiant, even when he was right.

My thoughts drifted toward my father, and I wondered if he felt the same frustration about my recent choices—basketball, Sequoia, journalism—as I did about Charlie's. I started to wonder what the divorce had been like for him. Did he hate my mother the same way Tanya seemed to hate me? Did he admire my mother's resolve the same way I'd admired Lucienne's? Was he angry at himself? Was he happy for her?

These were the ideas running through my mind when he walked in. "I'll pretend I didn't see that," he said, glancing at the tumbler as he passed into the kitchen, carrying a sack of groceries. "It's not easy to build an argument for lawfulness around here if I don't apply it consistently."

I drank off the rest and followed him into the kitchen. "I talked to Charlie."

He stopped unpacking groceries to glance at me, taking in my stretched collar, my torn sleeve, the rug burns on my cheek and forehead. I touched the goose egg on my crown, then turned to show him.

"That bad, huh?"

"It was pretty bad."

"Well," he said, reaching into the bag again, "that doesn't mean it'll have no effect. You never know how these things are going to settle once a little time has passed. What'd you tell him exactly?"

"Just that we're worried and trying to help."

"What did he say?"

"It's kind of a blur. I think he feels like we're trying to control him."

He laughed. "It's like your granddad used to tell me: *As long as you're living under my roof*—" He yanked the fridge open and threw in a carton of yogurt.

"I've just been thinking about what it's like from Charlie's perspective." I rinsed the tumbler and put it in the drying rack, then turned to him. "I've also been thinking about what it's like from your perspective."

"Trying," he said. "Very trying."

"I mean all of it. Are you happy for Mom, or do you hate her, or what?"

In the hesitation that followed there was a barrier between us that hadn't been there a moment earlier. "I don't think I'm ready to talk about that yet," he said.

"Sorry," I said.

"Not a problem," he said.

He gave a tight smile, and I gave one back, but it was clear we could both feel the new space between us. I searched for another topic to cover up the gaffe, but I couldn't think of anything except the private sorrows we all preferred to nurture in secrecy, so we just stood there, locked in tense, uncomfortable smiles, until my father said, "I just remembered something I have to do."

A moment later his office door clicked shut.

18

I pushed aside the refrigerator to reveal grimy pennies and a layer of filth I couldn't scour away. I pushed aside the couch, the beds, the bureaus, and after cleaning beneath them, I pushed them back. I even cleaned Charlie's room, expecting it to result in another shouting match, but if he noticed he kept it a secret. Then there was nothing left to clean that didn't cross the boundary into home improvement: landscaping, painting, repairs. I looked around, trying to take satisfaction in the immaculate condition of the place, and I did take some. But the house still felt wrong, and I had to confront the truth that it wasn't because of any mess I could clean.

I started wondering if I should try calling my old friends. If things could shift so quickly between us, why couldn't they shift back? But these thoughts were dangerous. It was like Andrews wishing for his old surfboard. But then I got an image of Andrews riding it on his belly, his chest propped up on two locked elbows, his triceps cutting horseshoes into his upper arms. I got another image of him rocketing around a basketball court in a wheelchair, doing tricks, sinking shots. It was exactly what he'd said he hated, this heroic new life he was supposed to embark on, but it was also his old life, in a way, and I liked imagining that his spirit had returned.

So rather than returning to Sequoia for finals week, I started going to the local YMCA, where for three dollars a day I could join the basketball games pounding from one end of the court to the other. The players were older guys with bellies and body hair and knee braces, but it felt good to run up and down the court with them, to focus on something as straightforward and unambiguous as a ball falling through a hoop. It felt so good that whether it fell through was almost beside the point. I shot wild misses. I lost my dribble. I sent passes straight to defenders. I was happy anyway.

After dating Lucienne, though, the three-dollar entry fee was a strain on my bank account. My next loan installment wouldn't come until the new year, assuming it came at all. You had to be in good academic standing, and I was currently missing final exams. Still, on the way home from the YMCA one afternoon, I couldn't help swinging into a Christmas tree lot, where the attendant took my last eleven dollars for a runty fir that was supposed to cost twenty. At home I dragged it inside, leaving a swath of needles across the carpet, then set it up in its stand, strung the lights, and hung the ornaments. The decorations accomplished what my housework couldn't, adding warmth and spirit to the stark material fact of the cleanliness. The feeling from previous years returned, the holiday joy we'd taken for granted, less like a memory now than a physical presence, as if those times were soaked into the carpet and walls, suffused into the air like the scent from the tree and the soft auric glow of its lights.

When my father came home, he sniffed the air, then shuffled into the living room and drew in a long breath through his nose. "It *is* nice having a tree," he admitted. Charlie had stomped past the decorations without giving them a second glance, but that night I found him sitting cross-legged in the living room with the lights off, chin cupped in his palm, lost in thought as he stared at the glowing tree. I wondered if he could feel it too—the collapse of time, the past touching the present, the return of what we had lost.

He left for Maryland at the end of the week. I followed him and my father to the garage and said, "Tell Mom hello for me."

As Charlie turned from the Volvo's open trunk, his face crumpled into its familiar squint of disgruntlement. "You're not coming?"

"No."

"Why not?"

"I guess I'm mad at Mom."

"Why?"

It was the first time I'd confronted the question aloud, and the mess of complication drifted away like a cloud uncovering the sun. "For leaving," I said. "Same reason you're mad at me."

Charlie opened his mouth but then seemed to remember himself, or maybe realized that he couldn't defend our mother without defending me too. "Whatever." He threw his bag into the trunk and closed it. "You should be coming."

I stood there after they'd disappeared around the bend, looking at the shadows slanted across the driveway, thinking about what he'd meant by that.

During dinner that night, I told my father, "I think I need to go back to school."

He looked up from his plate, worry on his forehead. "It's almost Christmas."

"Next semester, I mean. Assuming I can find a place to live. You mentioned you might have an idea?"

He closed his mouth over a forkful of peas and nodded, a flush of competence rising into his face. "What do you think the freshman retention rate is at Sequoia?"

"I have no idea."

"A hundred percent?"

"My roommate dropped out freshman year, so it couldn't be."

"And what happened to his housing?"

"Our dorm room? Nothing. I got it to myself."

"And do you think other students might be in similar situations this year?"

I took his meaning and thought it over. It was our old style of conversation, and I settled into it comfortably. "Can the college really sell that space again though?"

"Why not?" he asked.

"You pay a big lump sum up front, so you're still technically renting the space even if you move out."

"But will they hold that space for someone with no affiliation to the school? Say some forty-year-old plumber in town decides he wants a dorm room just for the heck of it but isn't taking any classes. Will they let him?"

"What if he *is* enrolled in classes but just isn't going to them?"

"Even so, won't those classes have expired by next semester?"

I smiled and nodded at the conclusive logic, and so did he, and whatever barrier had been between us vanished as suddenly and mysteriously as it had descended.

"Well, do you think you could come help me sort it out?" I asked him. "I know you have your job and everything, but you know how all this stuff works better than I do. Besides, I could show you around."

"Of course," he said. "I'd love to."

"Maybe we could also wait till Charlie's back so he can come too."

He gave me a sober look. "And if he refuses?"

"What if we don't give him the opportunity to?"

"I don't see how we can avoid it."

"What if refusing is a physical impossibility?"

"As in restraining him?"

"In a way."

"He's a pretty strong kid, Ed. You saw what happened when I tried grounding him for the marijuana."

"What if we don't do it with muscle? What if he's relying on you for a ride, and you drive him to Conrad Park instead of coming home. What could he do about it?"

My father smiled, impressed. "I'll check what day his flight comes in."

***

I was surprised and a little disappointed at how quickly my car sold. I still wasn't sure I wanted to part with it when a high school girl showed up on a bike and pushed five crisp hundred-dollar bills at me. She'd barely glanced at the Corolla, so before taking her money I led her through an inspection and had her drive it around the block, half hoping she'd find something wrong and let me keep it.

My father was off work that week for the holiday, so he drove me to the YMCA for basketball and the mall for Christmas shopping. Otherwise I was stuck at home. I spent a lot of time shooting hoops in the driveway. I plucked a Kerouac novel from my father's bookshelf, then another. They were wild books, but there was also something quiet and holy in them that moved me.

Christmas morning was socked in with fog, but with the tree and the lights, the smells of coffee and toast I conjured in the kitchen and the carols playing softly on the radio, the fog only made it feel cozier inside. I stood at the window, looking at the lights I'd strung along the eave and the colors they cast into the mist, thinking about Tanya and Lucienne. I wondered where they were, what they were doing, whether they were happy.

When my father came down in his bathrobe, he poured himself a mug of coffee and came straight to the living room. "Merry Christmas."

I smiled and said it back, then took his gift from under the tree and handed it to him. After unwrapping it he thumbed through the slim volume, smiling at the pages as if at old friends. It was a copy of *Howl* signed by Allen Ginsberg. After a time, he looked up and asked, "Ever read it?"

"I looked at a few pages before wrapping it up. I don't think I understood most of it. I'd need to read it again."

He went to his office, and I wondered if that was the end of Christmas morning, but he came back carrying a tattered old book. "Let's talk about it when you do," he said, handing over his own copy of *Howl*.

I thanked him, assuming he'd neglected to get me anything else, but then he handed over an envelope too. Inside was a gift card to a department store.

"I know it might not be the most exciting gift in the world," he said, "but if all your things are out in a yard somewhere, I thought you might need something practical."

I thanked him. I told him there was a lot I would need.

He went to his office afterward and stayed there. I poured myself more coffee and stood at the window, thinking of my possessions moldering on Tanya's lawn, what would be salvageable and what would be ruined, and then I thought of Tanya having to see the mess every day and how lonely a sight it must have been. It made me glad she had Paris with her, at least for now.

***

Eight days later I waited beyond the security gate until Charlie came staggering down the airport corridor like a big animal who'd been shot with a tranquilizer. He towered a full head over the fast-moving mob that flowed around him, his face loose, his eyes half closed. I ushered him toward the baggage claim, where he collapsed against the wall, dozing, his long legs splayed so that other travelers had to alter their course or step over him. I searched the carousel for his duffel.

Our father was waiting at the curb in the Volvo, headlights on, the sky behind him silvering into dawn. Charlie dumped himself into the back seat and huddled against the door with his eyes closed. As we headed north, the orange sun flared through the gaps in the foothills, and Charlie jerked awake every time his head fell from the fist it was propped on. When he finally rubbed his eyes and looked around, the sky had deepened into daytime blue. A flat panorama of dusty cropland drifted backwards, the low brown mountains in the distance bisected by electrical cables that disappeared over their top.

"Where are we?" he asked.

"Just past Salinas," our father said.

"Isn't that the wrong direction?"

"We're taking Ed back to college."

"Right now?"

"Yes."

"I've been on a plane all night. I want to go home."

I twisted in my seat. Charlie was hunched against the door, his eyes bloodshot, arms folded, legs extended diagonally across the car. "I have to find a new place and move out of my old one," I explained. "I'm not looking forward to it, and I could use some help."

"I'm supposed to be your personal mover now?"

"I don't mean physically. I mean, you know—moral support."

"What about Dad?"

"His too."

Charlie looked out the window, his face grim and full of resistance. "I want to go home," he repeated.

After San Francisco the sun tipped high and everything was showered in a hard white glare. We opened the windows as the heat mounted and then closed them in favor of the air conditioner. Charlie still brooded, refusing to respond to questions, even when I asked about our mother's civil union. It made the familiar drive feel tense and strange.

The feeling grew as we came into Conrad Park, passing the cracked asphalt of the car dealerships, the dumpy grocery with its hand-lettered promotions, the streets that led to the places where my life had unfolded. The weather was bright and freakishly warm. On campus students were sunbathing and chasing Frisbees like when I'd first arrived, and having Charlie and my father there gave me the disorienting sensation of two different lives touching. It might have been a pleasant sensation, like the one I had putting up the Christmas decorations, but Charlie's silent hostility just made me feel the empty spaces in both lives.

After lunch it was a long afternoon of arguing with the people at campus housing, waiting while bosses talked to other bosses and then searched spreadsheets and contacted my loan agency and made copies of contracts, agreements, identification, and keys. My father handled all of it on my behalf, alternating between toughness and patience while I stood gratefully aside. Charlie never said anything, never even came in. He just waited in the car, listening to fast, angry music he'd found on the radio, his head back, eyes closed, as if the breakneck drums and screaming calmed him.

By the end of it I had acquired a dorm room but no place to keep a dog. I asked my father if he would mind taking Paris until summer. He agreed, and I pictured him waving at neighbors and whistling while Paris tugged him forward on the leash. I saw Charlie hurrying in from the school bus to wrestle Paris affectionately to the floor. It seemed like some small reversal of everything that had happened to us since London went missing, and to be the one providing it instead of taking it away was like hearing a minor chord resolve itself into the major.

The low winter sun was about to slip over the horizon as we headed for the bungalow. I drove the Volvo with Charlie in the passenger seat, my father trailing in a boxy little U-Haul he'd insisted on renting, even though I'd assured him I owned nothing that wouldn't fit in a car. When we pulled to the curb, the bungalow windows cast pale yellow squares on the darkening lawn, where the shaggy grass grew around my possessions like old wreckage. Charlie waited in the car while my father and I loaded it all into the U-Haul, not bothering to distinguish what was salvageable from what was ruined. A lot of things were missing: the computer, some of the food, some of the clothes. I also noticed a few additions, such as Paris's leash and dishes and a bag of his kibble. It made me worry, and when everything was loaded, that worry helped push me to the front door and knock.

Tanya answered wearing her waitress uniform and smoking a cigarette. She looked gaunt and nervous, and she used the cigarette to gesture at the depressions around the lawn. "Took you long enough."

"I know. I'm sorry."

She laughed. "I was pretty pissed."

"You had a right to be."

She dropped the cigarette on the stoop and ground it out with her shoe. "I kept forgetting how young you are. Maybe it was wrong of me to get involved."

"It wasn't wrong. It was the best thing that happened to me since I came here."

She looked at me and flattened her mouth, as if what I'd said was a cheesy pickup line that needed to be retired. "Your mom called a couple weeks ago."

"I know. Did you—what did you tell her?"

"Relax. I told her you weren't living here anymore, and then I told her about Paris. That's it."

I would have felt relief, but there was still the matter of Paris to attend to, and I wasn't eager to ask Tanya for something she didn't want to give. "Do you think I could get him back now?" I said.

She let out her breath and ran her fingers through her hair, looking past me, as if noticing the figures in the Volvo and the U-Haul for the first time.

"I'm sorry I had to leave him here," I said, "but he's my dog, Tanya."

"He used to be."

"He still is," I said, and I was about to call for him when I realized how strange it was that he wasn't already wedging his black snout past Tanya's knee. I wondered again about the dishes, leash, and food in the yard. "Paris?" I called, but there was no scratching or barking, no sound at all.

Tanya looked at me grimly. "Didn't your mom tell you?"

"Tell me what?"

"Paris is gone."

"What do you mean *gone*?

"I mean gone. Not here."

"What happened?"

"You didn't come back to get him is what happened."

"Okay," I said. "But what happened?"

She looked out toward the street again, this time for so long that I turned around to see if my father or brother was approaching. They sat in their separate vehicles, my father reading a slim book beneath the U-Haul's dome light, Charlie reclining in his cocoon of noise, the sky behind them a golden sheet.

When I turned back to Tanya, she was lighting another cigarette, the flame carving her face into a dramatic portrait of concentration. She dragged, flicked the ash, and picked something off her tongue. "Derek came by again," she said, as though I could guess everything that must have followed.

"Yeah? And?"

"And he saw your stuff all over the yard and wanted to know what was going on."

"And?"

"And I said you were evicted. And he kept asking why, why, *why*. So finally I said, fine, you really want to know? Because he was fucking some other chick, so I threw his ass out, just like I did to you." She paused to drag from her cigarette, and I felt a fresh bout of disappointment in myself. "We got into another big fight, obviously. He started pushing things over. I went inside to call the cops, and while I was on the phone he took Paris. I ran out and screamed at him to stop, but he just drove off, same as he did with Romeo."

It took me a moment to recall that they'd had a dog together. "So Derek has him."

She shook her head. "I had Sharon drive me out. Paris wasn't there. All Derek would tell me was that he got rid of him. He looked pretty bad," she added.

"You think he hurt Paris?"

"Or worse."

I wasn't convinced. Derek had a dog, and I didn't see how someone who had one could hurt one. Maybe he had Paris locked in a room. Maybe he'd dumped him in some neighborhood or had taken him to the Humane Society. "Why didn't you call the police?"

"He's on parole," she said, as if the explanation in this was self-evident.

"Have you checked the Humane Society?"

"I don't think that's what he meant."

"But you aren't sure."

"Not a hundred percent," she admitted. That was all I needed. I knew what it was like to lose a dog, and I didn't intend on returning to those awful months of not knowing what had happened.

"Where does Derek live?" I asked.

"Why?"

"I want to talk to him."

"Right. I've seen how men *talk*. If you wanted to talk, you would've asked for his phone number."

"Do you want to find Paris or not? What if he's out in the forest somewhere, starving and terrified—"

"Then we'd never find him anyway."

"How do you know unless we try?"

She looked away, as if maybe an answer would emerge from the darkening streets. And maybe it did, because she threw down her cigarette and said, "I'll give you directions in the car."

"Don't you have work?"

She looked at me with her eyebrows up, as if asking what work had to do with anything. I gestured at her uniform, but I was thinking of my father and my brother, to whom I wasn't eager to introduce her. "You don't have to come," I explained, and she practically sang her response, drawing out the final consonants so they rang like a bell:

"*Wrong.*"

19

Tanya went back inside while I went to the U-Haul, where my father was sitting with his reading glasses perched on his nose, his thin book spread over the steering wheel. When I knocked on the window, he looked up, then searched the interior for the window controls.

"There's somewhere else we have to go," I told him.

"Where?"

"To find my dog."

"I thought your dog was here."

"So did I."

He closed the book, and I saw it was the copy of *Howl* I'd given him for Christmas. "Is this something you have to take care of right now?"

"Yes. The Humane Society closes in fifteen minutes."

"Well, maybe Charlie and I could start unloading your things while you take care of it. We have to hit the road before too much longer or we won't make it back tonight."

"If my dog isn't there, we need to go somewhere else, and I don't know how long it's going to take. I can't lose another dog,

Dad. It was really hard for me when you took London back to the shelter."

He gave me a look of guilt and surprise over the tops of his glasses.

"Isn't that what happened?" I asked.

He took off the glasses and gazed down at his lap. "Yes, but what you have to understand, Ed——"

"I'm not blaming you. Mom was leaving, and you had enough to worry about. I get it. I'm just telling you why I need to go find my dog."

"What you have to understand," he repeated, raising his eyes to meet mine, "is that it was your mother's idea to get that dog. She thought it would help fill the void she was leaving, and every time I saw it, all I could think about was how she thought a goddamned dog was going to replace her." He didn't say anything else, but he kept looking at me, a terrible expectancy in his face, as if he hoped I might explain how she could have thought such a thing.

"Sometimes it just feels good to play with a dog," I said. "It doesn't have to replace anything."

My father let out his breath and pushed his bangs aside. "You're probably right. It probably would've been good for Charlie, actually, having a pet. It hasn't been easy, you know, having just the two of us there. What did you say your dog's name was again?"

The door to the bungalow thumped shut. Tanya was locking it behind her, a puffy coat over her waitress uniform and a purse strap slung on her shoulder.

"Leave the truck here," I told my father. "Let's take the Volvo."

He put up the window and turned off the dome light, and we converged at the car the same moment as Tanya. Charlie, sensing our presence, lifted his head, and they all spent a long moment regarding one another.

"So you're the father and the brother," Tanya said.

"This is Tanya," I told them. "My landlord."

"Ex-landlord," she corrected.

"Her husband took my dog."

"Ex-husband," she corrected.

"We have to go find him."

Charlie gave me a long look of protest, then accepted the errand without complaint, just like he'd accepted everything else that day—not out of patience or generosity, but because he was determined not to participate, not even in the conversation.

When he stood from the car, Tanya tilted her head back. "Holy fuck," she said. "No wonder he thinks you're some kind of basketball star."

Charlie glanced at her, then at me, and then moved toward the backseat. Tanya brandished her forearm to block him, looking straight up. "Hey. Hasn't anyone ever taught you to take a compliment?"

He gave a look that meant she wasn't worth the effort of a real sneer, then pushed past her without much trouble, opened the car door, and dumped himself into the backseat. Tanya grinned at me. I didn't know what it meant except that she was enjoying herself.

By the time I got behind the wheel, the smell of whiskey had bloomed inside the car, and I saw Tanya pass something to Charlie in the rearview. I would have objected, but I already had a sense of the whole enterprise getting away from me, and I knew how little my objections mattered to Tanya and Charlie. The next time I looked, Charlie was grimacing and wiping his mouth.

Once we were at speed, Tanya tilted the flask herself and asked, "So what's it like to be so tall?"

Charlie's voice was surly but he answered immediately, "Sucks." It was the first word he'd said since we arrived in Conrad Park.

"Try being short some time," Tanya replied. "See how that feels."

"It's pretty much the same thing."

"You ever have to ask a stranger to grab something off the shelf at the grocery store? It's a real treat."

"Look at your leg room right now and look at mine," Charlie countered.

"Try having to look up at everyone you talk to."

"Try having everyone look up at you."

"I'd love to. It'd make me feel like a boss."

"No," Charlie muttered, "it'd make you feel like a freak."

I thought of my mother, her back hunched, shoulders pitched forward, looking down as she listened to other women and some men, including my father. I'd always believed she hated her height because she was a woman. I'd never considered the possibility that it was something a boy like Charlie could feel, too. For boys I'd thought of it only as an advantage.

Tanya said, "Except in basketball, right?"

Charlie tipped the flask. He slumped in his seat to hide it from me, or maybe just to put some room between his head and the roof of the car. "I don't like basketball."

"Why not? People usually like things they're good at."

"I was only good because Ed made me practice all the time."

I stayed quiet. I wanted to see what else Tanya would say.

"He made you, huh?" she said.

"Yeah."

"Whips and chains and all that?"

"I was a little kid. I didn't know any better."

"And then you became a big kid, and you had to show everyone how big and different you were, right?"

There was no response. When I glanced into the rearview mirror, Tanya was holding the flask at his chest while he looked out the window, refusing to take it.

"Christ," she said. "You might be a giant, but you're still a little kid. You Garrison boys. You think you're so different, but Ed's the same fucking way. Couple little kids trying to play grownup."

When I glanced at my father, he was smiling at the windshield. Tanya's hand came between us, shaking the flask. We declined, but my father wrenched around.

"So how long have you lived in Conrad Park?" he asked Tanya.

"Since I was sixteen."

"Did your family move here, or did the college bring you?"

"Neither. I was fucking an older guy and he kidnapped me. Or I ran away. Same difference. They got him on statutory, but we're still friends."

My father looked at her a moment longer, then glanced at me and turned back to the windshield, his smile gone, mine not.

***

We made it to the Humane Society with only a few minutes to spare. When I pushed through the jangling doors I found Danielle jabbing a broom into the corner. She turned her head, then her whole body, the surprise on her face quickly replaced by warmth. "Well hi there, stranger!"

She straightened her back and propped the broom beside her. Her cheeks were flushed from the sweeping, and a few wispy strands of brown hair had come loose from her French braid. She looked as lovely as ever, and though it hurt to see her, it also felt like seeing an old friend.

"Sorry to bother you," I said, "but do you remember that poodle I bought?"

Her smile dimmed. She gripped the broom handle with both hands. "Yes."

"He's lost. I was wondering if he might be here."

She glanced toward the ledger and then the back door, as if to confirm the bad news she suspected. "Sorry," she said. "We haven't had any poodles."

"I'm sorry too. But he's my dog now. You know? I just want to find him."

It was as much as I could manage, and she looked at me a moment, as if to determine whether it was enough. "That's what happens with dogs," she said finally, her face relaxing into the tenderness that seemed so much more natural on it.

"I'm sorry he's lost," she continued. "Do you need help looking for him?"

"No. My dad and brother are here, plus another friend."

"That's nice."

"It is," I agreed.

Her eyes slid sideways as the door jangled open behind me. I turned, expecting to see someone from my car, but it was a dark-haired man in a fleece jacket covered with animal fur. He was tall and handsome and several years older than us, with a broad, blue-shadowed jaw and a kind smile. "D?" he asked. "Ready?"

"Almost. I just have to finish sweeping." She gave him a smile of infinite goodwill before turning back to me. "Want me to call if a poodle comes in?"

I scribbled my father's phone number on a scrap of paper. I didn't have the heart to admit that if Paris wasn't there already, he never would be—not to someone as sensitive as Danielle. But as I traded places with the man and moved into the parking lot, I realized that she probably faced little tragedies like this every day, taking down reports of missing animals like Paris, taking in abandoned animals like London, and it occurred to me that tenderness wasn't the same as blindness. Why had I ever thought she was incapable of handling a little bad news?

***

The landscape was darkening under silver skies and the chill was starting to bite. "Not here," I said, sliding in behind the wheel. The smell of whiskey was strong, and the silence had a quality of fresh-ness and restraint, as if the conversation had been cut short by my return. I wondered if they had been talking about me.

My father passed the flask to Tanya as I started the ignition, and Tanya leaned forward to shake it at me. "There's a little left."

I turned on my lights as I pulled out of the lot. "Just tell me where Derek lives."

At her instruction I followed a highway north until she directed me onto another highway. Trees crowded the shoulders, darkening the road, turning dusk to night.

"How far are the Redwoods from here?" my father asked.

"An hour or so," I said, "but there are sequoia groves all over the place."

"Maybe we'll go through one," he said.

"Not on this road," Tanya responded.

"Do you remember that camping trip we took?" he asked me.

I nodded. "We used to have that picture on the mantle. That's actually what I thought the campus here was going to be like—out in the middle of some forest."

"Is that why you came?"

"Probably. That and basketball."

"Do you remember that camping trip?" he asked Charlie, tipping his head back, but Charlie only stared out the window. "You were pretty young," he added.

It was quiet except for the drone of the engine, the sticky sound of the tires ripping over the road, the occasional tapping of bugs, which spiraled whitely though the headlights before their black smudges appeared on the windshield.

"There was that fire," Charlie finally grumbled.

"That's right," our father said.

I'd forgotten all about it, but I remembered instantly. During one of our short attempts at hiking, a fire crew with equipment loaded on their backs had come up the trail at a jog. We'd thought it was a training exercise until we came across a tree shaped like a horseshoe, the center hollowed out. It looked like it had been that way a long time, but the scorching around the base—black and dripping—was obviously more recent. I remembered my parents debating why the crew would bother putting a fire out, since these trees had surely weathered a few since the Iron Age. I remembered all four of us standing inside the tree together, touching the crust of wet black charcoal, trying to sense the life behind it.

Our headlights skimmed the trunks as I swung us around the curves. We gained some elevation and then lost it. The forest thinned, then gave way to piles of manzanita, which pulsed and whipped in the wind. The smell of saltwater and kelp crept through the car. Houses started to appear, weathered old structures repaired with blue tarps and particleboard. I started to wonder how far we were going—and what I was headed toward.

"What's Derek on parole for?" I asked Tanya.

"Assault. Bar fight. Not a big deal, but the guy pressed charges and Derek had a prior. Never laid a hand on me, if that's what you're thinking."

"He fights a lot?" I asked.

"No, but sometimes."

I remembered him pointing the plunger at me. He hadn't looked very intimidating, but then again, neither did some of the guys who could throw a baseball a hundred miles an hour.

"Ed," my father said. "I want you to let me handle your dog."

"That's not necessary."

"Has it occurred to you that this could be the whole reason he took it? To entice you into a confrontation?"

"I'm not going to confront him. I'm just going to ask for Paris."

"He might not be reasonable enough to field that kind of request, not from you. The fact is, however Derek and I may differ, we've both lost a wife. I might be able to use that common ground to reason with him."

I appreciated the offer, but this wasn't campus housing. I wasn't going to hide in the car while my father worked things out on my behalf. "Please just stay in the car," I said.

We passed a country store with battered ice machines, a hotel with river-rock siding, a gas station blazing with light where a man with no shirt was filling a red gas can. The first stoplight we hit swung like a lantern from its long metal arm, and the street sign beside it was on hinges, flapping in the wind.

"Take a left," Tanya said. Half a mile later she said, "Left again."

I took us down a dark residential street webbed with black tar, no center line or sidewalks. Blackberry vines spidered low to the ground along the shoulder, the leaves flashing their silvery undersides. On the left was a row of decrepit Victorians with porches and colonnades, on the right a row of prefabricated houses that looked like they might go tumbling down the bluff at any moment, blown off their foundations by the heavy wind. Straight ahead was a dead end piled with more manzanita and beyond that the black immensity of the ocean.

"There," Tanya said.

I followed her finger past the last Victorian. On its far side, at the very end of the street, was a boxy add-on with a separate entrance. The paint was peeling, its color indistinguishable in the porch light's cold glare, which segregated everything into sharp distinctions of silver-blue and black. A jacked-up Chevy was parked on the road out front, the right hindquarters bashed in.

I pulled in behind it and cut the engine. The wind rocked the Volvo on its loose suspension, whistling in the door seams. Beneath the add-on's entrance was a concrete landing. It was level with the big scabby yard, which disappeared into the structure's black shadow around the side, and it was from this shadow that a brindled, short-snouted pit bull emerged. Even from a distance I could see its broadness, its wide head and thick muzzle, its knots of muscle at the shoulder and jaw. It stood with the shadow bisecting its back, motionless and alert, ears perked, eyes trained in our direction.

"Is that your dog?" my father asked.

"No."

"That's Romeo," Tanya said.

A heavy chain trailed from the its collar, but there was no telling how far it reached, just as there was no telling whether the eagerness in the dog's stance was for human company or the opportunity to do violence. But then Tanya got out, gripping her shoulders as if to hold in the heat, her hair flying sideways, and the dog cowered beneath the immensity of its joy. It came crawling over on its belly, trembling and whining, lips peeled into a menacing parody of a smile. She met it halfway, and the dog writhed with pleasure, snuffing and snorting, pressing itself into her shins as if trying to burrow beneath her, while she crouched and petted it, asking, "Who's a good boy?"

I got out, wanting that reception from Paris, and wanting to give the feeling of it to my father and brother.

There was no walkway, so I moved across the yard. It was littered with chewed up scraps of plastic, gutted toys, beef ribs gnawed into pale blades. A blond baseball bat, pitted with tooth marks, was splayed halfway to the landing. I paused over it, recalling Derek's threat and his conviction for assault. But carrying a bat to the door seemed like an unnecessary escalation, so I left it behind and did my best to think of Derek charitably. My father was right— his divorce had probably been equally painful, his sense of abandonment equally strong. He had made mistakes, but who hadn't? The opportunity to correct one was precious, and that was what I could offer him. I stepped up and knocked.

When the door opened, I wished I had the bat. Derek's eyes took on a beady intensity that made the back of my neck prickle, as if he couldn't believe his luck but knew better than to show it. His stubble was dark and an oversized T-shirt billowed around him like a sail. His pants were made of windbreaker material and his pale feet were splayed beneath them like two nocturnal creatures. Behind him there was only an economy-sized bag of pretzels next to a jug of Wild Turkey and a dented beanbag chair, all of it bathed in the shifting blue light of a television. There was no sign of Paris, and I knew that someone who kept his own dog chained in the yard wouldn't keep mine inside.

"I'm here for my dog," I told him.

His eyes moved to Tanya, then the Volvo, pausing briefly on each before returning to me, his expression flat and inscrutable behind his oversized glasses. He stepped over the threshold and closed the door, and I felt my body register the breach of space between us.

"Could you please tell me where he is?" I asked.

Derek offered only a cruel smile.

"I'm sorry about what happened," I told him. "I didn't mean for it to hurt you."

"Well if you didn't mean it then I guess it didn't happen."

"I just want my dog back," I repeated.

"You think I give a fuck what you want?"

"I think you want to do the right thing."

His hand came up, two fingers pistoled toward my chest. "I told you not to touch her, and now you're standing here telling me about the right thing?"

"If you want to hate me, fine. But you need to tell me where my dog is."

The two fingers came forward, landed on my shoulder, and shoved. My shoulder snapped back, and I became aware of the attention from the Volvo the way you become aware of attention from the bleachers as you concentrate on a free throw.

"Or what?" he asked.

"Quit it," Tanya said, as if it was part of an old argument between them.

"The dog doesn't have anything to do with this," I said.

"The dog is gone." Derek shoved me again, and my shoulder snapped back again. He seemed to know just the right amount of pressure to use, enough to snap my shoulder back but little enough for it to make me look weak. I thought of my father and my brother again, watching me be pushed around by this ridiculous man, waiting patiently for the dog they should've had since my mother left. My heart was pounding and my limbs felt weightless. I made myself take a breath.

"I'm not going to fight you," I said.

"Won't keep you from getting your ass kicked." He shoved again. "Didn't I warn you what would happen? Didn't I?"

Then my father was calling across the yard, "Everybody just calm down." He staggered toward us on his bad leg, shoulders seesawing from the effort to hurry, palms in the air. Behind him, Charlie was pale-faced in the far reaches of the porch light, watching from the Volvo's window. Closer, Romeo looked at us eagerly from the end of his chain, his tail swinging a slow rhythm until he pounced on a soggy-looking rope toy and shook it violently.

I was annoyed at my father for breaking his promise to stay in the car, and I forgot to strip the aggravation from my voice when I turned back to Derek and said, "Would you just give me back my dog?"

"Forget the dog, man. You're never gonna see that dog again. I got rid of it."

I pictured him leading Paris toward the dark beach, a rifle slung over his shoulder, and my chest clenched. I remembered what it felt like—never seeing a dog again, not knowing what had happened or whether there was any chance at reversing it, and I felt as powerless now as I had then. If Derek didn't relent, what could I do except send my father and brother back to their lonely house in San Seguro without me or the dog I had promised them? A feeling of wildness opened up in me, one I recognized, and black shapes billowed up at the edges of my vision.

"But I'm here," Derek said.

His smile was like an invitation, and when his fingers landed on my shoulder again, a charge shot through my arms. They almost seemed to be acting on their own as they knocked his hand away and drove themselves into his chest, wrenching a cry from my throat too long and desperate to be only from exertion. It sounded miserable even to me.

Derek recovered his two fumbling steps, then planted, pivoted, and sent a quick straight fist into my field of vision. It came as a surprise, not only because of its speed and impact but also because of its grace. It landed below my eye and sent sparks exploding across my vision, left pressure and numbness spreading across my cheek and into my sinus, and allowed everything that encumbered me to break cleanly away, leaving me free, unobstructed, empty of everything except a steady, focused, homicidal tranquility.

I charged him, running straight through a second punch at my ear and a third to the back of my neck as I drove a shoulder into his stomach and lifted him with wrapped arms, bringing him down hard on his back. I felt the impact of the ground through the meaty pad of his body, heard the deep involuntary "*unh*" of the air leaving his lungs. My momentum sent me somersaulting over the top, and I scraped my shoulder and hip on the concrete landing, then scrambled to my feet while Derek writhed on his back, mouth moving like a fish pulled from the water, trying to take in oxygen he had no access to.

Then Tanya was between us, palms out, restraining me the way referees and umpires do when one player pursues another in wordless fury. She was shouting words that collected at the back of my attention like a television playing in another room as Derek got up, looking strangled, still trying to draw a breath that wouldn't come. His eyes looked small and angry without the glasses covering them, and they locked on me with the same brutality that coursed through my veins. My father grabbed at Derek's shoulders while Tanya grabbed at mine, but we both broke away, rushing at each other again, swinging and slipping and grasping, until Tanya and my father intervened again.

We circled each other as we struggled from them, until I noticed the chewed-up bat lying a few feet away. I broke toward it, but Romeo pounced, pinning it with his front paws, rump in the air, tail wagging, and the three of them seized me. I grunted, struggling to loosen myself, or maybe to drive all four of us across the yard—anything in my power to reach the bat. But they overpowered me, driving me backward until my feet got tangled and I went down. That was when things got bad.

Nobody was restraining Derek anymore, and so nobody could prevent him from jumping on me, pinning each of my shoulders with a heavy knee, or raining down one blow after another. I thrashed, trying to throw him off, and when I couldn't, a feeling of helplessness settled over me like cold snow. Not even the sight of my father above him, fist raised awkwardly, showing the spiral where his pinkie curled into his palm, could relieve the hardening fear that I was in real trouble.

My father brought his fist down, driving from the elbow like a man trying to hammer home a stubborn nail, landing it atop Derek's head. It had no effect other than to distract him a moment, and to throw Tanya into action. She stepped between my father and Derek, as if to defuse their skirmish before addressing ours, knocking my father off balance, and he couldn't get his bad leg under him fast enough. It looked almost involuntary, the way he grabbed the tail of Tanya's untucked work shirt and pulled her after him, so that they both went spinning to the ground. Derek, his elbow flared, his neat row of knuckles still angled by his ear, his face calm except for the crease of concentration between his eyebrows, was free to return his attention to me.

The blows were like shots of Novocain. I got another in the cheek, one in the ear, the mouth, the other cheek, until my whole face felt thick and dull. The one to my nose made it feel tight, out of place, and then the blood came warmly down the sides of my face, filling my mouth with the taste of pennies. I wasn't worried about the blood, though, or even the pain, as much as I was worried about the damage he was inflicting, because the part of me being battered was full of important equipment I would have liked to keep intact. But there was simply no way to keep the blows from coming. All I could do was squeeze my eyes and clench my jaw and turn my head from the place the last one had landed, but again and again they emerged from the darkness to send white pinwheels exploding across my vision.

And then they stopped.

And suddenly I was released from Derek's weight.

And when I opened my eyes, I didn't believe what I saw—Derek floating above me with startled eyes. I wondered if it was a hallucination until the black tunnel of my vision opened. I took in the two massive hands clenched over Derek's biceps, the dark figure looming overhead, blotting out the pin-pricked sky. And when Derek went flying across the yard with such force that he bounced and skipped and nearly regained his feet before face-planting, I knew who had done it.

Derek was moving his limbs like a late sleeper being asked to get out of bed. Tanya was sitting near him, hair flung over her face, an arm propped behind her, grimacing and touching her forehead. My father, nearer still, got to his feet, panting and discombobulated. Charlie was kneeling beside me. "Ed? You okay?"

But I was already on my feet, blind with rage and humiliation, rushing for the bat. Pain pounded through my skull, and the ground tilted under my feet, making me lurch from side to side like a drunk. The pit bull was already there, handle between his back teeth, flexing his powerful jaw. "Drop it," I said, my tongue as thick and foreign in my mouth as a dentist's gloved fingers, but he understood the command and obeyed.

The wood was gouged, the handle slick with warm saliva. As I lifted it, the dog backed up a couple steps, eager, ready for me to toss it, as if this was all an elaborate game for his amusement. It helped me understand that the dog had nothing to do with any of this, that the dog was every bit as innocent as Paris was. But Paris was gone, and my face throbbed from the beating I'd just received, and my heart was too full of fury to care.

I raised the bat like an axe, feeling the weight of the barrel, the strength in my muscles, the invigoration of my hatred and pain. In the moment it stopped ascending, the dog seemed to understand what was happening. He cowered, ducking its head and looking up at me with disbelieving eyes, as if asking what I intended and if I might consider mercy instead. But it didn't keep my muscles from tugging, my arms from straining, my hands from pulling down with all the strength of my rage and longing and grief.

As I pulled, however, something else pulled back. The bat didn't budge.

I looked back and saw Charlie towering behind me in the cold blue light. He was gripping the barrel with two huge hands, his hair wild in the wind, his bare arms etched with muscle. Behind him, on the wraparound porch of the adjacent house, a brown-haired family stood watching, the father holding a little girl and covering her eyes while the mother pressed a cordless phone to her ear. I could already hear the distant sirens, though it might have only been the howling wind, which plastered my clothes to my chest and dove down my collar, frigid and moist and laced with the ancient odors of the ocean. It lashed Charlie's hair, threw it over his eyes and then lifted it away, and his face, swimming in the black sky above me, showed gentleness and concern. He looked like my brother again as he said, "Let go, Ed."

I did, then sat on the ground and wept.

20

The motel room was a shabby place that smelled of orange-candy chemicals and smoke-soaked upholstery. A few coin-sized bald spots were burnt into the carpeting, and a big beige stain was ror-schached over the ceiling. There were two beds, one each for my father and Charlie, and jammed between the far bed and the window was a slim rollaway cot wrapped in tight white sheets for me. Not trusting the floral spreads to be sanitary, we'd peeled them away before sitting down, our elbows propped on our knees, facing one another in the space between the beds. My father's bangs fell over his forehead, making him look boyish. Charlie was next to him, holding a swirl of blue and yellow glass, a little green bud tucked in its ash-blackened bowl.

"See this hole?" he was saying. "On the side here?"

"Yeah," I said.

"Hold it like this so your thumb covers it."

"Okay."

"But at the end of the hit, uncover it and keep inhaling. It'll help keep you from coughing. That's basically all there is to it."

He handed me the pipe and the lighter. I positioned one thumb against the flint and the other over the vent, as Charlie had instructed, and put the stem to my mouth.

"Don't put your lips around it so much," Charlie said. "It's not like sucking a straw. You just give it a little kiss. Like this." He bunched his lips.

Mine were too swollen and tender to make such a shape, but I kissed it the best I could, then looked to Charlie for feedback.

"Just make sure you get a good seal," he said.

I tightened my lips, then positioned the lighter over the bowl without striking it. "Now I just——?"

"Just put the flame down in the bowl," he said, "and take a puff."

"Into my mouth? Or my lungs?"

"Your lungs. And hold it in as long as you can. Don't breathe too deep though or you'll cough."

It was more complicated than I'd imagined. I went through it in my mind.

"Just take it slow," our father said.

I kissed the pipe, spun the flint, and raced through the steps in a clumsy manual panic, my attention required in more places than my mind could accommodate.

"Keep your thumb over the vent," Charlie coached.

I kept inhaling, then uncovered the vent and took the pipe from my lips and held my breath. When I exhaled, there were only a few thin traces of smoke.

"Not bad," Charlie said. "Next time try holding the flame closer, like all the way down in the bowl, and make sure you press your thumb over the vent so no air gets in until the very end. I'll tell you when."

I positioned my thumb securely over the vent, rehearsed the steps in my mind, and took a deep breath to steady myself. I thumbed, kissed, fired, and this time I could feel the hot smoke filling my lungs as I inhaled and inhaled, waiting for Charlie's signal. "Okay," he said, but at the same moment my throat grabbed, my diaphragm convulsed, and I coughed out a ragged white cloud. The pressure changes throbbed though my aching face. My eyes felt as if they might pop from their sockets. My nose, which I'd just had reset in the emergency room, ballooned with pain.

"Here," our father said. "Drink some water."

But I could only hold the flimsy plastic cup while I hacked and hacked. I could hardly get a breath. When my nose started bleeding, Charlie swiped up a few tissues and stuffed them into my fist, first removing the pipe and lighter. I pressed them to my nostrils and tipped my head back, still coughing.

Our father held out his hand and said, "Let me have a hit."

Charlie turned his head, eyes widening.

"I don't want you to get the wrong idea," our father said, "but come on. I grew up in the sixties. I studied poetry in San Francisco."

Charlie handed him the pipe and lighter.

Our father chuckled. "It's been a while," he said, looking at the tools, as if he might not remember what to do with them. But he accomplished the task with small, expert movements, stirring the flame over the bowl while he filled his lungs. I studied his technique.

He handed the instruments back to Charlie, who also took a hit. After a long pause, they exhaled thick streams toward the ceiling.

"The thing about drugs," our father said, leaning back, arms propped behind him, "is that you have to keep them at the edge of your life. You get what I mean?"

He was speaking to Charlie, and Charlie's face darkened, as if awaiting further criticism. None arrived, however, and his eyebrows unknit. He hesitated, as if truly considering the question, then nodded. "That makes sense."

"I still can't believe you got it through the airport," our father said.

"Both ways," Charlie reminded him.

By then I had taken some of the water. My nosebleed had nearly stopped. "All right," I said. "I think I'm ready."

The bud was charred but still held its shape. I ran through the steps in my mind, remembering our father's timing and patience, and then executed the attempt with clumsy success.

"Nice," Charlie said. He accepted the pipe and lighter from me. "Now hold it in as long as you can."

While the oxygen in my lungs dwindled and the burn increased, my father said, as if it had just occurred to him, "You probably shouldn't tell your mother about this." He let his head bob as he laughed with his eyes closed.

I exhaled a stream of thick smoke.

"Pretty good," Charlie said. "Especially for your first time."

"It's not my first time. My first time I had a bad experience."

"Paranoia?"

"No. Someone passed me a joint at a party and I did it wrong. Everyone laughed at me. Then I went inside and saw my date making out with another guy." I nearly chuckled. Everything that had happened since then made the memory almost funny. There was a corresponding brightness in Charlie's face that made me hope it was okay to say what occurred to me next.

"I think that's part of the reason I freaked out that day," I said. "At our pickup game. It felt like it was happening all over again. I overreacted."

Charlie's face dimmed, but not in anger. He dropped his eyes. "I was already on my way to the bathroom, so—" He shook his head and shrugged, as if it was a sentence he'd never figured out how to finish.

"Don't worry about it," I said. "You were going through a hard time."

"So were you," he said.

"We all were," our father said.

After that there didn't seem to be anything left to say. We passed the pipe again, taking big hits, and then we all sat there with our chests full, glancing at one another, smirking to acknowledge the unlikeliness of what we were doing. Charlie and my father were a strange match on the opposite bed, one looking rumpled but respectable in his pleated slacks and polo shirt, the other looking like a maniac with his purple hair and nose ring. Even sitting,

Charlie towered over my father, and when he tilted his face down to share a flash of happy disbelief, it reminded me of what he'd told Tanya in the car.

I let my breath out, coughing a little, under control. "Does being tall really make you feel like a freak, Charlie?"

He shrugged, examining the pipe.

"It's just height. It's not who you are."

"It's fine," he said, smoke pouring out behind the words. He dragged a wrist over his mouth and said, "In punk everyone's a freak, so it's not necessarily a bad thing."

"Is that why you like it?"

"I don't know." He tapped the ash into his hand but didn't get up. He sat there holding the black cinders in his big cupped palm. "I just like the music."

"You want to know what makes *me* feel like a freak?"

He looked at me. So did my father, still holding his breath.

"Not going to Berkeley, like I planned. I don't know why I didn't. It seems so stupid now."

Our father's exhalation was quick and clipped, without the luxurious streaming effect, as if there was something he was eager to say. "The longer you live," he said, waving a hand at the smoke, "the more there is to feel that way about. Believe me." Then his face went sober, and his eyes slid away, as if to some private memory. He looked at me, then at Charlie. "Did I ever tell you that I was engaged to another woman when I met your mother?"

For a moment we could only sit in astonishment and disbelief. "Shut up," Charlie said, as if it was an old joke he wouldn't fall for again.

"Sally Trussoni," our father told us, nodding. "We were engaged for almost three years but never set a date, mostly because I didn't want to be a grownup, though that wasn't the way I saw it at the time. I had all kinds of excuses. Then I met your mom at—well, you know the story. At the conference where we were presenting our Jack London papers. 'Canine as Bodhisattva,' mine was called. What you probably didn't know is that I was still engaged to Sally. Things got complicated pretty quickly. It was a confusing time for everyone. *Very* confusing for your mother, as it turned out. She never told me just how confusing, you know. Not until she'd already decided to leave." He tightened his lips, as if to endure the pain it cost him to recall it, then brought over the trashcan for Charlie, who brushed the ash from his palms.

"I have fond memories of that time," he went on, "when your mother and I were first getting to know each other. But I also have regrets. I didn't behave very admirably, and I really did love Sally Trussoni. But the thing about regret is that after a while, good things start to come along that wouldn't have otherwise. You boys, for example. Then you're not so quick to wish the regrets away. I think that's what people mean when they say they have no regrets. Everyone has regrets, but it's a way of saying your regrets have value to you."

His eyes searched the ceiling while he talked, but now he looked straight at me and gave a great belly laugh. It was so incongruous with his solemn philosophizing that I couldn't help laughing too. It came as powerfully and automatically as the coughing, and like the coughing, I couldn't stop. It went on and on. My nose throbbed with pain, my swollen lips felt like they might split, and I had to hold my aching diaphragm while I laughed and laughed.

When it finally died down, Charlie was grinning at me, as if with secret knowledge. "Feeling it?"

"Not yet," I answered, and I was about to ask what the feeling would be like when it arrived, but Charlie and my father burst into hysterics again, and I couldn't help joining them.

21

None of my professors from the previous semester asked for any kind of note from a doctor or parent. They moved their eyes over my purple, misshapen face, then changed my grade to "incomplete" and set new deadlines for tests and assignments. One professor with a thick brown beard and expressive eyebrows held his forehead tight with concern the whole time I was in his office. As I was leaving, he said, "Are sure you're all right? The reason I ask is because you get free sessions at campus counseling, and every student I've ever referred there has always found it—"

"Really," I told him. "I'm all right."

While my face ascended from shades of night toward colors of dawn, I worked like mad to learn the materials I'd missed while keeping up with my new classes, two of which were upper-level literature courses that required heavy reading. By the time I was fully healed, I had done enough to pass my old courses, and the rest of it I just let go.

My new roommate in the dorms, Ashok, was a thin Nepalese boy with crooked teeth and a quick smile. He was studying engineering and his ambition was to be rich. His face was round, his skin dark, his wiry black hair parted carefully on the side. Over his narrow chest he wore T-shirts that displayed their brands prominently: Nike, Levi's, Abercrombie & Fitch. He was quiet and studious and in love with America, he said, though I got the sense he saw a different America than I did. When I asked what he loved, he named the variety of soft drinks available, and the sidewalks laid in places where nobody walked, and the absence of bribery in law enforcement. On the dorm walls he had put up a poster of two red Mustangs, new and old, angled toward each other on a salt flat, and a poster of Mickey Mouse waving in front of the Disneyland castle. "In America," he explained, "you can have anything and do anything. Nobody tells you no. This is a very great opportunity."

What he didn't like, he said, was how hard it was to make friends with Americans. When he got homesick, he cooked big, fragrant pots of curry in the dorm kitchen and invited me to eat with him. During these meals, he told me about his father, a government official, and his mother, whom he referred to mostly by her household duties, and his seven younger siblings, and his home village of Bhadrapur, which he pointed out for me on a map. He showed me how to eat with my hands, scooping food with three fingers and then pushing it into his mouth with the back of his thumb, a maneuver he performed with neat elegance. I made a terrible mess but enjoyed trying it.

Eventually I told Ashok about my own family, including my parents' divorce, my mother's civil union with Jane, and my brother's fledgling punk band, whose debut I wouldn't witness until May. Ashok listened with polite interest, but I could see the struggle in his face. "In Nepal we have no families like this," he said, dropping his eyes, but kept any other disapproval to himself.

By then Paris was living with Tanya again. Danielle had discovered that the Humane Society in Damerow, where Derek lived, had a beige poodle turned in around the time mine had gone missing. I'd called Tanya, and we made the trip together, smushed into the front seat of the Datsun that had always picked her up for work. The driver was a woman named Sharon with orange hair foaming from her scalp. She explained to me at length, pausing now and then to deliver a single propulsive cough into her elbow, her plans to take night classes and become a nurse as soon as her social security kicked in or her son started paying rent, whichever came first. The poodle was indeed Paris. He trembled and peed and whined desperately when he saw us—or rather, when he saw Tanya—and this time I didn't argue whom he belonged to. Tanya was right. Paris had become hers while I was away, and it felt good to allow her—and Paris—the companionship I had been unable to provide.

I was also working for the newspaper again. Gilbert Platt had reclaimed his rightful place as sports editor, but I'd returned to the newspaper office to ask if he'd like me to take on an assignment, mostly as a gesture of contrition, laying my ego upon his altar so it could be ritualistically murdered. But his only retribution was to ask my assignment preference, which was baseball, and then give me a different one, track and field. I didn't argue. I liked watching the runners. I covered it diligently, dropping off my articles on time, without need for edits. The other editors eventually lost their coldness, except Lucienne, who continued to pretend she didn't notice me.

Then in April, at Sequoia's lone track meet, she came over to ask for consultation on her shots, flipping through them on a fancy new digital camera. She showed me a fallen hurdle, an unlaced shoe, a chain-link fence in sharp focus while the runners behind it blurred. I complimented the artistry and interpreted what each shot might represent, and I could see her fighting to keep the smile off her lips.

When she was finished, I asked what had happened with the A.C. Sullinger exposé I'd abandoned. She told me that Yusuf Alrahmani had pursued the article on his own, but his understanding of collegiate athletics was dim, and the basketball team had banded together to freeze him out. The article, therefore, had been brief and confused, and it was almost killed when Eli Duncan asked why they were targeting an underprivileged Black student for his academic scholarships in the first place. Yusuf broadened the focus of the article, then published it as everyone was leaving for winter break. Since then it had been largely ignored.

I saw Sully around campus sometimes. He gave me a friendly nod but no other greeting, and I wondered how much he knew about my role in the article.

I saw Knute Buhner often at open gym, where I was playing pickup basketball every weekday at noon. Sometimes I had to guard him, and he was a handful, big and shifty and skilled—the way I imagined Charlie would've been if he'd continued playing. But I was there often enough that my dribble started to come more easily and my shots started to fall, and Knute wasn't much of a defender, so I got a few on him too. Other times we teamed up and controlled the court, winning game after game together. I began to recognize the other regulars, learn their tendencies, appreciate the rhythm and nuances of their play. Sometimes we exchanged a few words between games or high-fived after a win. We started to nod at each other on the sidewalk and sit together in the cafeteria, and I wondered why I hadn't started attending open gym much, much sooner.

I saw Tanya only once more. I had no car and rarely went into town, but one day I spotted her marching down a campus sidewalk in her blue blazer, the one she'd been wearing when she rattled her divorce papers and told me to grab a condom. She looked as brash as ever but also vulnerable, out of place, working hard to look comfortable. It stopped me from calling hello, both because it was so unlike the Tanya I'd known and because it gave me the sense that she would be unhappy to see me right then. She didn't have to explain herself, I decided. She didn't have to provide updates on her life and Paris's just because I wanted them. I stayed where I was and watched her stride down the sidewalk, one moment wondering what I'd seen in her, the next moment wondering how I could have let it go. More than anything, I felt tender toward her and hoped she was all right.

***

For Mom's Weekend there was a wine-tasting, a chemistry magic show, a baseball-softball doubleheader, a faculty art exhibition, a choir concert, a President's breakfast, and, the crown jewel, at least in my eyes, "Shakespeare: Ten Epic Plays at Breakneck Pace!" I planned to attend all of them. I had a schedule drawn up, the whole weekend accounted for, complete with slots labeled "free time" and "sleep." I also had a tentative plan for each of our meals together—where we would go, what we would eat, how it might provide opportunities for conversation. But my careful planning was thrown into jeopardy the first evening when the time for the wine-tasting approached, then arrived, then passed, and they still hadn't shown up.

To take my mind off it, I tried working on a term paper about Hemingway's icebergs but found myself getting up every few sentences to glance out the window, even though I had no idea what their rental car would look like. I just peered at the parking lot below, where other mothers hugged my classmates. I wondered if they had gotten lost, or if their flight had been delayed. I turned on the evening news to make sure there hadn't been another hijacking, and the noise drove Ashok out of the room gripping two heavy textbooks. I checked my watch every few minutes, adjusting our dinner plans so we could still attend the Shakespeare performance, though that deadline was also approaching.

I was just beginning to convince myself it would be okay to show up late when I saw them snaking their way between cars in the low evening sun, my mother holding a map with both hands while another woman pointed at my dorm building. I rushed down to meet them, and by the time I'd made it outside they were moving into a different entrance. I had to call out, "Mom!"

She looked around until I waved my hands, and then a smile split her face.

It was the first time I'd seen her since she'd left for Maryland, and even from a distance I was surprised by the amount of gray laced through her black hair and by the weight she'd gained back. I was also startled by how familiar she looked otherwise, with the same height and hunched posture and designer black pants.

"We have to leave right now," I called, jogging over. "We missed the wine-tasting, but there's this Shakespeare thing, and if we leave right now—"

"Hey," she interrupted. "How about giving your mom a hug?"

"We just need to hurry."

But then I stepped toward her, and her arms closed around me. I stared down at the curb, where I could see the striations left by the mason's scraping tool, and then I put my arms around her.

When it was over, her smile was muted, her face creased more deeply than I remembered, with lines etched in little bursts from the corners of her eyes and prongs that ran from her nostrils. Even so, it looked brighter than I remembered those last few months of high school, when she'd been solemn in a way I'd interpreted as sternness and disapproval. It helped me see her as someone apart from her role as my mother, someone without special powers, vulnerable to weakness and confusion, groping her way toward happiness just like the rest of us.

She laid a palm on my cheek and studied my face for several more moments. "Look at all this stubble," she said, then took her hand away and stepped aside. "Ed, I'd like you to meet Jane."

Behind her was a small woman, short and slender, her mouse-brown hair cut shorter than my father's. She wore a collared shirt with the sleeves rolled up her hairless forearms and oval-shaped eyeglasses that she adjusted, gripping the rim of the lens, as she chopped out a stiff hand for me to shake. I had spent a lot of time worrying over this moment, but my discomfort was different than I'd expected. As we shook, she gazed up at me with such nervous deference that I felt like a parent meeting a prom date, and it invested me with an authority I wasn't sure I wanted. To give approval to a parent seemed backward and unnecessary. You're the adults, I wanted to tell them. My opinion doesn't count.

"It's very nice to finally meet you," Jane said with grave formality. "I've heard a lot about you."

"Likewise."

We pulled our hands back and slipped them into our pockets.

My mother said, "Jane's been dying to take someone to—shoot, tell me the team's name again?"

Jane rolled her eyes. "I'd rather not."

"There's a basketball team in D.C.," my mother told me, "and she's been dying to take someone to a game. I told her you're the one to talk to."

"The Wizards?" I said.

"I've been watching since they were the Baltimore Bullets," Jane said. "I've been watching since Earl the Pearl."

"You don't like the new name?"

"Guns to Klansmen. Big improvement."

"I didn't realize that's how they meant it."

"It isn't, but that doesn't take away the associations. At least it's not as bad as D.C.'s football team, which I can't even say the name of."

"I would go to a game," I told her. "They've got Michael Jordan."

She adjusted her eyeglasses and peered up at me with an awkward, endearing smile. "They've got Michael Jordan," she confirmed.

"Maybe we should skip the Shakespeare thing," I told my mom. "Do you want to come see my room?"

"I want to see everything. I never know where to picture you when we talk on the phone. It's nice to see you in a real place."

We ended up skipping everything the next day too. Instead, we spent the morning touring my life. I led them around campus naming buildings, pointing, trying to characterize my experiences in them with a few brief, inadequate facts. I showed them the classrooms, the gym, the cinderblock headquarters of the summer camp, the newspaper Quonset hut. I drove them by the Humane Society, the bungalow, the bowling alley, the fire road. Jane and my mother listened patiently, peering hard where I pointed, as if the nature of my experiences might be glimpsed through the windows. And then they described their own college memories, laughing fondly—the shabby apartments they'd rented, the pretentions they'd nurtured, the friends they'd expected to remain in their lives forever.

We had lunch at a chain restaurant we used to visit in San Seguro, which made it both familiar and incredibly strange. My mother and I ordered milkshakes like we used to. Jane got a beer. As we waited for our food, I braced myself and asked how the civil union had gone.

My mother took her lips from her straw, and after a few moments of reflection said, "The women who filed the original lawsuit in Vermont, they'd been engaged for twenty-seven years. Think about that. And of course, that's nothing compared to those who came before them. So to get this opportunity—it was incredible, Ed. I wish you could have been there."

She laid her hand on Jane's, and they looked at each other with tight, complicated expressions of happiness and pain.

Jane picked up her beer and said, "It's much more than a legal contract."

"It is," my mother agreed.

I made sure to keep my voice neutral and curious when I asked why.

My mother laced her fingers together and looked down at them a moment. "People think love creates commitment," she said, "but what I've experienced over and over again in my life is that the opposite is just as true. When you commit yourself, it makes you more capable of love."

I was glad my mother had found things as important as love and commitment in Maryland. I was glad for the new stability and legitimacy in their relationship. But the lines felt over-polished, as if she'd been practicing them in a mirror, and objections banged around inside me.

I tried coaxing the conversation from the dangers of philosophy to the safety of facts. "Did you wear a wedding dress and say vows and everything, or just fill out some paperwork?"

"We filed for a license at the courthouse, then said our vows before the justice of the peace." My mother laughed, then patted Jane's hand. "I'm sorry. I was just picturing you in a wedding dress."

"We're not really the wedding dress type," Jane informed me.

I waited for my mother to offer a correction, but she only chuckled again, and this time I couldn't help myself. "Then why'd you wear one when you married Dad?"

"I thought I had to." She looked at me and sobered. "Maybe I can wear a dress if Jane and I ever get to have a real wedding. Would that make you feel better?"

"I don't care what you wear. I just don't like it when you say things that make your marriage to Dad seem—I don't know. Wrong. Fake."

I could see the objection in her expression as clearly as I'd felt my own, but all she said was, "I understand."

We concentrated on our milkshakes after that. Jane was looking into her beer as though trying to divine our fortunes from the foam. I felt bad for her, and for my mother, but I didn't regret saying it. You had to say what you meant. Tanya had taught me that.

***

After lunch we drove out to the Redwoods, which Jane had been dying to see. We did a short tour of fallen giants, the root systems standing up like twisted wooden galaxies, dwarfing us as we posed for photos. Plenty of trees were still standing, and gazing up at them reminded me of the photo that had disappeared from the mantel, the one of Charlie and me as children, heads tilted up. It made me miss him, and my father, and as we came off the trail and into the parking lot, I found myself mulling what my mother had said about love and commitment.

Back in the rental sedan, my mother behind the wheel and Jane in the passenger seat, all of us enjoying a moment of relaxation in the shade of the big trees, I asked, "Mom?"

She tipped her head back to let me know she was listening.

"If commitment creates love, like you said, wouldn't you have kept loving Dad if you'd just stayed committed to him?"

There was a moment of silence as we adjusted to the sudden pressure change in the car, then Jane muttered something about bottled water and went striding toward the visitor center.

"Come up front," my mother said.

I did, closing the door Jane had left open. Beyond the windshield was a woodland tableau: split-rail fence, dirt path edged with ferns, colossal crimson trunks. The windows were open to admit a heady mixture of chlorophyll and pollen and decay. The only noises were birdsong and a soft rushing sound like a distant highway or waterfall.

"I never stopped loving your father, Ed." She turned to me with an expression of sadness and pain, as if she didn't like remembering her love for him but accepted it as the price of my comprehension. It made me believe her, and I wondered if it would've had the same effect on me if I'd been able to see it during our phone conversations.

"Even now?" I asked.

She nodded. "Even now I love his mind, I love his compassion, I love his sense of wonder, and the way I used to feel around him, and how happy it made him to offer my love in return. That's always been true, and none of it changed, and there was never anything false about it. But something was always missing, Ed. In the beginning I told myself it *had* to be missing, and that it was a tiny thing compared to all the huge things I just described. But a lot can shift inside you over two decades."

"Like what?"

"Well, the tiny thing grew into this huge emptiness. And then the world around us changed, and it started dispatching messages to me that what was missing didn't have to be, that the place where I felt empty could feel full. I never wanted to give up your father or to break my commitment to him, and I miss him almost as much as I miss you boys. But I also couldn't live with the emptiness anymore."

She looked me over carefully. "I know that to someone on the outside of all this, these things probably sound like contradictions.

And maybe they are. But contradictions are part of love and part of life. Is any of this making sense?"

I nodded. I didn't know if I'd been in love with Danielle or Tanya or Lucienne, but I'd been on my way, and I had come close enough to recognize what she was describing, the emptiness it answered, and the impossible choices it created. "You had to choose between two wrong options," I said.

"That's a perfect way of putting it."

"But it still hurts to be the option you chose against. It doesn't get rid of that."

"I would take it away if I could."

"I'm not asking you to take it away. I'm just saying it was wrong."

She put her hands in her lap and cast her eyes through the windshield, where a hummingbird paused in a shaft of light and darted away. "It would've been wrong to continue denying who I was, like you said. But I suppose you're right. It doesn't excuse me from breaking my commitment to your father—or you boys." She looked at me. "I'm sorry, Ed."

Which allowed me, finally, to offer a phrase so strangely adult that it ached in my mouth like new orthodontia: "I forgive you."

She smiled, and we sat there a moment longer, letting our new understanding settle through the car. Then we got out and joined Jane in the visitor center.

***

In the late afternoon we visited a beach along the northern coast. We bought churros from a sidewalk vendor after smelling the cinnamon and sugar from a quarter mile away, and then we walked the hard-packed sand at low tide, not talking, just enjoying the chewy dough and mild sunshine and breeze. My mother and Jane held hands. It was strange to see, and it hurt me in all the old ways, especially when I thought of my father at home by himself. But I knew how much it meant to have a hand you could hold, and I was glad my mother had

Jane's. It made me wish I had one too, and then I found myself wishing, as I often did, that Paris was with me. I wanted to show them that part of my life too, but mostly I wanted to throw a ball and watch him go tearing over the sand to retrieve it, all joy.

I knew that eventually, probably after college, I would adopt another dog, this time from a shelter, and that I would love it just as well. It made me wonder, as I often did, about that future version of myself, the Ed who existed just over the horizon, as if he were a stranger I was eager to meet. Except this time, walking the beach with my mother, I remembered trying to imagine the version of myself that I had now become, and it occurred to me that it wasn't some other version at all. It was still me. And it would always be me, the same me, looking out from these same eyes as I moved through the world—just calmer, maybe, and wiser, and more understanding of others.

We had dinner at a chowder house, then returned to the beach intending to watch the sun drop into the ocean, a miracle for Jane, who had never seen the Pacific. But the horizon became a gray band, making it hard to distinguish where the sky ended and the earth began. Before long a haze blew in off the water, and the sun disappeared in the gray murk, and then there was nothing to watch, no flares of pink or violet, no sky at all, just a gray curtain pulled shut in every direction.

My mother and I knew the coast well enough to have come prepared with coats, hats, and scarves. After we had bundled up, we walked the beach again, taking pleasure from the dense white air, the sound of hidden waves hurling themselves onto the sand, and also from the knowledge that it was a cloud around us. We were seeing a cloud from the inside, and this was another kind of miracle. We knew the world was still out there behind its screens—we could smell the salty ocean, we could hear the waves crash and effervesce, we could see the shells and driftwood and half-crumbled castles emerge from the mist—and we felt warm and well-protected as we walked, enjoying ourselves in the diminishing light of a sun that still shined brightly somewhere beyond our observation.

ACKNOWLEDGEMENTS

I'm deeply grateful to the people who helped this book into the world. Everyone at Ooligan has left me in awe at the time, attention, and talent they've invested in helping me improve it: Alyssa Schaffer, Joanna Szabo, Ari Mathae, Taylor Thompson, Des Hewson, Kim Scofield, Melinda Crouchley, Emma Wolf, Hazel Wright, Anastacia Ferry, Abbey Gaterud, and Robyn Crummer-Olson. Thank you for believing in this book and working so hard on it. Isabelle Brock, Claire Carpenter, Cai Emmons, T.K. Dalton, Jeremy Simmons, Wayne Harrison, and Rob Drummond read early versions and provided immensely helpful feedback. Jordan Hartt of Centrum was generous in allowing me time and space to work at The Port Townsend Writer's Conference. Roby Conner and Mike Copperman provided early support that was crucial in getting it off the ground.

Because this is my first book, I also owe gratitude to the teachers and mentors who have stoked my passions and helped me pursue them: Lora Nordquist, Samra Spear, Rand Runco, Will Lingle, Dave Gilbert, Ann Whitfield Powers, Kim Barnes, Daniel Orozco, Mary

Clearman Blew, Laurie Lynn Drummond, David Bradley, and Ehud Havazelet. Many thanks to my mom for reading to me endlessly and to my dad for telling me stories, and to both for the encouragement and opportunity they provided during my childhood and beyond. Thank you especially to Katie Bushnell for the patience, generosity, and support that made this book possible.

ABOUT THE AUTHOR

J.T. Bushnell grew up with three brothers in Sisters, Oregon, and San Luis Obispo, California. He teaches at Oregon State University in Corvallis and lives in Eugene with his wife and two daughters. This is his first novel.

OOLIGAN PRESS

Ooligan Press is a student-run publishing house rooted in the rich literary culture of the Pacific Northwest. Founded in 2001 as part of Portland State University's Department of English, Ooligan is dedicated to the art and craft of publishing. Students pursuing master's degrees in book publishing staff the press in an apprenticeship program under the guidance of a core faculty of publishing professionals.

Project Managers
Anastacia Ferry
Hazel Wright

Editorial
Emma Wolf
Melinda Crouchely

Design
Morgan Ramsey
Denise Morales Soto

Digital
Chris Leal
Megan Crayne

Marketing
Hannah Boettcher
Sydnee Chesley

Publicity
Alex Gonzales

Acquisitions
Jennifer Ladwig
Michael Shymanski
Des Hewson
Kimberly Scofield

Social Media
Alix Martinez

Book Production
Jenna Amundson
Sarah Bermudez
Jill Bowen
Cole Bowman
Andre Cole
Glorimar Del Rio

Rachel Done
Kendra Ferguson
Ivory Fields
Frances Fragela
Alexander Halbrook
Denali Helicki
Alexandra Magel
Vivian Nguyen
Bailey Potter
Emma St. John
Annie Stein
Courtney Young